ENOCH

ENOCH

ALTON GANSKY

ReAlms
A STRANG COMPANY

Most Strang Communications/Charisma House/Christian Life/ Excel Books/ FrontLine/Realms/Siloam products are available at special quantity discounts for bulk purchase for sales promotions, premiums, fund-raising, and educational needs. For details, write Strang Communications/Charisma House/ Christian Life/Excel Books/ FrontLine/Realms/Siloam, 600 Rinehart Road, Lake Mary, Florida 32746, or telephone (407) 333-0600.

Enoch by Alton Gansky
Published by Realms
A Strang Company
600 Rinehart Road
Lake Mary, Florida 32746
www.strangdirect.com

Scripture quotations are from the New American Standard Bible. Copyright © 1960, 1962, 1963, 1968, 1971, 1972, 1973, 1975, 1977 by the Lockman Foundation. Used by permission. (www.Lockman.org)

The characters portrayed in this book are fictitious unless they are historical figures explicitly named. Otherwise, any resemblance to actual people, whether living or dead, is coincidental.

Design Director: Bill Johnson
Cover Designer: studiogearbox.com

Library of Congress Cataloging-in-Publication Data
Gansky, Alton.
  Enoch / Alton Gansky. -- 1st ed.
    p. cm.
  ISBN 978-1-59979-344-3
  1. Prophets--Fiction. I. Title.
  PS3557.A5195E66 2008
  813'.54--dc22
                           2008019112
First Edition

08 09 10 11 12 — 9 8 7 6 5 4 3 2 1
Printed in the United States of America

Alton Gansky's *Enoch* kept me up past midnight more than once and made me late for an appointment. One moment I didn't want the story to be over, and the next I had to stop myself from skipping ahead to find out how it all ends. What a ride!

—ATHOL DICKSON
CHRISTY AWARD–WINNING AUTHOR, *WINTER HAVEN*

Over the years Al Gansky has established himself as master of the Christian thriller; with *Enoch* he nails down the lid. The book moves like a rocket on crystal meth, packed tight with twists and turns and jaw-dropping moments of crystalline prose so transcendent you'll weep. It's also chock-a-block full of finely limned characters you couldn't forget if you tried. So strap down and hang on. You're in the hands of a professional here.

—JOHN ROBINSON
AUTHOR, JOE BOX AND MAC RYAN SERIES

Enoch is…chilling, because of the truth he tells. Alton Gansky knows how to take a message and drive it home with such grace that you don't know it's happening until it already has. Excellent book. Highly recommended.

—HANNAH ALEXANDER
AUTHOR, THE HIDEAWAY SERIES

I had an idea of what *Enoch* was about from the title, but I have to say the story was nothing I expected. Thoughtful, heart-tugging, powerful thrilling…I was drawn in from the first page. *Enoch* is a story you'll want to read in one sitting and that you'll pass on to a friend just so you can talk about it!

—TRICIA GOYER
AUTHOR, *A WHISPER OF FREEDOM*

Alton Gansky's *Enoch* is wonderfully imaginative, sometimes a little unnerving, and never predictable. I can't wait for the sequel.

—DeAnna Julie Dodson
Author, *In Honor Bound*

Take a five-thousand-year-old man so holy that God lets him bypass death—not even grow old, even. Mix in a maniac, demon-possessed false evangelist with a lust for power. Stir in several armed thugs and federal investigators. You have *Enoch*, another gripping Gansky thriller of the supernatural.

—Eric Wiggin
Author, *Blood Moon Rising*

HE FIRST THOUGHT OF HIS FEET.
It seemed an odd first thought, but there it was. His gaze drifted to a pair of soft-topped shoes, each with a symbol stitched to the side.

"N." He wondered why anyone would stitch a letter on footwear.

He raised a foot, then wiggled it. The shoe felt good. He dug a toe in the sandy dirt, then raised his head. A field surrounded him. No crops, no buildings, no people. Just a wide expanse of rugged scrub that shivered in the cold wind.

A full-circle turn revealed nothing but the same: miles of empty land. He blinked against the wind and the bits of dirt and dust it carried. To the west the sun lowered itself to the horizon. In the opposite direction, darkness crawled up the sky, keeping pace as if the descending orb pulled a curtain of night behind it.

Turning to face the sun again, he saw a break in the expanse of near-barren ground. At its edge ran a thin fence. He moved toward it, amused at the soft crunch the earth made with each step of his N-shoes.

Something scampered to his right. A covey of quail sprinted away and then took to the air, flying a short distance before making contact with the earth again. The sight made him smile.

Henick wrapped his arms around himself to ward off the chilling breeze. The material of his multicolored shirt felt soft against his arms and palms. He kept his gaze down, protecting his eyes from the sun's glare and looking up only long enough to get his bearings and check for holes or rocks that might cause him to stumble.

The fence was a simple series of metal stakes supporting four strands of metal wire punctuated with evenly spaced barbs. He extended a finger, touched one of the points, and frowned. The knife-sharp tip drew a drop of blood. He stuck the offended finger in his mouth. A quick scan of the fence's length revealed no gate.

A short distance from the fence ran a wide, smooth, black surface with a series of white dashes down the middle. He marveled at its unerring straightness.

He returned his attention to the fence. He wanted to be on the other side but preferred to arrive there with skin and clothing intact. Placing a hand on the top strand, he pushed down. The metal wire moved, but not enough to make straddling the thing acceptable. He tried again, this time using both hands. The wire fence gave more but still too little.

Henick decided on a different approach. He stepped to the nearest metal upright and tested it. It looked old, as if it had spent a lifetime stuck in that one spot. Seizing it with both hands and careful to avoid the stinging wire, he shook the thin metal pole. It wiggled. He leaned into it and then pulled back, repeating the motion twenty or thirty times. The metal felt cold against his bare hands, and gritty rust tinted his flesh.

When he had worked the pole loose, he lifted its base from the ground, then moved to the next upright and reenacted the procedure. With two posts loose, Henick could step across the barrier without injury.

Once on the other side, he replaced the posts, stomping the surrounding dirt with his foot until the soil was as compact as he could make it. In time, weather would reseal the posts to their original strength.

The exertion had warmed him enough to raise a film of perspiration on his brow and beneath the black hair that hung to his shoulders. The breeze found each moist area and chilled it. He could expect a cold night.

Stepping to the middle of the black path, he bent and touched the surface. It appeared smooth but felt coarse beneath his fingers. The black material radiated gentle warmth. He straightened and looked up and down the long road. It seemed to have no end in either direction. Deciding that one direction was as good as the other, Henick began to walk, choosing his course so the wind would be at his back and not in his face.

When the last of the sun's disk fell beneath the horizon, Henick had made two or three miles. He passed the time by counting the white dashes in the middle of the strange path or wondering about the letter *N* on his shoes. He liked the shoes; they made walking easier.

A quarter moon replaced the sun in the sky but offered little light. Soon the final light would follow its source below the distant horizon. If he had remained in the open field, he would have had to stop his journey. Walking over uncertain and irregular terrain with no light would be foolish, but the hard path with its white lines made it possible for him to continue.

Just before the sun said its final good-bye, Henick saw a black and white sign with a puzzling, irregular shape and the words RANCH ROAD 1232. Sometime later he saw a sign that read DON'T MESS WITH TEXAS.

The air moved from chilly to cold, but the breeze had settled.

Henick kept moving.

Lights and a rumble approached from behind. The light split the darkness and gave Henick a shadow that stretched impossibly long before him. He stopped and turned, raising a hand to shield his eyes against the glare.

The roar grew louder. The lights neared.

A sudden blaring assaulted his ears, but Henick stood his ground.

"What are you? Nuts?"

The voice came from behind the glare. A large metal device pulled alongside. The words *pickup truck* entered Henick's mind.

The vehicle stopped. "Have you plumb lost your mind, boy? I coulda run you down and not even known I hit ya. What are you thinking?"

In the dim light, Henick could see two people seated in the truck: a man in his sixties and a woman of the same age.

"Go easy on him, Jake. He looks confused. Maybe he's lost." The woman's voice rode on tones of kindness.

"That it, boy? You lost?"

"I am just walking," Henick said.

"In the dark? Where you headed?"

Henick thought for a moment. "That way." He pointed down the long stretch of road.

"Ain't nuthin' that way but Blink, and there ain't much reason for going there unless that's your home. I'm guessin' it ain't. Pretty small town; I think I'd have seen you before."

"I don't live there."

The man the woman called Jake exited the truck and eyed Henick. "It's a bit cold to be out in nuthin' but blue jeans and a flannel shirt. It's supposed to drop into the forties tonight."

"It is true. I am cold."

"Give him a ride, Jake." The woman had slid closer to the driver side door. "We can't leave him out here. He's liable to step in some pothole and break a leg."

"More likely he'd step on a rattler. They like the warm asphalt."

"Either way, Jake, we can't leave the man out here."

"All right, all right, just keep your shoes on." Jake looked at Henick. "Turn around."

Henick raised an eyebrow.

"Turn around, boy. I jus' wanna make sure you ain't packin'."

"Packin'?"

"Totin' a gun. You sure you haven't wandered off from some kinda home for the slow?"

"Jake!"

"All right, Eleanor, I don't mean no disrespect." He motioned for Henick to turn in place. Henick did. "OK, here's the deal. I'll give you a ride, but that's all. Me and the wife were going into town for a meal. Friday night is our evening out. Been doing that for thirty-five years."

"I would like a ride."

"Yeah, well, don't have no room for you up front, so you'll have to ride in the back. I got some blankets to keep the wind off you. It's the best I can offer."

"Thank you." Henick climbed into the bed of the truck and leaned against the cab.

"Blankets are behind my seat. I'll get 'em."

A few moments later, Henick, snug in two wool blankets, turned his face heavenward, gazed at the stars, and wondered what a "Texas" was.

2

"Hurry up, it's about to start." Millie Moskos sat on the sofa and worked her back into the cushion. She reached for a china cup of orange spice herbal tea.

"Settle down, woman, I'm coming, although I don't know why you want me to watch this nonsense." Harry Moskos, Millie's husband of nearly thirty years, carried what had once been a white cup, now yellowed by age and a thousand washings. He sipped his coffee. Harry always drank coffee, a habit chiseled into his character by twenty-five years spent as a navy doctor.

"It's not nonsense. You love this show as much as I do. And you should stop drinking so much of that stuff; it's bad for your blood pressure."

"So you said this morning and at lunch. Coffee has never done me any harm. Besides, I'm a doctor; I know what is and what isn't good for my blood pressure." He took another sip and smacked his lips. "Ah, man-milk. A guy like me needs it."

"A guy like you needs to find a better excuse."

Harry settled into his La-Z-Boy chair, squirmed until his body matched the well-worn depressions, and then pulled the handle that raised his legs. "Yes, sir, if the navy had recliners like this on the ship, I'd still be serving instead of working ER."

"Sometimes I think you love that chair more than you do me."

"Just sometimes?"

Millie studied her husband. His gray hair lay flat on his head, and stubble decorated his jowls. He never shaved on his days off.

Over the years he added over sixty pounds to his frame. Middle age had not been kind to him. Of course, she carted an extra thirty pounds herself. They both were victims of aging in a Western society filled with every fattening food a person could desire.

"I hope she has the same spirit-guide as last week." Millie raised the teacup to her lips.

"What, the one that talks about alien life?"

"Yes. Isn't it exciting to know that people like us live on other planets?"

"We don't *know* that, Millie. All we know is that Mary-Martha said it."

"Not Mary-Martha; Lustar, her spirit guide, and he should know. He lived and died on another planet."

"If you say so."

"Mary-Martha says so, and I don't think she'd lie to the world."

Harry chuckled.

"Laugh all you want, but I believe her."

"Ease up, old girl. I'm just having some fun with you. Haven't I sat here each week with you and watched her show on television? Don't I send her money each time I pay the bills?"

"It's starting. Turn up the volume."

"You keep me around just to operate the remote, don't you?"

"It gives you a sense of purpose. Now hush."

Willie Lennox stood to the side of camera three, unmoving and veiled in the penumbra of white stage lights. He felt comfortable in the dark, just a step or two from the activity of others. Mr. Behind-the-Scenes, always present, seldom noticed. He thought of the stage musical *Chicago*. A character named Amos—another husband of a famous person—sings about his own invisibility. *Mr. Cellophane shoulda been my name...* The words churned up the tune in Willie's mind.

Around him cameramen worked the large, commercial video

cameras. In a room down the hall a director gave commands to the technicians over headsets while recording everything the cameras saw. The middle camera—camera two—was attached to a small boom and began to rise slowly until camera and operator hovered ten feet above the floor of the private studio.

A man who had yet to see thirty summers raised three fingers and wiggled them at the woman seated on a high-backed white throne with gold trim. Potted trees framed her seat, and plush cobalt blue carpet covered the dais. Tiny lights like fireflies sparkled on the serene, ocean background rear-projected on a screen. The flickers came from a cheap disco ball hanging overhead.

The rest of the studio held nothing but darkness and the discards from previous sets. Willie felt more connected to the detritus than to the stunning woman who sat upon the throne and stared through unblinking eyes at things only she could see.

Willie had seen every taping and live show over the last ten years. Every year, more people tuned in. Every year his wife grew more lovely and popular. He should be happy.

He wasn't.

His discontent wormed another inch into his soul, spreading tiny barbs to anchor its position should Willie come to his senses and decide to give up the doormat lifestyle. There wasn't much chance of that.

Returning his attention to the woman on the throne, Willie forced himself to listen. These days it was an act of supreme will.

Her body was rigid, eyes wide, and head tilted a few degrees to the left as if someone were pouring information in her right ear.

"A new chasm threatens to divide the cosmic personhood, to rend it as one tears an old cloth…the dangers of the chasm are real. The enemy approaches. Already several worlds have given in to its greed, have sipped from its fountains of lies and been drugged into compliance…Earth residents are warned. Love and hope alone can prevent this encroachment. Belief in the eternal good that is in everyone is the only power that can keep your planet from falling into the abyss.

"Be seekers of truth, searchers of honesty. Beware the false teachers with their fancy churches and promises that can never be fulfilled. Beware and be warned. The future belongs only to those who listen to the voices of the Cosmic Council. All others are pretenders, and pretenders earn their own punishment. But you are a different breed. You are an evolutionary step beyond the others. You are true believers, the ones who can send the dark, starless abyss back to its evil beginnings.

"Listen to us who have gone before you, we who have lived countless centuries and seen all. Accept our love and guidance. Follow our anointed one. The future of your world and countless others…countless others…countless…" Her voice faded and her head wagged from shoulder to shoulder.

"…countless other worlds depend on you."

With the last words, Shirley Lennox, known to the world as Mary-Martha Celestine, ceased speaking, and her head dropped forward as if she had fallen fast asleep. No one moved. Movement wasn't needed. They had all seen it before. Without looking, Willie knew camera two was pushing a close-up as the boom operator lowered it to the floor again as if whoever was speaking through the woman on the throne descended to the humble earth.

Slowly, as if her skull were made of concrete, Mary-Martha raised her head and stared into the glass eye of the camera. "Our…" She swallowed hard. "Our celestial brothers have brought this message to you through me, their humble servant. We must be wise and listen to their warnings, heed their words. Nothing less than our world and countless other worlds depend on your faithfulness. That's why we at Sanctuary so need your continued support. We are only as strong as our worldwide ministers. Your positive thoughts and financial support allow us to take the message throughout this tired world, bringing hope to the hopeless and moving the human race farther along the road of evolution—"

Willie stopped listening. He saw the financial books; he knew the figures. The Church of New Revelation was flush…very flush. And that referred only to the money the IRS knew about.

The floor director held up ten fingers and began lowering one with each tick of the second hand.

"Remember, your positive thoughts make a world of difference. Until next time, may the power of the universe be yours in every area of your life."

The red light on camera two blinked out.

"And we're clear," the floor director said.

Mary-Martha stood and stretched. "Can't someone get better padding on this chair? My back is killing me."

"I'll see to it," the floor director answered.

"Thanks." Mary-Martha descended the five steps from the raised platform to the studio floor.

"We'll be on tape for the rest of the program. We have the interview you did earlier this week."

Willie met her as she stepped from the last tread. They married straight out of college, and Willie thanked the stars a thousand times that the ebony-haired beauty with hazel eyes had agreed to a lifetime with him. Most days, that lifetime seemed a life sentence, but when she leaned forward and kissed his cheek, he felt as he did when a smitten junior at the University of California at Riverside. That was over fifteen years ago.

"A wonderful performance." He regretted the words before the last syllable escaped his lips.

The space between the two iced over. "How many times do I have to tell you not to call it a performance?" She lowered her voice. "Especially when others are around."

They already know, Shirley. These guys are the insiders. You can't fool them for long. "I'm sorry, sweetheart. I'm a little under the weather and not at my best."

"You're sick?" She took a half step back.

"No, just a headache. It'll pass. Maybe some dinner will help."

She shook her head. "You go ahead. I want to look over the books. The month is about to close out." She walked away from the set. Willie stayed in tow.

He would eat alone again tonight.

ONE OF THE GREAT THINGS ABOUT BEING A FILM STUDENT at UCLA, Ray Tickner thought, was all the movies he got to watch without guilt. If a man had to have homework, then movie watching made the best kind. Tonight, however, he made no pretense about watching a flick for class. He had come to the High Manor Multiplex Theater to spend time with Jocelyn Spencer, a twenty-one-year-old theater student. Blonde bouncy hair, large eyes, full lips, and skin as smooth as polished marble had caused scores of male students to pull a muscle in their necks when she walked by. If Ray hadn't decided as a child to be a movie director, he'd switch majors just to create a film for Jocelyn.

"This isn't going to be a guts-and-gore movie, is it?" When she spoke, Ray was certain any birds that heard her would swear off singing.

"Not really. There is some intense action and violence, but it's worth seeing." They stepped from the concession stand and started for the theater in the multiplex that played *Danger's Street*. Ray juggled a large soda, bag of popcorn, and a package of Twizzlers. He also had a coat draped over his arm.

"Why?" She held a medium diet soda.

"Why do I want to see this? Two reasons. First, it stars Thom Blake. He's one of the fastest-rising leading men in this decade. The ladies love him for his looks, but I like him because he's a good actor—scratch that, he's a *great* actor."

"And the second reason?"

They passed through the art deco style double doors and into the theater. The place had begun to fill. Ray hated crowded theaters. He preferred the Monday crowd. On several occasions he had been one of two or three in the theater. Perfect viewing.

"Mitchell Tabor was the DP. I think he's the best in the business."

"What's a DP?"

Ray smiled to choke down a sigh. Jocelyn might be the most beautiful woman on campus, but she was not the brightest light in the projector. She knew little of movies, stating the Broadway stage was her calling. There had always been a dichotomy between those who loved the "legitimate" stage and those who preferred movies and television. All Ray cared about was telling stories. He chose film, but he appreciated the other mediums.

"DP is shorthand for director of photography. He's the guy responsible for the camera work. The director tells him what he wants; the DP uses his skill to make it happen."

"Oh. Sounds interesting." The words would have been more believable if she hadn't yawned immediately after speaking them.

They found a pair of seats dead center and two rows from the back. In theaters with stadium seating, Ray liked to sit where his eyes were level with the middle of the screen.

Once seated, Ray offered his date some popcorn. She shook her head. "Too much starch, and the artificial butter gives me skin problems."

"Ah." He shoveled a handful of the treat into his mouth. Directors didn't have to worry about such things as skin conditions.

"Don't tell anyone, but I have a copy of the script."

Jocelyn furrowed her brow. "You have the script? Isn't that supposed to be, like, secret or something?"

"Yeah, it's, like, secret."

"How did you get it?"

Ray smiled. "I know a guy who knows a guy." He offered nothing more.

The lights dimmed, and after six trailers advertising upcoming movies, the film started.

Once the theater was dark, Ray removed a small video camera from his coat pocket and pointed it at the screen. Fortunately, no one sat to his right. He set the camera on the armrest.

Thom Blake looked good and delivered a great rendition of a drug-addicted FBI agent, sympathetic yet unforgivable. When his partner died in a shoot-out, a death that Blake's character could have prevented, Thom delivered a heartrending scene of remorse. Ray blinked back tears. It wouldn't do to get weepy on a date with Jocelyn. He stole a glance at her. Her eyes were dry and her expression broadcast boredom.

Oh, brother. An Arctic cod would be cuddlier. He refocused on the screen. Thom Blake had tears on his face, and Ray felt certain they were real and not something artificial from the makeup crew. Blake's dark hair hung in his face, making him look like an orphan lost on the mean streets of Philly. The tears gave way to anger. Picking up his partner's weapon and drawing his own, he rose and turned toward the small shop that harbored three thugs, thugs who shot and killed his friend. His intent was clear—he planned to walk into a hail of gunfire that would certainly kill him. For Blake's character, it was the only means of redemption. With a 9mm Glock in each hand, Blake's FBI character turned his back on the camera and started forward.

Ray leaned forward, waiting for the sacrificial moment that would seal the plot. He knew what would happen next. He hadn't told Jocelyn this, but he saw the film last week. He planned to spend his time studying the DP's approach to shooting the scenes but found himself caught up in the plot again. Blake was amazing.

One step. Two steps. Gunfire from the store. Muzzle flashes. Blake's character didn't flinch. He would make amends for the death of his partner—

Blake stopped. On the movie screen the action continued. The sounds of gunfire poured from the large theater speakers, but Blake had stopped moving.

"What…?" Ray leaned forward. This didn't happen the last time he saw the film. Before, Blake let loose a blood-chilling scream and charged through a storm of bullets, his gun spitting bullets.

Instead, the screen character turned and faced the camera. Actors never faced the camera. It was the quickest way to break the illusion and short-circuit the audience's suspended disbelief.

Yet there he was, America's newest and biggest star at the age of twenty-eight breaking the most basic rule of filmmaking. And why had the director and film editor left the faux pas in the release version? Someone messed up big-time. The only thing Ray could figure was that this reel was from a blown shot but somehow made it off the editing room floor.

"This is nuts—"

"Shush. I'm trying to watch the movie."

Sure, now you're interested.

Ray studied the images. For just a moment, it looked unreal, like computer-generated animation.

Blake blinked, smiled, tilted his head, and then straightened. The smile flattened as he pursed his lips.

"Time grows short. Look for the one I send you. He walks among you."

Blake turned, faced the action again, raised his guns, let out the blood-chilling scream Ray had heard the first time he saw the movie, and charged forward, bullets belching from the handguns.

A moment later, the character lay dying in the street.

The credits began to roll.

The lights came up, but no one in the jammed theater moved.

"What was that supposed to mean?" Jocelyn looked at Ray. "I mean, the movie was good, but I didn't understand the final dialogue."

"I don't know. It's not in the script, and it didn't happen when I saw the movie earlier."

"You saw this before?"

"I'm a film student, Jocelyn. It's natural for me to study the better movies."

"So tell me what it means. Who walks among us?"

"I have no idea."

THE TOWN OF BLINK ROSE FROM THE DUSTY FLATLANDS.
Dark had settled on the landscape, making the lights of Blink
stand out against the ebony of evening. When Henick got a
glimpse of the illuminated town, he pushed aside the blankets,
knelt on the ribbed base of the truck bed, leaned over the side,
and gazed in wonder. Excitement poured from his heart, electri-
fying every limb and charging his thoughts. He stood, using the
top of the truck cab to steady himself. The motion of the vehicle
as it clipped along the two-lane road made him sway on otherwise trustworthy legs.

"Sit down!" The voice oozed from the cab and mingled with
the sound of tires on the road and wind in Henick's ears.

The truck slowed and moved to the right. It came to a complete
stop, and the driver emerged. His lips were tight, and in the dim
cab light Henick could see the man's face had turned red.

"Have you lost your senses? You wanna get killed or somethin'?"

"No. Why would I want to do that?"

The man the woman called Jake rubbed his face with both
hands as if waking from a nightmare.

"You can't stand in the back of the truck while it's moving
down the road. If I hit a bump or have to dodge some coyote,
then you're gonna go flying out and land on your ear."

"My ear?"

"Look, buddy, just sit down. We'll be in town soon."

"I wanted to see the lights. There are so many of them."

"So many…? Have you been holed up in some cave or somethin'? Blink is a small town; it ain't no big city."

"I want to see a big city."

"And I want you to put your fanny down on the truck bed."

Henick blinked several times.

"Sit down." Jake pointed.

Henick lowered himself, sat, and pulled the blankets over his shoulders.

"Just stay there. We'll be in town in ten minutes, and you can look at all the lights you want. Understood?"

"Yes, I understand."

The truck began to move.

Three minutes later, Henick was on his knees again, leaning over the edge, his face pressed into the cold wind.

Once in Blink, the truck moved along narrower roads. Light poured from lamps on poles evenly spaced along the path. On two occasions all forward progress stopped at a white line with a red-yellow-green set of lights hanging above the ground. When the red light blinked out, replaced by a green one, the truck started again.

Another turn led to a wide street with buildings on either side. Other vehicles, many of them similar to the truck in which he rode, were left to stand empty, angled to the edge of the road and positioned between a pair of solid white lines. It seemed an organized way of keeping unused vehicles from hindering the progress of others.

Some of the buildings had lights of many colors, but unlike the street lamps, these were long tubes that someone had twisted into shapes and words. To his surprise, he understood the letters although he couldn't recall ever seeing the strange squiggles.

Jake pulled the truck between two white lines, and the roar from

ENOCH

the front died. The lights dimmed then blinked out. Jake exited the cab on one side, as did the woman Eleanor on the other.

"You can get out now." Jake's face was no longer red. The anger he expressed earlier had settled over the last minutes, and Henick was glad. He did not want to anger the man who took time to help him. "This is as far as we go."

Henick stepped over the side of the truck and dropped to the ground. "You have been kind. It would have taken me much longer to walk here."

"You would have made it by morning." Jake laughed. "So what now?"

"What now?"

He sighed. "Yup. What are you gonna do next? Do you know anyone in Blink?"

Henick shook his head. "I do not know anyone in any town— except you, Jake."

"Well, I'm not a townie." Eleanor came to Jake's side. Her face wore kindness well. "We have a ranch about ten miles from where we picked you up."

"If you don't know anyone in these parts, then what will you do?" Eleanor's words rode on currents of concern.

"I do not know, but my path will be made straight."

She chuckled. "I don't know what that means, but I do know a hungry man when I see one. When was the last time you ate?"

The question drew a laugh from Henick. "A very long time ago, Eleanor."

She slipped her hand around Jake's arm. "Ask him to join us, hon."

"The man has his own business to attend."

Henick saw her squeeze Jake's arm. "We should at least ask, don't you think? Just because he ain't our neighbor doesn't mean we can't be neighborly."

"I suppose you're right." He faced Henick. "How about it? You want to break bread with me and the missus?"

"Yes. I would be honored to share your table."

"You know what, partner; you sure have an odd way with words."

"I will get better."

"Somehow, I don't doubt it. Well, they ain't gonna serve us out here. Let's go…" He stopped. "You know, I don't think I ever caught your handle."

"Handle? I have no handles."

Jake guffawed. "Sure ain't nuthin' wrong with your sense of humor. I'm askin' about your name. I assume you got one."

"Yes. Henick."

"Henick what?"

He thought for a moment; then the answer flashed in his mind. "Henick Jaredson."

"Well, Mr. Jaredson, I'm hungry. Let's grab some grub."

Before Eleanor let go of Jake's arm, she said, "And we're paying." Jake sighed.

"God is good to provide."

Eleanor nudged Jake. "See, I told you there was somethin' spiritual about the man."

Eleanor led the way into the restaurant. Henick looked at the thin glowing tube of light over the door: CHARLIE'S TEXAS STEAKHOUSE.

The air inside was warm against Henick's cool skin, and he relished its touch. Music filled the space, but he could see no musicians. Still, it seemed right to him, although he didn't know why.

Tables and chairs populated the room like mushrooms in a field. A row of covered benches with long tables between them lined one wall and reminded Henick of animal stalls. Just like animals in stalls, men, women, and children put food in their mouths, talking between bites.

Near the back wall a couple danced on a small, checkered

wood floor. The rest of the floor was covered with unrecogniz-
able squares of material.

"Hey, Jake. You and Eleanor want your usual place? I've been
saving it for you." A young woman in jeans similar to those Henick
wore and a shirt of tiny red and white squares greeted them with
a wide smile. Her hair was the color of barley, and she had bound
it in such a way that Henick thought of a donkey's tail. She held
some kind of documents in her hands.

"What made you think we were going to be here tonight? Are
we that predictable?"

"How many Fridays have you missed?"

"Not many, I suppose."

The young woman led them to one of the padded benches
separated by a table. "Here ya are, folks, your usual booth."

"Home sweet home." Jake let Eleanor slip in, then he sat next
to her. He motioned for Henick to take the other bench.

"And just who is this you have with you?" She laid the documents on the table. She wore a small sign on her shirt that read
TRIXIE.

"A new friend," Eleanor said. "His name is Henick."

"Can't say I ever heard that name before. You from around
these parts?"

"No. I am…new to the area."

"Blink doesn't have much to offer, but Charlie serves up the
best T-bone in West Texas."

Jake rubbed his hands together. "Anything special tonight,
Trixie?"

"Charlie whipped up a mess o' catfish that's to die for."

"Hush puppies with that?" Jake asked.

"Of course. We also have butter beans with ham hock. We
serve that with cornbread. Whatcha want to drink?"

"Lemonade for me," Jake said.

Eleanor added, "Me too."

"What about you, mister?"

"Water."

"That's it? Just water."

"Yes. Just water."

Trixie laughed. "You must be from California."

"I don't understand," Henick said.

"She's just teasing you," Eleanor said. "Look at the menu. See what you want, although I think I'm gonna go for the catfish myself."

"Good as that sounds, I think I'll stick to my usual steak," Jake said.

"Why am I not surprised?" Eleanor placed her hand on his.

"I may be stuck in my ways, woman, but I know what I like. How about you, Henick? You want a steak?"

"I like vegetables."

"It comes with veggies and a large baked potato." The waitress winked at Jake. "Unless you want mashed potatoes with gravy."

"A man can't turn that kinda offer down," Jake said. "Fix us both up with the T-bone, mashed potatoes, and gravy. Eleanor says she wants the catfish."

Trixie nodded. "I'll bring a basket of rolls unless you want an appetizer."

"No appetizer. I'm trying to watch Eleanor's waist." He snickered, then said, "Ow!" and rubbed his shoulder.

"You just leave my waist to me."

"I was just teasin'. No need to get violent." Both smiled.

Trixie looked at Henick. "I hope you're a good referee." Before he could reply, she was gone.

"Referee?"

"Not a sports fan, eh?" Jake said.

"No."

Henick started to speak when the door to the restaurant swung open and two young men staggered in. Jake turned.

"Uh-oh. Here comes trouble."

KATHERINE ROONEY'S ANGER HAD SUBSIDED SOME, BUT the heat of it still boiled in her stomach. She closed the door to her Los Angeles apartment harder than necessary and immediately felt guilty for disturbing the neighbors. At least it wasn't late, not even seven o'clock.

She dropped her handbag on the side table near the front door and set the keys to her Nissan Sentra next to it. Above the table hung a mirror framed in walnut. Her father, a woodworking hobbyist, had made it and presented it to her when she moved into her first apartment. She was twenty-one then. Nine years had transformed her. She no longer wore her hair straight and bleached. Instead her hair hung to her shoulders in a loose perm, and the natural reddish-brown complemented her light skin and pale blue eyes. The blue eyes in the mirror were narrow and flashed with rage.

The lids of her eyes fell shut, and she drew in a deep, noisy breath, held it, then let it slip through her lips.

The scene still played in her mind. It shouldn't. Her mind was more disciplined than this. She repeated the breathing exercise.

All she wanted was a quiet dinner and a chance to read the latest Ken Follett novel. The day had been long and tedious, filled with enough paperwork to level an acre of forest. Her office desk had been her daytime home for the last two weeks, and she hated it. It came with the job, she understood that, but understanding didn't mean she had to like it.

She had left the office at ten after six with a hunger for southwestern cuisine, and she knew just the place. On the Border was a franchise restaurant that served up spicy meals—the kind of meal she had been thinking about all day.

Leaving the office late had put her in the middle of the dinner rush. Hungry families hunkered outside the entrance, clutching pagers that vibrated and lit up like a Christmas tree when a table was available. Inside was worse. What few seats were available in the lobby were filled with impatient people.

"It looks like ninety minutes before we have an open table, ma'am." The hostess looked all of sixteen and already bored with life.

"You're kidding."

"I'm sorry." She paused. "You can check out the bar area. They serve the same menu and seating is open."

Katherine suppressed a sigh. "I'll do that."

"Shall I take your name just in case?"

"No thanks. If I can't get a seat soon, I'll have to go somewhere else."

"OK."

She worked her way through the crowd, and five "excuse me pleases" later she was in the lounge area. The place was packed with people at the bar, seated around tall, small, round tables and filling the booths that lined two walls.

Just as she was about to surrender the search, an elderly couple wiggled out of a booth and stood. Katherine wasted no time in crossing the obstacle course of humans and chairs and plunked down on the bench seat. A moment later a busboy cleared the table and brought a basket of chips and salsa. She had been lucky.

The noise of fifty different conversations mixed with the sounds of a basketball game being shown on four televisions hung high on the walls and spaced around the room. The noise wouldn't be a problem. She could lose herself in a book even if a hurricane battered the window next to her.

The harried waitress appeared and offered her a margarita, but Katherine chose iced tea instead. She seldom ate in the bar sections of restaurants. Each time she did, the server seemed surprised that she wanted tea instead of beer or a mixed drink. Growing up, her home had been alcohol free, and she never developed a taste for it. She tried a couple of drinks in college but couldn't find the attraction.

Katherine had already perused her choices online so had no need for a menu. She ordered.

It took fifteen minutes before the plate of Enchilada Suizas with black beans arrived, and in that time Katherine had almost finished the chips.

The meal was everything she hoped. The gooey cheese, spicy sauce, and flavorful beans couldn't have been better.

She cleaned the plate. Guilty about eating the whole thing, she comforted herself with the fact that she had a very small breakfast and no lunch. Plus, it was Friday. She never dieted on Fridays…or Sundays.

She leaned back and sighed with satisfaction. Raising the book, she hoped the waitress would take her time with the bill.

"I like a woman with an appetite."

Katherine raised her eyes to the man who stood by the table. "Excuse me?"

"A good appetite shows character and strength."

He slipped into the booth and faced her.

"Do I know you?"

Laughter drew her attention to the bar. Two other men stared back.

"No, but this is your lucky day." The pungent smell of beer floated across the table. The man's eyes had a sheen to them that indicated he had been lubricating himself for some time.

The satisfaction she felt a moment before evaporated. She closed the book and set it on the table.

"Let me guess. You and your pals have made a bet. You said you could pick me up with your rugged good looks and witty banter, and they said you couldn't."

"So you think I'm good looking."

Katherine closed her eyes for a moment, then opened them again. No luck. He was still there, reeking of booze and looking like one more beer would put him under the table.

"I hate to break it to you, but you're going to lose the bet."

"Oh, come on, sweetheart. You're as beautiful as the night is long and I'm the best offer you're going to get tonight."

"No offer would be better."

His face darkened. "Listen, missy. I've been watching you all night—"

"Forty minutes."

"What?"

She leaned over the table. "I've only been here forty minutes."

"I don't understand…doesn't matter. I can show you a good time, sweetheart." He reached over the table and stroked her hand.

She smiled. "You like your hand? Because if you do, you'd better pull it back."

"Why is that?"

Katherine, in a move so fast a sober man wouldn't have seen it, seized the pest's index finger and bent it back. She felt his knuckle slip in the socket. He started to pull away. "Don't move. Don't say a thing. Not if you ever want to use this finger again. Got it?"

Sweat dotted his brow. She glanced at his friends, who sat slack-jawed. Several seconds passed before they closed their mouths and rose from the bar stools.

Katherine reached into the left-side pocket of the dark pantsuit coat she wore and removed a thin leather holder and flipped it open, showing it first to the approaching men. They stopped mid step, then slinked back to the bar. She turned the case to the man whose finger she bent close to the snapping point.

"Are you too drunk to read this?"

"Um…no, ma'am."

"What's it say?"

"It says FBI, ma'am."

"That it does. Now how do you want to do this? I can arrest you here and now, or we can forget this happened and you can tuck your tail between your legs and return to your friends."

"Arrest me?" He started to pull his hand back. Katherine added a few more pounds of pressure. The grimace that twisted his face told her she had found the sweet spot. "On…what…charge?"

"I can think of several, but it doesn't matter. When the police arrive, they'll compare the word of a drunk to that of a sober FBI agent. Who do you think they'll believe?"

She took a glance at his buddies. Both were still glued to their stools. She also noticed that several people in the bar were staring at her. The waitress stood with a woman she assumed to be the manager.

She bent the finger another eighth of an inch. "So what's it going to be?"

Sweat dotted his forehead. "I think I'll go back to the bar."

"Wise choice. One last thing. I have a long memory. You had better hope your name doesn't cross my desk. Clear?" It occurred to her that she didn't know the man's name, but she saw no reason to mention the fact.

"Yes, ma'am."

She let go and the man withdrew his hand, cradling it close to his chest. He slid from the booth and returned to his pals. No one laughed. Seconds later, the three were gone.

The waitress and the other woman approached.

"That was amazing," The waitress said. "I don't know how many times I've wished I could do that."

"It helps to have a badge."

The other woman spoke. "I'm the restaurant manager. I'm so sorry this happened."

"It's not your fault, although the bartender might have cut the guy off about three drinks ago."

"I'll speak to him. Also, your meal is on the house."

Katherine shook her head. "Thank you. That's very kind, but it would be unprofessional for me to accept a gift."

"I understand," the manager said. "How about a piece of cheesecake?"

"No, really, I couldn't…raspberry cheesecake?"

The manger grinned. "That can be arranged."

Katherine slipped from her business attire, setting her service pistol on the nightstand. Five minutes later she had changed into an old pair of sweats and walked barefoot from the bedroom, across the apartment to the small kitchen. She tossed a bag of Orville Redenbacher's finest into the microwave and waited for the kernels to stop popping. She then found the remote to her television, plopped down on the sofa, and turned on the set, resting the bowl of popcorn on her lap.

She felt miserable. She had eaten a whole plate of southwestern food, followed by a monster slice of cheesecake—which never appeared on the bill—and now she was stuffing starchy food into her mouth. It was the confrontation at the restaurant. It had all turned out well, and she had done everything right; still, the adrenaline demanded payment, and for Katherine, payment came in the form of food. There would be an extra half-mile on the treadmill tomorrow.

She flipped through the cable channels but found nothing to capture her attention and opted for something mindless and safe: an *I Love Lucy* rerun.

Halfway through the program, her nerves began to settle, and she laughed at a tipsy Lucy attempting to sell Vitameatavegamin.

"Now if that drunk had been this funny, I might have let him stay awhile."

Watching the show, she wondered how old she was when she first saw it. Maybe eight or nine, and even then the program was considered a classic. Since then she had seen the episode a dozen times and could almost recite the monologue.

She mumbled the words along with Lucy when Lucy stopped and stared into the camera.

"Time grows short. Look for the one I send you. He walks among you."

It was Lucy's mouth that moved. It was Lucy's voice that spoke, but gone were her tipsy monologue and comedic antics.

Katherine stopped mid-chew. "What?"

As if answering her question, Lucy repeated the words. "Time grows short. Look for the one I send you. He walks among you."

The set hadn't changed. The props were in the same location, the lighting unchanged. If this was computer generated, then it was the best she had ever seen.

The action returned to normal with Lucy taking yet another draw on the alcohol-laced vitamin juice.

Katherine snatched up her remote and pressed the record button. The DVR on the top of her television flashed a red light, indicating it was recording. The digital video recorder would be able to save the whole program, even the part she had already watched.

She sat on the edge of the sofa, rewound the DVR, and watched the scene again.

The bowl of popcorn fell to the floor.

Henick watched Jake and Eleanor consume their food using a knife and handheld, pronged tool. He learned the name of the pronged device when Jake motioned for Trixie to come back to the table.

"My fork is dirty. Can I get a clean one?"

"You know whatever you find on the fork is free." Trixie lightly punched Jake's shoulder, but the humor she had displayed earlier was gone.

"Tempting as that is…"

"I'll get you a clean one."

On the table before Henick rested a plate with a near black slab on one side, a mound of white material bathed in a thick, light brown fluid, and a mix of vegetables on the other. He picked up his knife and poked at the black slab.

"Something wrong with your steak?" Jake asked.

"What is it?"

"What ya mean, what is it? It's a T-bone steak. It's meat."

"Meat?"

"From a cow."

"This is cow flesh?" He set the knife down.

"Of course. It comes from Texas cattle. Don't tell me you've never seen a steak." Jake looked at Eleanor.

"I've never eaten the flesh of any animal," Henick said.

"You're a vegetarian?" Eleanor seemed stunned. "You should have told us earlier. We could order something different for you."

"You really don't eat meat?" Jake sliced off another bite and shoved it in his mouth and chewed for a moment. Before swallowing he said, "Sounds like a miserable life to me. No wonder you're so thin."

"We'll get you a salad." Eleanor seemed concerned. She caught Trixie's eye.

Henick shifted his gaze to the woman who brought their meals. The smile she had worn when they first arrived had gone missing. It disappeared the same moment the two young men entered. The two had taken seats at one of the small tables that ran down the middle of the open room. Since arriving, they had been loud, demanding, and tormenting Trixie at every opportunity.

As she moved past their table, one of them slapped the back of her thigh. Henick could hear it, and Trixie's face flashed with the pain she felt.

"Something wrong with the food?" She clipped her words.

"Nope," Jake said. "Great as always, but it turns out our new friend doesn't eat meat. How about a—"

"You've been ignoring me, baby." One of the men stepped behind her and placed his hands on her hips.

Trixie spun and pushed him back. "I told you not to touch me, Eddie. I also told you to never come in here drunk."

"I ain't drunk, baby. I only had a few beers."

"A few is too many. Now go sit down. Better yet—leave."

"Come on, sweet thing, you know you want me to hang around. You miss me."

"I can't stomach the sight of you."

"That's not what you said a few weeks ago." His grin became a sneer. "You want me to tell everyone here what we did? Maybe I'll stop by and visit your parents. I'm sure they would be interested."

"Time to back off, Eddie." Jake slipped from the booth, but before he could stand, Eddie put a hand on his head and shoved him back to the bench. Jake cracked his elbow against the table and let out a yelp.

"Stay out of this, old man."

Jake rubbed his elbow and started to rise again. "I ain't young no more, but old is still a good ways off. I still got enough man in me to handle a punk like you."

Eddie backhanded him. Trixie stepped back, but Eddie seized her arms and jerked her close. "I'm not done with you. Not done by a mile. You and me got some business. A man has yearnings, you know." He leaned forward to kiss her then stopped.

Henick stood by Eddie's side and placed a hand on his chest.

"What do you think you're doing, long hair? You want a piece of me too?" He released Trixie.

Eddie's friend stepped to his side. "Eddie. This is a pretty public place. Maybe you should sleep this off."

"Shut up, Burt. I know what I'm doing."

Eddie knocked Henick's hand away, seized him by the front of his shirt, lifted, and pushed, driving him back a half dozen steps until Henick felt the unyielding block wall. It was hard like stone and nearly drove the wind from his lungs.

"Leave him alone!" Trixie sounded close to tears.

"Not until I'm done with this long hair."

"Eddie?" Burt began.

"I told you to shut up, Burt, or I'll give you the same. Got it?"

"Yeah, Eddie, I got it."

Henick looked over Eddie's shoulder and saw Jake rise from the booth. Henick shook his head and Jake settled back into the booth.

"So what's it gonna be, boy? You and me gonna have it out right here?" Spittle flew from his mouth.

"Please, Eddie, let him go." Tears streaked Trixie's cheeks.

Eddie was big and strong and had pinned Henick to the wall. Henick raised a hand and placed his palm in the center of Eddie's chest. He closed his eyes for a moment, then opened them. Moisture flooded his eyes. "You miss her."

"Who? Trixie?" Eddie laughed. "She's just one more notch in my belt—"

"Not Trixie. Your mother. She died. Two months ago."

"What...? How...?"

Henick pressed the man's chest a little harder. "It was a long death. Painful. You stayed by her side."

"Shut up. Shut up! You don't know nothing 'bout me or my life."

"Your father used to beat her...used to beat you...until he left. You believe it is your fault."

Eddie pulled his prey from the wall, then slammed him back. He did it again with enough force that Henick's head hit the block wall, sending bolts of pain firing down his neck. "SHUT UP!" The command came with a sob.

Words came to Henick's mind. "My boy. My little boy all grown up. At least I got to see you grow into a man, but—"

"No, no, you can't know that."

"—but I worry about you, son. I fear you've lost your way—"

Eddie slammed Henick into the wall again. "Stop. Please stop." He began to weep. His hands began to shake.

Henick pressed on the man's chest harder still. It was the only thing holding him up.

"I don't have many hours left on this earth—"

"No, no, don't...please..."

"—come back, sweetheart, come back to the faith. I want to see you in heaven."

Eddie drew back a fist and let it fly at Henick's face.

Henick moved his head to the side and heard knuckles breaking. Eddie screamed and jerked away, clutching his wrist with his good hand.

The entrance door sprung open, and two men in uniform entered. Henick reached for Eddie, who stood doubled over, weeping from a ragged gash in his soul.

Before Henick could touch Eddie again, one of the men seized his wrist, twisted his arm behind his back, and forced him to the wall again, this time face first. Before being turned around, he saw the second man take Eddie to the floor.

"Ow, my hand. Take it easy; my hand is broken."

The man holding Henick released his wrist. "Hands on the wall. Spread your feet." The man kicked Henick's feet apart, and then with one hand clutching Henick's shirt, he began searching his pockets. "You got anything that might stick me like a needle or knife?"

"No," Henick muttered. "I have nothing in my pockets."

"Deputy?" It was Jake's voice. "He's the victim. It was Eddie who started it all."

"Just sit still. We'll get to that in a second." The deputy released Henick, who turned and watched as the other man lifted Eddie to his feet.

"What happened to your hand, Eddie?" the deputy nearest Henick asked.

"I hit the wall."

"That sounds about as dumb as anything I've ever heard. You been drinking, boy?"

"Yes, sir. A few beers."

"How many is a few?"

Eddie shrugged. "I dunno. Maybe six or seven."

"And you call that a few?" He turned to Henick. "What about you? You been drinking?"

"Water."

"What's your name?"

"Henick Jaredson."

"OK, Mr. Jaredson. Do you have any ID?"

Henick looked at Jake.

"He means identification."

"No."

"No driver's license? Nothing?"

"No."

"What about money?"

Henick shook his head.

"No money. No ID. Where do you live?"

"Very far away." Henick smiled.

"No money, no ID, and no home. That makes you a vagrant."

Jake spoke up. "He's with us."

"You know him?"

"Well, not really, Deputy. We found him walking in the middle of the road and gave him a lift to town. Thought it only right to feed him."

"Picking up strangers isn't all that wise."

Jake shrugged. "I suppose you're right, but I know he didn't start the fight."

"OK, who's going to tell me how the fight started?"

Henick listened as Jake explained what happened, and as Trixie, still in tears, told of Eddie's attack. The deputy listened occasionally, interrupting to ask questions.

Henick said nothing.

"OK," the deputy said. "Mr. Jaredson, I need you to turn around and place your hands behind your back."

"Why?"

"Just do it. Let's not have any more trouble."

Henick turned and did as told. He felt something metallic and cold circle his wrists.

"What are you doing?" Jake asked. "The man did nothing more than protect Trixie, and you're arresting him?"

"He's a vagrant. I'm just holding him until I can get some positive ID on him and to be sure there are no warrants for his arrest."

"What about me?" Eddie said.

"You get a trip to the hospital to get that hand looked at, then you'll be our guest too."

"This is crazy," Jake complained.

The deputy shrugged. "In case you haven't noticed, the whole world has gone crazy."

THE SIGN OVER THE DOOR OF THE SMALL BUILDING READ: SHERIFF SUBSTATION BLINK, TEXAS. The building was white with a red tile roof and arches that marked off the porch area.

The drive from the restaurant to the substation had taken a short time. Henick made the journey in the back of a patrol car, his arms still bound behind him. The metal cuffs chewed at his wrists. He shifted his weight, twisting beneath the belt the deputy had placed across his lap.

The driver pulled the car around the building and parked near a blue, metal door. The driver slipped from behind the wheel and opened the door nearest Henick. He leaned in and released the lap belt.

"OK, slip on out here." His voice was firm but not unkind. The other deputy had taken the man called Eddie in another car and disappeared into the night.

Henick complied, swinging his legs through the opening, scooting along the seat until his feet were firm on the ground and then stood. For the first time, he noticed a brass tag over the man's right pocket: PARDEE.

"Pardee."

"That's my name." He placed a hand on Henick's elbow and led him from the car. They stopped at the blue door, and he removed a ring of keys from his leather belt. A yellow light shone from a bright lamp over the door. In the light, Pardee's brown hair seemed lighter, and his sun-darkened skin tinged gold.

Pardee swung open the door and, taking Henick by the arm again, led him over the threshold. Inside, rectangular lights illuminated pale green walls. To Henick's left were three areas marked off by metal bars. On his right were three metal doors with windows in them. He glanced in one of the rooms and saw only empty space.

"What is this place?"

"What's a matter? Never seen a jail before?"

"No. You keep people in the cages?"

Pardee chuckled. "That's the idea. We put the better-behaved folk behind the bars. Those that can't control themselves we put in the cells."

"Cells?"

"The rooms. Keeps them isolated and keeps them from spitting on the deputies and others."

"People spit on you?"

"It's been known to happen. They usually only do it once, if you catch my drift."

Henick thought he understood.

At the end of the hall was a wide room populated with several desks and a table with metal chairs around it. A tall and wide counter separated the room from a smaller space just inside the front door. Henick guessed that most people entered through that door.

They stopped at a desk. "Hang on a sec." Pardee stepped behind Henick. The metal band on his right wrist came loose, but the one on his left took an extra bite of his flesh. "Sit down."

Henick did, and Pardee snapped the loose end of the metal bindings to a metal ring attached to the side of the desk.

"That is unnecessary. I will not harm you."

Pardee dropped into a wood chair in front of the desk. The chair swiveled. "No doubt about that. Others have tried and regretted it. The cuffs stay on for now. It's procedure."

"Cuffs," Henick repeated.

"Yeah. Somehow I don't think handcuffs are new to you."

"I've never seen them before."

"If you say so." He turned his attention to a glowing device on the desk and placed his hands on a wide, boardlike instrument with buttons that bore the image of letters. He pressed the letters in sequence, and words appeared on the glowing box. "OK, name."

"Name what?"

"Your name, pal. Don't get cute with me."

"My name is Henick. What are you doing?"

Pardee pounded the buttons. "What's it look like I'm doing? I'm filling out an arrest form on the computer. Last name?"

Hearing the word *computer* unleashed information in his mind as if it had been held in a pitcher and just now poured out. "Jaredson. Henick Jaredson."

"Interesting last name. Interesting first name, for that matter."

"Jaredson means son of Jared."

"Ya think?" He shook his head. "I get all the wacky ones."

"Why am I here?" Henick studied Pardee's face.

"Because you were in a fight, because you were part of a disturbance, and most of all, because you have no identification. How about a driver's license number?"

"No."

"Social Security number? You have to have one of those."

"I don't."

Pardee swiveled to face Henick. "No DL and no Social Security number." He sighed. "How about a birth date? I know you have one of those."

"Yes, but…it is difficult to explain."

"Try."

Henick took a deep breath. "It would make no sense. The…context is different."

"The context? Were you born in this country?"

"No."

"Are you here legally?"

"I do not know. I am just here."

Pardee ran a hand across his eyes. "What country?"

Henick chuckled. "That too is difficult to explain."

"OK, pal, I'm growing weary of this game. The law requires that you identify yourself to a law enforcement officer."

"I have told you my name."

"Not enough. Not enough by a long shot. How about your address?"

"No address."

"That's it." Pardee sprung to his feet, his chair skidding behind him. He removed a small key from his belt and unlocked the cuff attached to the ring on the desk. "Stand up and turn around."

Henick did, and a moment later his hands were bound behind him again.

"This way."

"I have told you the truth."

Pardee shook his head. "I doubt that. Maybe some time in the jail will help your memory. At very least it will allow me to see if there are any wants or warrants out for you."

A dozen steps later, Pardee pushed Henick into one of the barred spaces and closed the door. "Let's see your hands."

Henick raised his hands.

"No, I mean put them next to the bars. I'm gonna take the cuffs off."

Henick turned and wiggled his fingers.

"Thank you," Henick said.

"If you want my thanks, then you had better get serious with the answers."

"I don't know what else to tell you."

"OK. When you have anything to say, just holler."

Pardee walked down the hall.

Gene Manford wanted to be home instead of stuck in his two-year-old, "inferno red" Dodge Charger. The Washington DC traffic had become sludge, a coagulation of cars, delivery vehicles, and limos. It was nearly ten, a mere two hours before midnight, and here he was stuck in traffic that should have cleared hours ago.

He had worked in DC long enough to know slow traffic was a way of life. Still, a man had the right to expect something better at this hour. Granted it was Friday, which meant partygoers were out and migrating from social gathering to bar to party. Manford preferred a quiet evening in his Virginia townhouse. Let the denizens of the dark have the streets. Give him a good book or television mystery, and he would be content.

The enormous black SUV in front of him moved five feet then stopped. It also blocked his view of what lay ahead, making the drive all the more frustrating. He had tried to pull into the lane to his left, but an unyielding line of cars hemmed him in. Despite running his turn indicator for ten minutes, not one driver offered to give him the space necessary to make the transition. *There's a reason DC isn't called the friendliest city on Earth.*

He turned on his radio and tuned to a local news station known for frequent traffic updates. He glanced at his watch. The station gave reports every ten minutes. He just missed one.

Taking a deep breath, Manford tried to relax. Fighting traffic was like fighting a young Michael Tyson—a guaranteed loss and a painful beating.

He ran a hand through his hair, an act that reminded him he needed a trim. He hated haircuts: sitting passively while some young woman wielded sharp scissors around his head and ears. Then there was the matter of the growing crop of gray hair. His locks still held the color of coal, but more and more of the gray strands appeared each month like weeds in a garden. Every time he sat in the stylist's chair, she asked, "So, shall we do something with that gray today? I have some excellent products." He always declined. Always. But maybe next time—

The radio announcer brought the bad news. An accident three miles ahead had brought traffic to a near standstill. He listened as the newscaster told of a truck versus sedan accident that left one dead. With a death, the amount of information the police needed to gather tripled. He'd be lucky if he made the three miles in less than an hour. Bedtime would come late tonight.

An advertisement about Sleep Comfort beds replaced the announcer. "Great, just what I need." He rubbed his eyes. The ad faded, and for a moment there was nothing but soft static. Dead air. Someone forgot to punch a button. Radio stations hated dead air. Silence meant that someone searching for the station could shoot too far down the dial, landing on the competition's frequency.

The soft static gave way to a voice. "Time grows short. Look for the one I send you. He walks among you." The static returned.

"What the—"

The newscaster's voice poured from the car's speakers. "Sorry about that, folks. We seem to have experienced a short interruption of our signal, but we're back in operation now—"

The announcer's voice faded, leaving the vague static behind.

"Man, these guys are having a worse day than me," Manford said to himself. Then...

"Time grows short. Look for the one I send you. He walks among you."

Something about the voice caught his attention. Manford had heard every conceivable type of broadcast. His love of all broadcast media pushed him to join the Federal Communications Commission within a year of graduating college. This voice sounded a tad too smooth, a smidgen too fine to be real. Computer generated? Perhaps, but no matter how sophisticated a speaking computer might be, it always came across as a machine attempting to sound human.

Manford's first impulse was to dismiss the whole thing, but he couldn't. Someone might be playing a trick at or with the radio station. And since he worked in the enforcement department of the FCC, it was his obligation to find out. After all, he wasn't going anywhere at the moment.

Removing the Bluetooth earpiece from his shirt pocket, he placed it in his ear and tapped the button. "Name dial."

"Say the name," a true electronic voice said.

"Information."

"Dialing information."

A short conversation later he could hear the phone at WINF ringing. He doubted anyone would answer the public line at this hour, but it merited a try. On the eighth ring he heard, "W-I-N-F radio, your source for information all day long. May I help you?" The man on the other end sounded winded, as if he had to run for the phone.

"Yes. My name is Gene Manford. I'm calling about the odd message on your station—"

"You and everyone else. The phones have gone nuts."

"I can imagine. I wanted to—"

"I hate to be rude, pal, but we're a skeleton crew at this hour. I got my hands full. If you'll call back in the morning—"

This time it was Manford's turn to interrupt. "I work in the enforcement department of the FCC."

A moment of silence passed between them, then Manford heard quiet swearing. "Yes, sir. What can I do for you?"

"Well, for starters, you can tell me who you are."

Another pause. Manford could imagine the man agonizing over the situation. The FCC didn't call every day.

"My name is Nathan Buckley. I'm the night engineer."

"OK, Mr. Buckley. Can you tell me what happened?"

"I wish. I don't have a clue. I've checked everything here, and everything is perfect. I know it didn't come from here. Maybe someone's stepping on us."

"The signal came across clear and strong. You're a pretty powerful station; it would take a strong transmitter to overpower your signal. You say you're getting lots of calls?"

"You bet. Every line has someone on it."

"Are the calls coming from one location?"

"I've fielded a dozen calls already, and they came from listeners scattered around our broadcast area. I guess that rules out some local pulling a prank."

"I wouldn't rule it out yet. Has this happened to your station before?"

"No…"

Manford heard another voice on the phone. Someone was taking to Buckley.

"I…can't…hang on." Buckley's voice turned hollow, and Manford guessed the man had pulled the phone away from his mouth. Still, he could hear the conversation on the other side.

"What other station?" Buckley asked.

The new talker said, "I was listening to some tunes and heard the same thing."

"You were listening to another station—"

"That's what I'm saying, dude. I like the oldies, so I tune in to an FM station while I work. I heard the same message at the same time."

"Mr. Buckley," Manford prompted.

"Yeah, I'm back."

"I overheard someone say the message played on a local FM. Did I hear that right?"

"Yeah. That was Ricky. He's our janitor; cleans up around here at night."

"How could he hear both your transmission and one from an FM station?"

"I dunno. I'm not his supervisor...wait. He wears a headset all the time. He must have had his radio tuned to the other station. Our broadcast plays throughout the building, especially during the night shift. We need to hear what's going on at all times."

Manford understood. He earned his way through college working at a radio station. It wasn't unusual to hear the broadcast in the halls and even the bathroom.

"Your station is part of a network, right?"

"Yes, the AirWaves Network. They have about a dozen stations on the East Coast."

"Do you have a directory of those stations?"

"Sure. Somewhere around here."

"Do me a favor. Call as many of the others as you can. See if they have had the same experience."

"Oh, man. I'm slammed here."

"It would be a big help."

"Look, I have no problem with the FCC, and I hope we haven't done anything wrong, but my hands are full. I can't be doing errands for you."

"OK. I understand. I shouldn't have asked."

Buckley calmed. "I'm not trying to be a pain, but there's only so much I can handle."

Manford tapped the button on his earpiece, ending the call. Ten minutes later, the traffic began to creep forward. Manford pushed his way into the right lane and took the first side street he found. Before long, he headed in the direction he had come—back to the FCC building.

9

THE METAL BARS IN THE CELL FELT COLD AGAINST HENICK'S
palms. After a few moments, he released the bars and returned
to the small, metal bed on the opposite wall. A thin pad cushioned
the flat surface and kept the cold of the metal from oozing into
his flesh. A dark green, neatly folded blanket rested to one side.
A toilet and metal sink occupied the space between the bed and
one of the three block walls that made up the rest of the room.
The cell had no window. The only light came from the glass tubes
running down the corridor on the other side of the bars.

Henick sighed. In the few hours he had been confined in the
room he had examined every corner and found nothing of interest.
Deputy Pardee had checked Henick's pockets and found nothing.

He felt confused, unable to understand why Pardee kept him
behind a locked door. He had done nothing wrong. True, Pardee
wanted identification and Henick had none, but holding a man
against his will for such an unimportant thing seemed…unjust.
After all, he had been truthful about his name and the events at
the restaurant.

Henick lay down on the bed and rested his head on the coarse
blanket. The ceiling offered nothing of interest. He thought of
Jake and Eleanor. They must be home by now. He thought of
Trixie, and the image of her frightened face came to mind.

The back door rattled. Henick rose and moved to the bars. The
sound of footsteps echoed through the corridor. Pardee appeared
just as the backdoor swung open.

"I about gave up on you, Stu."

Pardee's partner stepped through the opening, pulling Eddie along by the arm.

"The ER is hopping tonight. Took longer to patch Eddie's hand up than I expected."

"That was three hours ago, Stu. We're supposed to have priority with prisoners."

Stu shook his head. "Not when there's been a heart attack. Weren't nothing to do but wait."

Pardee nodded and moved to the cell next to Henick's and opened the door. He faced Eddie. "How's the hand, boy?"

"It hurts, not that you care any."

"If I did care, would it matter?"

"No."

"I didn't think so. Step on in. You're our guest tonight. You can sleep off what's left of your drunk."

"I can do that at home."

Pardee chuckled. "Yeah, but where would the lesson be in that? Get in."

As Stu led Eddie past Henick's cell, Henick could see a white casing surrounding the young man's hand and wrist. Metal cuffs were around the other wrist and strung through his belt, tying the undamaged hand behind his back.

Stu led Eddie into the cell. The block wall separating the two rooms kept Henick from seeing what happened. He listened.

"What'd the doc say?" Pardee asked.

Stu answered, "He said ol' Eddie here busted up his hand real good. Broke a couple of knuckles and three bones. He'll be wearing that cast for the better part of two months. He might even have to have surgery to get everything right again."

"See what too much booze and too much anger gets ya, Eddie?"

"Save the lecture, pig."

Pardee's voice chilled. "I see he hasn't learned any manners yet. He give you any trouble?"

"Nope. Didn't get mouthy until we got here."

"It's him," Eddie snapped. "The freak in the other cell."

"I'm a pig and he's a freak, is that it, Eddie?"

"You really want to know what you are? 'Cuz I'll tell you. I'll tell you plain and simple."

"Shut up, boy," Stu said. "Lean against the wall."

"You lean against the—Ow!"

"Listen, son," Stu said. "A simple sharp twist of the cuffs and I can break your other wrist. You wanna walk around with both hands in a cast?"

"OK, OK."

"I'd listen to him, son," Pardee said. "Trifling with him would be a mistake."

"OK, just ease up."

A few moments later, Pardee and Stu stood outside the cell. Stu held the cuffs and Eddie's belt. Pardee closed the door.

"Sleep it off, Eddie." Stu closed up the cuffs and placed them in a leather holder on his wide, black belt. "Be good, and you might get to go home in the morning."

Eddie didn't respond.

Stu stepped to Henick. "What about him?"

Pardee joined him. "He's been no trouble. Gave me his name, but I can't find any record of him anywhere. No ID. No address. No nuthin'."

"Wants and warrants?"

"Not on the name he gave. That's about as far as I can go. I'll let the day crew fingerprint him. Maybe they can get a hit off of AFIS."

"AFIS?" Henick said.

Pardee said, "Automated Fingerprint Identification System. If you've ever been fingerprinted, the system will identify you."

"I have never been fingerprinted."

"Not even for a driver's license?"

"I do not drive."

"A man your age doesn't drive?" Stu looked puzzled. "You got some kinda medical condition or something?"

"No, I am well."

"So you're what…forty or so and you don't drive. Some judge took away your license?"

"Maybe a little older. I have never met a judge."

Pardee frowned. "He wouldn't tell me his age either. I can't tell if he's giving me the runaround or is just what he seems."

"Beats me." Stu looked down the hall. "Coffee fresh?"

"I made a pot about twenty minutes ago."

"I need a cup before hitting the streets again. I assume you want me out there."

"Of course. I'll keep an eye on the guests."

The two moved down the hall to the office area where Henick had been first led. Henick returned to the bed and sat.

Ten minutes crawled by when Eddie spoke. "So how did you do it? How did you know?"

Henick rose and walked to the barred partition. He could not see Eddie. "How did I know what?"

"About me and my mother. How could you know her words? How could you know how I…felt?"

"You were hurting. I could see that."

"But you knew her very words. I ain't ever seen you before. If you hung around with her I'd know it. Wait. Church. That's it, right? You musta gone to the same church."

"I have never been to your mother's church. Before now, I have never been in this village."

"Village? You mean town, don't ya? Blink ain't much, but it's a shade or two better than a village."

"I meant no offense."

Eddie laughed. Even though several feet separated them, Henick could smell the pungent odor he first experienced at the restaurant. "You are a piece of work, man. A real piece of work."

"Thank you…I think."

"It wasn't a compliment. Now, how about it. Tell me the truth. How do you know about my mother and what she said to me?"

"I just know. I am unable to tell you how. I'm still learning."

"What do you mean, learning?"

Henick took hold of the bars. "This place is strange to me. The language feels odd in my mouth, yet I know it well. Some things remain ill defined, like trying to recognize an animal through a thick fog. The fog is thinning."

"What ya do, beam down from some alien spaceship?"

"No. I have never seen a spaceship."

"You talk like a man from a different world."

Henick paused. "I suppose that is to be expected."

"So you're not going to tell me how you knew my mom's exact words."

"I cannot. I needed the words, and they were there."

"What about what you did to me? Touching my chest. It was like you were reading my mind, reading all about my mom and..."

"Father? He treated you and your mother badly."

"That's one way of putting it." Eddie's voice sounded weak. "It don't matter now, anyway. A man can't change his past."

"But he can change his future."

"Oh man, you ain't gonna preach at me, are you? I hate that. I hated it when my mother did it, so I'm not going to listen to the likes of you."

"Does it hurt?"

"Losing my mother? I guess. Ain't nothing I can do about it. People die all the time."

"I meant your hand. Does it hurt?"

"They gave me something for the pain at the hospital, but it throbs pretty good. The pain meds will wear off soon, then I suppose I'm gonna have a real problem."

Henick moved close to the block wall that separated them,

pushed his arm through the bars, and reached around the end of the wall. "Can you see my hand?"

"Yeah. Sure. What are you doing?" He sounded nervous.

"Touch it."

"Why?"

"You must learn to trust."

"Trusting people has never worked out for me."

Henick persisted. "Please. Touch my hand." He felt the light stroke of cool, damp flesh. "No. Use the hand that is hurt."

Eddie grunted. "I can't. The cast won't fit through the bars."

Pushing himself against the bars as much as possible, Henick stretched until it felt as if his joints would separate. His fingers felt the cold metal of the bars of Eddie's cell. He reached his limit. The tips of his fingers hung in the space between the bars. "Now."

"I don't know, man, this is weird."

"Do it." The strain forced droplets of sweat to the surface of his face. "Now. Please."

A touch. Just two fingers. Unlike the first touch of moist, cool flesh, these fingers felt warm and puffy. Henick didn't need to see to know that Eddie had laid the fingers of his damaged hand on the tips of Henick's skin.

Henick closed his eyes. A bolt of electricity fired in his mind and sparkles of light coruscated in his eyes.

"What...your hand—Ah!"

Eddie's touch disappeared, and Henick withdrew his arm.

"That hurt. What did you do to me?"

"Yes. It hurt. I must rest."

"I didn't mean you; I meant me. What did you do to my hand?"

"Rest. Must...rest."

Henick stumbled to the bunk. The room spun. The lights dimmed.

Blackness.

I'M TELLING YOU, IT REALLY HAPPENED. I SAW IT WITH MY own two eyes." Ray Tickner did his best not to sound desperate. He had no desire to give these guys any more ammunition.

"Hey, Ray, it isn't that we don't believe you, it's just that…we don't believe you." Ted Pulaski's words brought laughter from Jimmy Lender. Ted's thin frame earned him the nickname "The Stick," although no one called him that to his face. His pale skin looked two shades whiter in the dim light of the bar. He looked underfed and anemic in every way, but his mind carried a wit sharp enough to cut the hubris from any man.

"I'm not making this up, guys." Ray lifted his Samuel Adams to his lips and sucked down the last of the beer.

"Of course you are," Jimmy said. "We're film students. We live in a fantasy world. It's what we do. Your creative mind just got the best of you." Jimmy had never topped five-six, but he never let his short stature damage his ego. He had the look of a movie star and often reminded people that Tom Cruise is short.

Ray sighed. "Guys, I came here for a little support."

"I came for the beer and chips," Ted said.

Margarite's Cantina attracted more UCLA students than any other restaurant bar. A bowl of freshly fried tortilla chips rested in the middle of the tall table. A deep bowl of thick, rich, red salsa kept it company.

"I shouldn't have told you. I should have known you'd razz me about it."

"Of course we'd razz you about it." Ted ran a finger through the condensation on his beer bottle. "You're no better. If I fell over dead right now, you'd joke about how stupid I looked when my head bounced off the floor."

"That's because you always look stupid."

Ted laughed. "Now there's the Ray we all know and love."

"Guys, I'm serious. You know I've seen *Danger's Street* a dozen times. I know every scene in the movie, and what I saw tonight didn't belong. You can ask Jocelyn if you want. She saw it too."

"I've got a few questions I'd like to ask Jocelyn." Jimmy elbowed Ted, who winced at the jab.

"The whole student body wants to ask her—"

"Knock it off." Ray spoke louder than he intended. Several nearby patrons turned in his direction.

"Ease up, man." Ted's words were low but firm. "You see, that's the problem, isn't it? You're on a date with the hottest babe on campus, and you're watching a movie you can quote verbatim instead of watching her. I know where my eyes would be."

"I don't believe this. It's like talking to a couple of junior high students. Can't you give me a break?"

"OK, Ray," Ted began, "let me see if I have this. You saw Thom Blake step out of character, address the camera, and deliver some cryptic line about a messenger."

"Right."

"Then he steps back into character and finishes the movie?"

"Yes."

"And Jocelyn saw this?" Jimmy said.

"Yes, I already told you that. Everyone in the theater saw it. I have the script; I know that there is no such scene."

"How did the audience respond?" Ted asked.

"They didn't. They just sat there as confused as me."

Ted looked at Jimmy. "You're the special effects guy, Jimmy. You think someone could have pulled off a prank like that?"

"Probably, but it would be a huge prank. A good tech can

computer generate actors. They've been doing it for years. In *Titanic* they used CG to create people falling into the water. That was what—1997? *Jurassic Park* had a ton of CG work. They even pasted the face of one of the actresses on a stunt double who accidentally looked into the camera. Saved reshooting the scene. Of course, Gollum in *Lord of the Rings—The Two Towers* is completely computer generated."

"So it can be done," Ted pressed.

"Well, yeah, of course, but it would be a lot of work for a gag." Jimmy thought for a moment. "You see, CGI films render in at 1.4 to 6 megapixels. It takes about three hours per frame and goes up by a factor of ten if the scene is complex or heavily detailed. The software comes at a pretty hefty price. If it's a gag, then somebody had more time and money than common sense."

"That's never stopped practical jokes." Ted turned to Ray. "There ya go. It was probably a gag."

Ray rubbed his eyes. It had been a long day, and the clock had already passed midnight. "So someone swiped a master of the film, inserted a CGI scene, made a print, and snuck it into the theater so that it could be played. Not even the CIA could do that. Besides…"

"Besides what?" Ted said.

"I went back. I took Jocelyn home and then returned to the theater. I had to see if the same thing happened."

"Did it?" Jimmy asked.

"No. It wasn't there this time."

Ted said, "That means nothing. Once they knew someone had fiddled with their film, they would swap it out for another copy. You know, they often play the same movie with slightly different starting times. That requires a separate copy." He slapped Ray on the shoulder. "Let it go, man. It's not like a war started. I'll buy another round." He waved at the waitress, then made a circle motion over the table.

"Not for me," Ray said. "I've had enough of this day."

"Come on, Ray. Have one more. Technically, it's Saturday. No classes today, buddy."

Ray couldn't think of a response, so he just nodded. "Something is happening, guys. I can feel it."

"What you feel is the beer."

Jimmy and Ted laughed.

Ray didn't feel the humor. "I need to show you guys something."

KATHERINE ROONEY LAY ON HER BACK, STARING AT THE ceiling. In her lightless bedroom she couldn't see the flat surface overhead, but she gazed at it nonetheless. The bedside alarm clock showed 12:22 in green LED numerals. She had gone to bed at eleven but had yet to find sleep.

She closed her eyes and began the ironic ritual of forcing herself to relax. She tried to will the muscles in her legs and back to surrender. Using visualizations she had practiced over the years, she imagined herself reclined on an isolated beach with gentle waves caressing white sand. She called to mind the smells, the gentle warmth of the sun, the silence only broken by the lullaby of the sea.

Still she lay awake. Adrenaline, she told herself for the thirteenth time since crawling beneath the covers, adrenaline from her encounter with the drunk at the restaurant. That had to be it. But each time she closed her eyes she saw Lucy and heard the words about the coming messenger. The words upset her more than the restaurant confrontation, and she didn't know why. It made no sense.

Katherine kicked off the bed covers, sat up, and draped her legs over the edge of the bed. She hated fighting sleep. She never won.

She pulled on slippers and donned her terry cloth robe. The apartment felt cold, and she considered turning up the heat. Instead, she went into the living room, pulled a lap blanket across her legs, and opened the Sue Grafton novel she had started on Monday. Like sleep, reading wouldn't come.

Snatching the television remote, she turned on the set. Nothing caught her attention. Jay Leno still had a few minutes left on his show but not much. A band she never heard of was playing. Katherine seldom watched the show, but she knew that he ended each episode with a band.

Once Leno had finished for the night, Katherine channel-surfed until she came across a program promising fast wealth by working from home, selling goods over the Internet. "I should be able to sleep through this."

She pulled the blanket to her waist, held the novel like a child held a teddy bear, and snuggled in.

She tried to keep her eyes closed, but every few moments her lids would part and she would watch testimonials of housewives who made an extra $100,000 in cash working part-time. She hung on every word, not because of the promise she doubted could be true, but because…

…it might happen again.

Willie Lennox pretended to be asleep when his wife entered their bedroom. The bedside clock showed 2:15. He listened as she moved around the room like a cat searching for a way to annoy its owner. They had been married so long he knew everything she was doing without seeing her do it.

Two slight thumps—she had removed her shoes. A slight rustling sound—blouse and skirt removed and set on a dressing chair. The squeak of wood against wood. Mary-Martha sat on the chair to finish removing her control-top panty hose. A few moments later she slipped into bed and pulled the covers over her.

"The books must have been really out of whack."

"I thought you were asleep."

"No. Just lying here waiting for you."

"I decided to do a few interviews after we closed the books."

He rolled on his back. "Interviews? After midnight?"

"These were Internet interviews. You know, they send an e-mail filled with questions and I answer them. I had three to do. Sent them off then came right home."

She smelled of fresh perfume. "I see."

"OK, what's eating you?" Her tone darkened.

"Nothing. It's just…we're spending more and more time apart. You're working late more and more, and then there are all those trips out of town."

"I'm sorry. Time has been a rare commodity of late. Things will smooth out and everything else will be back to normal."

"Were you alone?"

"What?"

"I asked if you were—"

"I know what you asked." She pushed herself into a sitting position. "I was alone in my office. The two security guards were there, but they never came into my office. What are you suggesting?"

"I'm not suggesting anything." Willie rolled onto his side, his back facing Mary-Martha. "I just wanted to make sure you were safe. I don't like you being alone this late at night. Too many weirdos."

"Many people think I'm the weirdo."

He heard a smile in her voice. "Not to me."

She lay down and wiggled close to him, then rested an arm on his shoulder and fingered his hair. He could feel her smooth warm skin against his own. "You have nothing to worry about, baby. I'm yours now and always. I know my work demands a lot of you, but it will all pay off. I can feel it. Something good is going to come our way, and Sanctuary will be a reality beyond what we or anyone can imagine."

"I'm tired of eating alone."

"It won't be much longer, sweetheart. We're almost at the tipping point, and then I will be able to hire more help to do some of the things I have to do. I'll just focus on the general leadership and the television and radio broadcasts. You'll see. Things will be better than ever."

"I hope you're right."

"You just have to believe in me, baby. That's all. You do believe in me, don't you? Believe in me and the work I do?"

He had to force the words from his mouth. "Of course."

W HEN DEPUTY PARDEE APPEARED BEFORE HENICK'S cell, Henick stood and stepped forward. "I'm springing you, but I have a few conditions."

"Conditions?"

"I hung around to see if your fingerprints rang any bells in the AFIS system. I should have been home two hours ago. It didn't. The best I can tell, you don't exist. I can hold you for a while longer and charge you with vagrancy, but I can't see any sense in that. Mostly, I just want to put an end to this shift."

He inserted a thick metal key into the cell's lock and turned it. With a sharp pull, Pardee pulled the door open. "I'd tell you to get your things, but you don't have any."

"You said you had conditions." Henick stepped from the cell.

"Jake and Eleanor are here. I called them. I can't release you onto the street with no ID, no money, or no home, so I asked them to pick you up. They came to your defense when I arrested you."

"They are kind."

"They're good people, and that leads me to another condition. If you hurt them in any way, if you steal from them, if you even raise your voice, I will hunt you down like a rabid dog. The one thing you never want to do is tick me off. You got that?"

"Yes. I would never do them harm."

"See that you don't. Where they take you or what you do once you drive off the premises is no concern of mine unless you start causing trouble." He paused then. "There's one more thing.

You have the right to press charges against Eddie for assault and battery. Of course, if you do, you'll need to hang around for court. I doubt the county prosecutor will want to do much with it since no real harm was done. So what do you think?"

"Think?"

"Do you want to press charges against Eddie, or do you want to forget the whole thing?"

"If I…press charges—"

"We keep him a little longer, bail will be set, and if he can post it, we let him go. At some point, you two go to court. If you refuse your right to bring charges, then I let him loose."

"I wish him no harm."

"OK then. Jake and Eleanor are in the lobby." He started down the corridor. "I'll walk you—" He stopped in front of Eddie's cell. Henick stood by him. Chunks of plaster and gauze littered the floor. Eddie sat on his bed holding his right wrist in his left hand. "Eddie, what have you done?"

"I removed my cast."

"You idiot. Your hand is busted up three ways to Sunday, and you think it's a good idea to remove your cast."

"That's the thing, Deputy. It ain't busted up no more. Look at it." He held out his hand.

Pardee shouted down the hall. "Hey, Chet, got a sec?"

A round, uniformed man appeared at the end of the hall. "Yup. What's up?" He started down the hall.

"Eddie here thought he'd be smart and take the cast off his busted hand."

"Don't sound all that smart to me," Chet said. "How did you get it off, son?"

"I rubbed it against the rail of the bed. It's not very sharp, but I managed to cut a groove in the plaster. I just pulled it apart with my fingers."

"I've seen a lot of things, boy, but you take the cake." Pardee inserted a key into the lock. "I'm comin' in, Eddie, and I don't want trouble from you. If you're thinking of trying something, then you should know that I'll plant your head in the concrete. Are we clear?"

"You'll get no trouble from me, Deputy."

Pardee opened the door and Chet followed him in. Henick remained on the other side of the bars.

"We're gonna have to take you back to the hospital. I'm not giving you any cause to sue us for lack of medical care." He took Eddie's hand. Henick saw him push on the skin. Eddie didn't move. "It doesn't look broken."

"It's not," Eddie said. "It was, but it sure ain't broken now."

"How can that be?"

"Jake and Eleanor are waiting for me," Henick said.

"Yeah, yeah, go ahead." Pardee looked stunned.

Before Henick started down the hall, he made eye contact with Eddie...and shrugged.

Gene Manford had gone home at two that morning, slept, rose at eight, showered and shaved, then made coffee. At ten past nine, he held a steaming cup of coffee in one hand and rubbed his still weary eyes with the other. He crossed his Virginia townhouse to his home office and sat at his desk. The flip of a switch brought his computer to life. He sipped his coffee while waiting for the HP to boot and wondered if last night had really happened. He decided that he might be sleepy, but he wasn't insane. The voice came over the radio and he heard it, and the night engineer at the radio station heard it too.

Hours swept by as he did his best to contact employees of other stations to see if they had experienced the same unexpected insertion. At that hour, few stations answered, but those that did confessed to experiencing the enigma. No one had any idea how it happened.

Manford set his coffee down and started his e-mail program.

Eleven e-mails awaited his attention, with sixteen more in his junk mailbox. He deleted the latter with a couple of clicks of the mouse. Of the eleven legitimate e-mails, only one interested him—a missive he sent himself from the office.

He opened it and saw the notes he had made from the telephone calls. The notes included the name of the station, its location, its owner, its wattage, and its basic format. Then he opened Google Earth and plotted each station's location. Yellow pin icons marked the locations of each radio station. Thirty minutes later he had a visual picture that made no sense.

Most stations created their own content, playing music or broadcasting talk shows. But often, material originated elsewhere that local stations broadcast. Syndication allowed a program to be played over affiliate stations. Shows like Rick Dees' *Weekly Top 40*, *The Rush Limbaugh Show*, and *Coast to Coast AM With George Noory* each originated in one studio but were broadcast nationally. It was not unusual to hear a music program or talk show in San Francisco that originated in Dallas. Most listeners never knew the difference.

If the voice with the strange message had played on just one local radio station and no others, then Manford would assume someone couldn't resist playing a gag, but such wasn't the case. The message went out over several stations at the same time. For all he knew, it went out over every station in the DC area. That remained to be confirmed.

He studied the satellite map. The few people he could find to speak to last night represented stations broadcasting syndicated programs and original content. Since multiple stations were involved, Manford doubted a prankster could set up a situation in which stations unwittingly broadcast the message. The syndication factor proved that. Those programs came from outside the DC area.

If someone didn't set up an "inside" job, then the signal must have come from a pirate station, an illegal station that broadcast without license. It would have to be a powerful....No that couldn't be it. The station would have to broadcast on all the frequencies of the affected stations, both AM and FM.

So what was left? A conspiracy? Manford liked a good conspiracy theory as much as the next guy, but he couldn't fathom why anyone would go through so much trouble to deliver a fifteen-second message that made no sense and had no context.

The phone on his desk rang. He seldom received calls at home. A lifelong bachelor, he mostly used his phone to order pizza.

"Hello?"

"Gene, Alec Casey here. Sorry to bother you on a Saturday morning."

"No problem." Manford couldn't remember the last time the director of the Federal Communications Commission called him at home. "Did I leave the lights on last night?"

"What? I don't know. What were you doing in the office last night?"

"I heard something strange on the radio and thought I'd—"

"You too? I've been getting calls from congressmen and senators. Seems some of them heard an unauthorized broadcast and are screaming for answers. The only problem is—"

"They heard the same thing on different stations."

"How did you know that?"

"I heard the same thing. That's why I went back to the office." Manford explained what little he had learned.

"And what do you conclude from all of this?"

Manford chuckled. "I can't conclude anything. I'm going to make some more calls and see if I can get more information. I just can't understand how someone can step on a broadcast with such clarity and do so across spectrums."

"Well, find out what you can. If Homeland Security gets involved, we'll be doing paperwork for the rest of our lives."

"A terrorist attack?"

"Not every attack needs to end with something blowing up. If a

nation or terrorist group proved they could disrupt radio communications at will, then we'd have a real problem. This country runs
on electronic communications. Imagine losing radio, television,
Internet, and cell phones. What if someone found a way to broadcast their propaganda by every electronic means? We wouldn't be
having this conversation. We'd be hearing who knows what."

"I don't think that's possible."

"Neither do I, but we have some pretty paranoid people on
Capitol Hill, and sometimes they make sense. I'm afraid I'm going
to have to ask you to work this weekend. Did you have plans?"

"College football, that's it."

"That's it? You need a woman, Gene. There's more to life than
work and college football."

"I'm happy."

"Sure you are."

13

"YOU HAVE GOT TO BE KIDDING." PARDEE STOOD NEXT TO Patrick Anderson, MD. Both stared at X-ray films clipped to a wall-mounted light box.

"I'm not known for my scintillating humor."

Anderson stood tall, bald, and lanky. When he spoke, the words moved across his lips like December molasses. Every time Pardee dealt with him, he had to fight the urge to slap the man on the back of the head to get the sentences to emerge faster.

"I won't argue with that, Doc, but I might debate your findings." Pardee rubbed his eyes. He had finished his graveyard shift hours ago, yet he still wore his uniform. More than one person had accused him of having the emotional detachment of a bulldog.

"Argue all you want. I'm just telling you the facts."

"I cuffed Eddie myself. I saw his hand, and it was a mess, and when Deputy Altman brought him to the jail from the ER, he told me you guys said he busted knuckles and other hand bones."

"Not 'you guys.' I didn't come on duty until the morning."

"So you're saying the other doc messed up?"

Anderson shook his head. "I said nothing of the kind. Dr. Lyman is punctilious in his work."

Pardee gazed at Anderson.

"Punctilious...detailed, meticulous. If he put a cast on the patient, then the patient needed it."

Frustration percolated in Pardee. "Look, Doc, I'm not a physician, but even I can tell there is a big difference between this

X-ray," he tapped the black and white film on the left, "and this one." He pointed to the film on the right. "Even I can tell the first one shows fractures."

"It does indeed."

"And that is the X-ray taken last night?"

"Yes. You can see the date on it."

"Then how does Eddie's hand go from hamburger to healthy overnight?"

"I don't know. It's a miracle."

"I thought guys like you didn't believe in miracles." Pardee struggled to keep his voice low.

"I don't."

"Then how do you explain it?"

Anderson shrugged. "I can't. It is what it is." He turned from the light box and stepped to Eddie, who sat on the edge of an ER bed. "Your hand looks good to me. Are you having any pain?"

"No, sir. It feels great."

"Glad to hear it. Well, there's nothing more I can do here, and I have other patients to see." He started to walk away.

"Wait," Pardee snapped. "That's it? You just shrug and walk away?"

"What would you have me do?"

"You could...could...I don't know."

Anderson smiled. "Enjoy your weekend, Deputy." Anderson crossed the ER to the bed of an elderly woman with a cut on her forehead.

"What now, Deputy? Remember, no one has pressed any charges."

"Yeah, I remember, but I may lock you up anyway."

"For what?" Eddie's face flushed.

"For giving an officer of the law a headache during the course of his duty."

"I don't think there's a law against that."

"There ought to be. Come on, I'll give you a lift home."

"Can I ride in front?"

"Don't press your luck, son."

"Sure we can't change your mind?" Jake said as they passed the LEAVING BLINK—COME BACK SOON sign. "You're welcome to stay with us for a few days."

Jake was behind the wheel of his 1996 Toyota Camry. Eleanor sat in the back, Henick in the front passenger seat. Jake had told Henick that the car would be more comfortable than riding in the back of the pick up. "Besides, you can't stand up in the car like you did in the truck."

"You are kind, but I must say no."

"But why?" Eleanor asked. "Where are you going?"

Henick shrugged. "I am going to the next place."

"Which is…?

"The next place." Henick said with a slim smile.

"The next place is Oak Grove. It's a good bit bigger than Blink, but not nearly so homey." Jake drove slowly as if he didn't want the trip to end.

Eleanor asked, "What will you do there?"

"I will know when I get there." Henick looked out the passenger window. Miles of flat land and native shrubs created a bleak vista, yet he found a beauty in it.

"I worry about you, Henick." Eleanor said from the backseat.

"Worry? Why?"

"May I be honest?"

Jake piped up. "Eleanor, a man has a right to mind his own business. I'm sure Henick knows what he's doing."

"Please let her speak. A shared concern becomes half of a burden." Henick turned in his seat. "What worries you?"

"It's just that…you seem so lost, like you're in a strange country and can't find your way home. You have no money and only the clothes on your back. You're so…alone."

Henick saw tears in her eyes.

"You have known me such a short time, and yet you are concerned about my well-being." He paused. "Thank you. I will be fine. God provides. He always provides."

Silence.

"Look, Henick, my wife is a bit of a busybody, but she's right about most things. I can drop you off at the next town like you ask, but then what? Are you just going to continue walking west? Where will you sleep? How will you eat?"

"I do not know, but God does."

"OK, look, I'm just as religious as the next guy, but we need to have some common sense too. You can't go wandering around with no money or identification. You'll end up in jail, and the next deputy might not be so kind."

"Jail was good."

"What?" Jake almost drove off the side of the road. "Have you lost your mind? They locked you up when you done nuthin' wrong. That's unfair no matter how you slice it."

"I had a bed and warmth. God provided."

Jake snapped his head around. "Wait a sec; just wait a second. Are you blaming God for puttin' you in jail? I don't think I'd blame the Almighty for such a thing."

"I blame Him for nothing. I was warm and safe."

"But you weren't free, Henick," Eleanor said.

"I am free now."

"I give up," Jake said. "You are one weird cowboy, Henick. Are you sure your mother didn't drop you on your head when you was young?"

"Jake!"

"OK, Eleanor, OK. I shouldn't say such things. I know. I'm just flabbergasted."

"I suppose that's one word for it."

They made the rest of the drive to Oak Grove in silence. Henick continued to gaze at the passing scenery, Jake fidgeted in his seat as if it had been filled with rocks, and Eleanor fixed her eyes on the handkerchief she held.

"You have any place in mind?"

"I don't understand." Henick turned his sight upon Jake.

"Is there a particular place you want me to drop you?"

"Anywhere is fine."

Oak Grove seemed twice as large as Blink. There were more cars on the road, more people on the walkways. Overhead a blue sky graced with small clouds looked down upon them. The morning air had warmed, and the trees wore their best fall colors.

Jake pulled into an open parking spot in front of a Denny's restaurant. "How's this?"

"This will be fine," Henick said and reached for the door.

"Hang on a sec, pal." Jake touched his arm. "Listen, I don't feel good just dropping you off and driving away." He turned to his wife. "Eleanor."

Henick followed his gaze. Eleanor opened a small handbag and pulled several green slips of paper from it. She handed them to Jake.

"Um, this ain't much, but it's all we can spare." He extended his hand. "Here's five hundred. That's a lot for an old rancher like me, but we want you to have it."

"This is money?"

"Yes, Henick, it's money. You have enough there to buy meals and even get a few nights in a decent hotel."

"I do not need money."

"Don't argue with me, son. You need money. Everybody needs money. Take it. Make the most of it."

"You have already shown me such kindness. You two took me to Charlie's Texas Steakhouse to eat and took me to your home from the jail."

"That was nuthin'," Jake said.

"You also fed me today."

"All you ate was bread and fruit," Eleanor said.

"I enjoyed it very much. I should not take your money."

"You will take it." Jake's voice became stern. "I know it is hard for a man to take money from another man, but sometimes pride ain't all it's cracked up to be. Just take it. It will help."

"Yes, Henick, please," Eleanor pleaded. "Just put it in your pocket."

"If it will make you happy."

"It helps," Eleanor said. "I just wish we could see you again."

"You will," Henick said, then he paused. "Your son will be fine, and you will see him soon. He's coming home."

Eleanor gasped and Jake's face paled.

Jake almost choked on his words. "We never told you about our son. How do you know about him? Did Pardee say something?"

"Pardee did not speak of your son."

"Then how…"

"He loves you. He misses you." Henick slipped from the car and closed the door. Jake lowered the window.

"How can you know?"

Henick leaned in the opening. "Watch for the messages. Then comes the Messenger."

He straightened and walked away, but not before hearing Jake say, "He's as nutty as a can of cashews."

Tears laced his voice.

I NEED TO SPEAK TO HIM, MR. CLAYTON. IT'S IMPOR-
tant."

Jake studied Eddie but refused to ask the young man in. "I'm
afraid you come a long way for nuthin', boy. He ain't here." Eleanor
stepped by Jake's side.

"Do you know where he went?"

Jake said nothing.

"Come on, Mr. Clayton. I'm not out to harm him." Eddie
looked worn and in need of a long night of sleep. He also looked
desperate.

"Last time I saw you with him you were trying to take off his
head."

"I was drunk then. I'm cold sober now. He... he did something
for me. I feel like I should be with him."

"What'd he do?"

Eddie lowered his head and stared at the worn boards that
formed the floor of the front porch of the ranch home. "It doesn't
matter. I just need to see him."

"Let me see if I got this right. You come knockin' on my door,
wanting information, but you don't want to cut loose with a little
info of your own."

"He healed my hand." Eddie blurted the words. "I know you
won't believe me, but you can ask Deputy Pardee. He took me
back to the hospital this morning to get it checked. The doc there
will tell you the same thing."

"He healed your hand?" Jake didn't bother to mask his skepticism.

"I know it sounds like a load of...look." He held out his hand. "You were there. You saw me hit the wall. I was swinging for all I'm worth. I felt the knuckles break, Mr. Clayton. They popped like dry twigs. Even drunk, it hurt as bad as anything I've ever felt. Well, almost anything."

"I believe him, Jake."

"Eleanor, you believe everyone. For all we know, Eddie here is fixin' to track Henick down and do what he couldn't do last night."

"Jake." Eleanor's word carried an edge with it. Jake recognized the tone.

"Woman, let me handle this. Guys like Eddie don't change overnight."

"You did." Eleanor held her ground.

"What are you going on about, woman?" Jake snapped.

"When I first met you, you were maybe a year younger than Eddie here and just as cantankerous. Daddy swore he'd fill you with birdshot if you ever came by the house."

Jake chuckled. "Yeah, I had him a little on edge."

"A little. I had to sneak out to see you. I took a lot of grief for you during those early weeks. Daddy came around because *you* came around. Maybe it's time you passed on the favor."

Jake turned to Eddie. "I have your word you mean the man no harm?"

Eddie straightened. "Yes, sir. You have my word."

Jake narrowed his eyes as if it would allow him to read Eddie's mind. "I took him to Oak Grove this morning."

"What? Why would you do that?"

"Because he wanted me to."

Eddie flushed, and for a moment, Jake thought he would keel over. "How could you let him go?"

"Last I looked, son, he was a grown man. He doesn't need my permission for anything."

"How long ago?"

"We been home about six hours. Didn't pay attention to the clock when we left."

"Where did you drop him off?" Eddie seemed lost.

"There's a Denny's off the main road, about three miles into town."

"You just left him on the street?"

"Listen, son, we found him on the street. Besides, that's what he wanted."

Eddie looked at his '80s-something black Chevy pickup. Jake could tell he was doing some hard thinking. "You goin' up to Oak Grove?"

"Yes…if I can get enough gas."

"Hang on." Jake reached to his back pocket and removed a leather wallet that had seen ten years of sitting. He pulled two twenties from the bill pouch. "Here. These days that won't fill up most cars, but it'll get you close."

"I can't take your money, Mr. Clayton."

"Why not? Eleanor takes it all the time."

For the first time in Jake's memory, Eddie laughed. "I'll find a way to pay you back."

"I got a fence that needs some attention. A couple of hours will do."

"But…"

"Not now, boy. Later. Whenever you get the time."

"You're on, Mr. Clayton." He started to leave, then stopped. "Were you really like me at my age?"

"Let's just keep that between us, shall we? I know you're thinking, 'Man, this is what I have to look forward to?'"

Eddie grinned. "If I turned out like you, then I won't have wasted my life."

He walked away.

Jake's eyes began to burn.

GABRIEL HOAGLAND HAD SATURDAYS OFF. IT WAS THE only day he was guaranteed not to be interrupted. As Mary-Martha Celestine's head of security, he spent his days and nights accompanying her wherever she wished to go. Over the last few years her popularity had grown such that she was on the road, speaking several times each month. He had no doubts that soon she'd be traveling overseas. That would present new challenges.

With his sports bag slung over one shoulder, Hoagland entered the Barney's Community Gym and Boxing School, found an empty corner, and began stretching his muscles.

Barney's sat in the darker part of Albuquerque, New Mexico, and despite its billing as a "community gym," most people in the community avoided it. The place had been built in the fifties and had never changed. A regulation boxing ring sat in the center of the large space. The ring was the original and barely maintained. The ropes that marked its boundaries drooped as if the ring had shrunk over the decades. Along the long eastern wall were weight-lifting stations. Not fancy, modern equipment with elastic bands and intricate pulley systems—just barbells and dumbbells.

Near one wall hung heavy bags patched with duct tape and leather speed bags that had endured countless punches.

The place reeked, smelling of old cigarette and cigar smoke, beer, and sweat. An air conditioner that had been little more than a glorified fan for the last year shoved the air around, its fan clanking a complaint about failing bearings.

Hoagland spent ten minutes stretching, then worked up a good sheen of sweat with a jump rope. He moved to the speed bag and worked on his rhythm and reflexes. He planned time on the heavy bag and then on to the double end bag.

"Hey, you Hoagland?"

The question pulled Hoagland out of the zone. He stopped his rhythmic pounding of the speed bag and faced the squat, bald-headed man to his left. The man held an unlit cigar in his mouth. A stereotype.

"And if I am?"

"Larry said—you know Larry, don't ya? He owns the place." When the man spoke, his cigar jerked around like a conductor's baton.

Hoagland picked up a south Jersey accent. "Yeah, I know him."

"Well, Larry says to me, he says, 'Hoagland is the man for you. Go ask him.' So I'm asking."

The short man's voice felt like sandpaper on Hoagland's eardrums. "Precisely what are you asking?"

"Oh, sorry. The name's Emerson Tiddle. I know; it's a weird name. My parents wanted me to be a poet or something."

"You still haven't told me what you want."

"Right." He removed the cigar. "I'm the trainer for my boy over there." He motioned to the ring. A large, pale man with a chest as wide as the hood of Hoagland's Acura stared back. He bounced from one foot to another tapping his gloves together.

"So?"

"So, I had a training match set up. Victor—that's his name, Victor Tolopov—has a fight in a few days, and he needs a sparring partner."

"What happened to the guy that was supposed to be here?"

"Got drunk and stepped off a curb. Dummy broke his ankle. Anyway, Larry says you're our best bet. How much you weigh?"

"Two-forty."

"And you're what? Six-three?"

"That's right."

"Perfect. His opponent is about that size. Larry says you know your way around the ring. That's good, but not to worry, I'll have him go easy on you. I just want him to work up a good sweat." He paused. "I'll pay you…a couple of sawbucks."

Hoagland looked at Victor the wide-body, then back to the squat Emerson.

"OK, OK, I'll make it fifty bucks. How about it?"

"Sure. I could use the workout. Sounds like fun."

"I don't know about fun, but like I said, he'll go easy on you."

Hoagland answered with a smile. "You want me to go easy on him too?"

"Ha! No worries there. You're a big man, but I doubt you'll lay a glove on him. He's the best I've seen in years."

"If he's so good, then why are you training in this dive?" A bead of sweat ran down the side of Hoagland's face, and he wiped it away with his training gloves.

"I'm trying to keep a low profile. He's knocked out every opponent so far, but those were low-tier guys. This upcoming fight is different. After he KOs this guy, the major boxing publications will take notice. So, how about it? You ready to put on the gloves?"

"Sure." Hoagland removed the thinner, less-padded training gloves, tossed them on his sports bag, and walked to the ring. Emerson disappeared into the locker room and returned with a pair of regulation gloves and helped Hoagland slip them over his taped hands and wrists. He then tied and taped the laces.

Hoagland walked up the small set of wood stairs that bridged the distance between floor and ring canvas, slipped between the ropes, and took a place in the corner. He began to bounce on the balls of his feet and rotated his head to loosen the muscles in his neck.

A moment later he fixed his eyes on the Russian boxer. The man looked like a redwood tree with arms. Everything about him shouted strength and determination. Some boxers spent hundreds of hours building their upper body but ignored their legs. Victor hadn't missed anything. His legs rippled with muscles, his abs formed a perfect six-pack, and his arms showed well-defined muscles. In bodybuilding terms, the man was "ripped."

There was no ring bell. Emerson said, "Ready." When Hoagland nodded, Emerson said, "Go," and pressed a button on the stopwatch in his hand.

The bulldozer of flesh advanced. Hoagland met him in the middle. Hoagland tossed a jab to measure distance. Victor did the same, except Victor's jab stung.

More jabs were exchanged. Hoagland anticipated this. Smart boxers took a few moments, sometimes a few rounds to take measure of the man before them. Victor slipped a jab through Hoagland's raised hands, catching him square on the nose. Fire blazed through his face and head.

"Nice," Hoagland said. Victor didn't respond.

Victor's next three jabs missed, but the right cross didn't. The glove impacted the side of Hoagland's head. It felt like the business end of a sledgehammer.

Hoagland staggered to the side.

Victor pressed his advance, jabbing, jabbing, then another right cross. Hoagland bobbed; his opponent's glove passed over his head. He then countered with two body shots. A brick wall would have moved more.

Before Hoagland could think, a left landed on his chin. Fireworks flashed in his eyes. Another punch slammed his temple, another just above his left eye. Staggering back, Hoagland tried to put a little distance between them. Victor wouldn't allow it. Punch followed punishing punch. His mouthpiece flew across the ring.

Hoagland's legs turned to cooked noodles. A second later he lay on his back, looking at the glare of the overhead lights.

A shadow covered his face. The mountain named Victor Tolopov stood over him. He smiled, showing a bloodred mouthpiece. He spit it out, and it landed on Hoagland's chest.

Two blinks later Victor turned to Emerson. "You promised

me a man. Instead you give me this little girl. How can I train without a real opponent? Does America have no men who know how to fight?"

"It's the best I could do, Victor. How was I to know the guy had a glass jaw?"

Hoagland rolled on to his side, pausing to let his vision clear and let his brain stop quivering. He pressed himself to his knees, then to his feet.

"He stands!" Victor shouted. "Go away. You do not belong in the ring."

Hoagland stepped away, bent to pick up his mouthpiece, then faced Victor. "You spit on me. You shouldn't have done that."

"Did the little girl get his feelings hurt? You know what I think? I think you are not a man. Do you wear your mother's panties?" He laughed. The sound of it stoked coals in Hoagland's gut. The muscles in his back tightened, and he clinched his gloved hands so tightly he could feel the tape dig into his flesh.

"That's enough, Victor. Let the man be. At least he had the courage to step in the ring. Can't say the man doesn't have guts."

He walked to Hoagland. "You OK? How many fingers am I holding up?"

"Get lost." Hoagland whispered the words.

"Look, I know you're sore at me for this, but—"

"I said, get lost." Hoagland slipped the mouthpiece between his lips and over his teeth.

"You already took a beating, pal. I can't let you toe-up again."

Hoagland pushed the man aside. "Tell your boy to pick up his mouth guard."

"I do not need it," Victor said. "You'll never touch me."

"Your choice, buddy, but don't say I didn't give you a chance."

Hoagland raised his gloves, leaving enough space to watch Victor sneer.

They circled each other, Victor broadcasting his confidence by keeping his hands down and dancing just out of Hoagland's reach. It didn't matter. The man was a boxer; he'd move close soon enough.

Victor threw a long jab and missed. He threw another, but Hoagland pulled back in time. The jab missed by several inches. Victor laughed and took a step closer. It was a step too close.

Hoagland threw a left that caught Victor on the nose. He followed that with a right to the deltoid muscle in the man's right arm. He saw the arm go limp for a half second.

Victor retreated a step, but Hoagland advanced two. The next set of combinations started just below the ribs and worked their way up. The body blows landed so hard that he could hear the air forced from Victor's lungs. That was when he noticed that Victor no longer smiled.

Victor launched a series of punches; each landed, but with less force than before. Hoagland knew he had hurt the man. The coals of anger that burned in him blazed. Like a shark with its first sniff of blood, Hoagland advanced. He took a shot to the side of his head, and blackness flooded his eyes but disappeared a half second later.

"That's it? That all you got?"

Victor let go a roundhouse swing, a swing that could have knocked a door off its hinges had it connected. It didn't.

Hoagland lowered his head and moved forward with fists pumping like pistons in a race car. He landed half a dozen blows just above Victor's trunks, crushing the six-pack. Two of the blows landed just above the hip to the soft, meaty flesh.

Victor grunted and bent forward. Hoagland went into autopilot. The blows came without thought. Instinct guided each fist to its target. When Victor bent so much that Hoagland no longer had a clear target, he did what no professional boxer would do. Hoagland never claimed to be professional. He placed his gloves on the big man's shoulders and lifted him upright. He wasn't done breaking the man's body down.

Victor wrapped his arms around Hoagland, attempting to tie

him up. That pleased Hoagland. It meant exhaustion and pain had taken over.

Victor pulled him close, pinning his arms. Battered as he was, the Russian showed remarkable strength. Hoagland had no intent of letting the man catch his breath. He struggled to pull free, but Victor wouldn't budge. That left only one weapon available to Hoagland.

He head-butted him.

Victor screamed and backed away, shielding his face with his hands. When he lowered his hands, Hoagland saw blood pouring from a nasty cut on the bridge of the man's nose and from his nostrils.

"Hey, that's a foul," Emerson shouted.

Hoagland knew he was right, but then he didn't care.

Victor released a banshee's scream and charged. He met a vicious uppercut that stopped him, staggered him. Hoagland followed with a hard, straight right to the sternum. What air remained in his lungs came out in a single gush.

Hoagland's left landed on the man's neck, just below the right ear. Victor swayed. One more shot should do the job. Hoagland's right hand landed on Victor's jaw.

Something snapped.

The boxer fell hard, unconscious before his head bounced on the canvas.

Hoagland stood over the fallen man and spit out his mouthpiece. It landed on Victor's chest. Blood poured from the unconscious man's mouth.

"You really should have used your mouth guard."

"You almost killed him," Emerson said. He knelt by his fallen athlete.

"It was a temptation."

Emerson stood and looked at Hoagland. "Listen, have you ever thought of boxing as a career? With my connections, I could get you in the best fights in no time. Of course, we'd have to split the purse, but I can make—"

Hoagland walked away.

16

EDDIE HAD TO FIGHT TO KEEP FROM PRESSING THE ACCEL-erator of his 1984 Chevy pickup to the floor. He had too many speeding violations already. One more could cost him his license. At least he had been smart enough to dump the empty beer cans that normally populated the floorboards and space behind the seat.

Since he couldn't drive as fast as he would like, he bounced on the seat as if doing so would get him to Oak Grove all the sooner.

He took another deep breath, held it, then let it sigh away. The dash clock read 4:12 p.m. Time seemed to be the only thing moving fast. Jake Clayton had said they had been home about six hours. Oak Grove was forty minutes west of Blink. Assuming Jake drove somewhat close to the speed limit, then it took something like forty-five minutes to get there. Forty-five minutes plus the six hours they had been home meant Henick had been in Oak Grove for seven hours. Maybe a little longer.

Eddie clinched his jaw. A man could go a lot of places in eight hours. Why Oak Grove? Did he plan to hitchhike to some other town? If so, and he caught a ride, then he could be in any number of other towns.

His frustration churned in his chest. "How am I going to find one man in a town of fifty thousand?"

He pressed the accelerator. Surely the cops wouldn't stop him for doing five miles an hour over the speed limit. Like most of West Texas, the road was straight and flat, and he could see miles ahead and behind him. There were no vehicles that looked like a trooper's car.

He turned the radio on. Reba McEntire was crooning her latest hit single. Eddie turned off the radio. He fidgeted. This wasn't like him: impromptu, compulsive, driven. Yet here he was moving as fast as he could down an open stretch of two-lane road to catch a man he barely knew, a man who had made a broken hand well with a touch.

Oak Grove came into view. Eddie had to raise a hand to shield the sun from his eyes as he continued west. Things got dark early this time of year.

He slowed as he entered the city limits, being conscious of the forty-five-mile-per-hour speed trap, and pushed through slow traffic on Main Street until he reached the Denny's Jake mentioned. He pulled onto the parking lot and parked.

"Now what?" He doubted that Henick had spent eight hours drinking coffee in the restaurant. Where would he go?

He exited the truck and entered the Denny's. A forty-something hostess greeted him. "Hi, hon; just you this afternoon?"

"Have you been working all day?" Eddie asked. The smell of fried food made him hungry.

"Why?" She looked suspicious.

"I'm trying to find a friend. He was dropped off in front of the restaurant."

She raised an eyebrow. "Hon, I've been here since eight, and I've seen maybe three hundred people. I'll need a tad more to go on."

"I'm sorry. He's tall, maybe forty, long hair, and about a week's worth of stubble on his chin."

"That narrows it down to about fifty people."

"OK…um, he's wearing…" He called Henick's image to mind. "He's wearing a flannel shirt, jeans, and running shoes—Nike, I think."

"That could still describe lots of people, but I don't think I've seen anyone like that."

"Thank you."

Eddie walked outside, and the weight of the universe fell on his shoulders.

They ate their meal in near silence. Jake complimented Eleanor on the pork chops, mashed potatoes, and corn. She thanked him. Neither said more until Eleanor rose, moved to the refrigerator, and retrieved two pieces of apple pie.

"Do you want your pie heated?"

"Nah," Jake said.

"What about ice cream? Want a scoop?"

"No thanks. I'm so full I'll be lucky to get the slice of pie down."

"I can put it up for later. We don't have to eat it now."

"Don't be silly, woman. Of course we do. How do you expect me to justify another piece later if I don't eat this one now?"

"I don't know how you can eat so much and never gain a pound." She set the small plate in front of him and then took her place at the table.

"High metabolism. My body is a finely tuned engine."

"I think I hear your valves knocking."

That made Jake laugh, but the laughter died a second later. He took a bite. Eleanor poked at her small piece.

"What do you think he meant?" Eleanor said a minute later.

"Who?"

"You know who."

"Henick?" He shrugged. "I don't know. I keep thinking about it."

Eleanor raised her head and recited the words as if reading them off the dining room wall. "Your son will be fine, and you will see him soon. He's coming home."

Jake stopped mid-chew. "How did he know? I never said nuthin' to him. Never mentioned our boy."

"I don't know." She looked back at the plate. The pie remained intact. "It's like he read my mind."

ENOCH

"People can't read the minds of other folk. Maybe on some television show, but not in real life. I don't buy it for a minute."

"Then how did he know?"

"I don't know!" He slammed his fork down then regretted it. "I'm sorry. It's just that his words keep eatin' at me." He took a deep breath and dragged a sleeve across his eyes. "What's it been now? Five years?"

"Five years three months."

"Seems like an eternity."

"Two eternities."

Jake saw tears in his wife's eyes. He reached across the table and laid his hand on hers. "He'd be twenty-five now, I guess; a full-grown man." He paused. "I shouldn't have ridden him so hard. It seemed like I was always on his back."

"Don't blame yourself, Jake. You gave him a good home, and you did your fatherly duties just right. It's not your fault. He just carried more troubles in his mind than most people. Even as a child he was difficult. He seemed born to trouble."

"I guess you're right. I hoped the two years he spent in jail would straighten him out. It only made him worse."

"Why didn't he come home when he was released?" Eleanor's tears flowed as they had a hundred times before. "We would never turn him away."

Jake shook his head. "I've asked that question a thousand times and ain't never got an answer. I guess he just didn't need us." The words scorched his throat.

17

So far, Katherine Rooney had counted just fifty-two blog postings about the *I Love Lucy* episode. The number gave her some comfort, but it also discouraged her. Fifty-two of the millions of bloggers had seen the episode and had written about it. She had no idea how many others may have seen the show.

Last she heard there were 50 million bloggers worldwide—more than the population of California. People who followed such things argued about the real number, with some stating 70 million blogs existed. Most, she figured, had died within a few months of creation. Still, the number couldn't be ignored.

The comfort came from realizing she hadn't imagined the whole thing. But why so few posts? It had been over twenty-four hours. Did that mean only a select group had seen and heard Lucy's announcement? Maybe it meant that only a handful of people had seen the episode. That made sense. It aired on a Friday night. How many people stayed home on a Friday night watching reruns of 1950s' comedies? That question burned a little. She had been one of the people.

The blogs themselves offered little information with writers posting, "So weird." "It freaked me out." "I must've fallen asleep and dreamt the whole thing."

She had tried to forget the haunting image and follow her usual Saturday routine. Rise, run for three miles, shower, buy breakfast at a small diner six miles away, and settle in with the *Los Angeles*

Times. She managed the jog and breakfast just fine, but by noon what she saw began to eat at her. A little computer work was in order. By eleven, she sat at her dining room table with her laptop in front of her.

She worked through lunch, searching for and reading everything she could find about the event. That had taken several hours but yielded little information. She learned that the episode played in several states, making it larger than just a Los Angeles phenomenon.

An idea came to her. She went to the Google Web site and did a search for the words she heard Lucy say: "Time grows short. Look for the one I send you. He walks among you."

She put quotes around the message, directing the search engine to find only exact matches. A half second later her computer screen displayed a list of links to sites that contained those words. Many of the returns were blog sites she had already visited, but one caught her attention: FILM GURU. Katherine clicked the link.

The site replaced the Google page. "Nice," she said. The blog looked professional, laid out in an easy-to-read format with muted colors and easy-to-read font. Judging by the archives, the blog had been around for a couple of years. She glanced at the most recent posts and noticed the owner posted at least twice a week.

All good information, but Katherine really wanted the newest post titled "Blown Away." Her eyes drew in the words, puzzling her more with each line. This had nothing to do with the *I Love Lucy* episode. The author complained about a movie he had recently seen, one in which the actor stops midaction to address the audience.

"This can't be right." She clicked on the ABOUT link and read about the author. The author, Ray Tickner, studied film at UCLA and would graduate at the end of the school year. His picture revealed a young man in his midtwenties, good-looking, clean cut.

She returned to the article. Having searched for the message Lucy had delivered, Katherine expected Tickner to blog about the

I Love Lucy episode she had seen, but he made no mention of it. The message he heard in the film matched what she had heard on television.

How could that be? How could someone mess with both television and a movie and get away with it? UCLA wasn't that far away; maybe she would talk to him. She clicked on a tiny icon of an envelope and an e-mail window opened. She raised her hands to the keyboard.

> Mr. Tickner:
>   I saw something similar but in a different venue. I would
>   love to talk to you about the matter.
>   Katherine Rooney, 310-555-1345

She sent the e-mail.

Five minutes later, her cell phone rang.

The television played in the living room, but Jake's eyes were fixed to the top of the set where there rested a family photo taken fifteen years previous. Three people stood in front of Sleeping Beauty's castle at Disneyland. The photo encapsulated one of the few good memories of his son. That was the problem with photos—they always told the truth of the moment. This photo showed Jake and Eleanor with broad smiles; Ryan, just ten at the time, stood between them. He didn't smile. It wasn't long after that vacation that Ryan began to show signs of mental torment.

Jake tore his eyes away and turned his attention to his wife, who sat in a rocking chair with a magazine in her lap. She hadn't turned a page in thirty minutes.

A grinding sound from outside pressed into the house. A light flashed in the windows.

"Sounds like a car." The sound awakened Eleanor from her trance.

"You expectin' company?"

"No. I don't know who it could be." She rose.

"Better let me get it."

Jake moved to the front door and reached for the knob just as someone knocked softly on the wood. He opened the door.

"Hey, Pops."

A tall, thin man with a freshly shaven face stood on his porch. He stared back through gray eyes, gray eyes Jake had not seen in five years and three months.

Eleanor began to cry.

Jake pushed open the screen door and wrapped his arms about the thin shoulders of his son. Both began to weep.

A moment later, Jake felt the familiar form of his wife press against him and extend her arms around the two men.

The fresh darkness of night replaced the stale darkness of regret.

Ryan had returned home.

Ryan sat on the sofa. "This brings back memories," he said.

"It should," Eleanor said. "We've had it for over fifteen years."

"I've taken many a good nap on that sofa." Jake wiped at his eyes and sniffed. He felt full and empty at the same time.

"Are you hungry, son?" Eleanor said. "We just finished dinner. I can make something for you."

"Maybe later, Mom. I had enough money for a burger, so I'm good for now."

Eleanor nodded and took a seat in the padded rocking chair near the wood-burning stove. Jake returned to his leather recliner. Silence hung thick in the air.

"I suppose you're wondering what I'm doing here." Ryan shifted on the sofa and rubbed his hands on his pants. "Well, it's not for money or anything like that. I've taken too much of your money as it is, and I hope to pay it back."

"We're just glad to see you, son. It's been a long time since we exchanged a word." Jake's words came with difficulty.

"Yeah, I know. I'm sorry about that." He cleared his throat. "You know how I am—was. My head hasn't been screwed on right since I was a kid." His eyes flooded. "I've been a real burden to you over the years. You deserved a better son."

"No family is perfect, dear." Eleanor's voice cracked.

"Maybe not, but I made ours pretty tough."

"It's not all your fault, Ryan," Jake said. "You have...well, you know."

"Schizophrenia. The voices were just the beginning of the problem. I made things worse with drugs." He gazed out the window. "So many years gone. So many years wasted."

Jake looked at Eleanor. The gaze carried a truckload of thoughts.

Eleanor had to try twice to get the words out. "Where have you been?"

"Lots of places. California mostly, living on the streets of San Diego and Los Angeles. I stayed in homeless shelters when I could. Ate at rescue missions."

Eleanor raised a hand to her mouth.

Ryan continued. "Lately, I've been hanging out in Phoenix. It's warm most of the time there. Never could stay in one place very long. I kept moving. The voices kept following. Always following. Always putting bad ideas in my head. Until yesterday."

"Yesterday?"

He nodded. "I was panhandling the office workers downtown. I tell them I'm an Iraqi war vet injured overseas. That works better than anything. Some days I made a couple of hundred dollars— which I spent on drugs and booze."

"What happened to you yesterday?"

"I don't know, not really. I was working my corner like every day and doing pretty good. I got to thinking about knocking off for the day when this guy walks up to me. I put the move on him.

I tell him how I was hurt in Iraq, fighting for our country, and how I can't get a job and asked if he could help me out with a couple of bucks. That's when it got weird."

"Weird? How?" Jake leaned forward.

"Well, he looks me in the eye and says, 'I don't have money, but what I do have I give to you.' Then he grabbed my head."

"He grabbed your head?" Eleanor said.

"Yes." Ryan laughed. "I thought he was trying to rob me. I grabbed his wrists, but the guy's arms wouldn't budge, not an inch. I yelled for him to get off me, but he didn't move. The voices start telling me to kick him, scratch him, punch him—kill him. I started to fight back. I became furious. I wanted nothing more than to get my fingers around his pencil-thin neck. I have never been so angry. Then it happened. Lightning flashed behind my eyes. The voices screamed and then…then…a warm light filled me; it filled and warmed me."

Tears ran down his cheeks. "The voices were gone. I waited for them to return, but they didn't. I felt—clean."

Eleanor's hands cupped her mouth. Jake felt nailed to his recliner.

"I'm not lying. That's exactly how it happened."

"I believe you, son. I can see a difference, but I do have a question. What did this man look like?"

"Oh, I'll remember that face forever. He stood taller than me and was about as thin. He had dark hair with some gray. He wore it long—down to his shoulders. He hadn't shaved for a while."

Jake's heart stumbled to a stop. "Was he wearing sneakers and jeans—"

"And a flannel shirt?" Eleanor added.

"How did you know?"

"This happened yesterday?" Jake tried to get the bees in his brain to settle.

"Yes."

"About what time?"

"Just after dark."

"In Arizona?"

"Yes, what's going on?"

Jake folded his hands to hide his shaking. "Son, I think we may have a better story."

18

KATHERINE ROONEY AGREED TO MEET RAY TICKNER AT Starbucks near the UCLA campus. She slipped into a tan pair of slacks and a white blouse. A light tan coat finished the ensemble and also covered the small revolver she carried. She dropped her badge case into the coat's side pocket.

College students filled the coffee shop. Some sat in groups chatting with friends; others bent over laptops pounding keys and listening to music through earbuds attached to iPods.

Tickner sat in the back corner of the bistro as far from the others as possible. He stood when she approached, and Katherine struggled to remember the last time a man did that in her presence.

Tickner wore jeans, sandals, and a T-shirt with the words SUPPORT INDY FILMS emblazoned on it. Tickner seemed worried.

"You're Katherine Rooney?"

"Yes." She extended her hand. "You seem shocked."

"I expected someone older."

"Thanks…I think." She took a seat at the small round table.

"Can I get you anything?"

"Sure, if you let me pay. After all, you're doing me a favor by meeting with me."

"OK."

She ordered a straight latte with low-fat milk.

"Keep an eye on my backpack."

Tickner worked his way to the front counter and placed the order. A few moments later he returned.

"I appreciate you taking time to meet with me—"

"Are you a cop?"

The question caught Katherine off guard.

"Does it matter?"

"It might. I didn't do anything wrong."

Katherine smiled. "I never said you did."

"You e-mail me out of the blue after reading a post on my blog, then give me your phone number and ask to meet. That's suspicious."

"I told you on the phone that I have an interest in what you saw at the movie theater. I just want to ask a few questions."

"No questions until you answer mine."

So much for manners. "Yes. I'm a cop. Specifically, I'm with the FBI."

He turned white.

"Relax, Mr. Tickner...may I call you Ray?"

"Um, sure."

"OK, Ray. Call me Katherine. Let me put your mind at ease: I'm not here on Bureau business. This is personal research."

"I don't know if I should be talking to you."

"Look, I'm not here to bust your chops. I just have a few questions. You act like you've committed a crime."

He shifted in his seat. "I've done nothing wrong."

"Good, then there's nothing to worry about."

"Do I need a lawyer?"

"You're not under arrest, Ray. We're just having coffee."

He sighed and looked around the room.

"Look," Katherine said. "I know that sitting across the table from an FBI agent can be daunting, but I'm not on duty, I just need to ask a few questions about what happened in the movie theater. Trust me. Have I ever lied to you before?"

"I've only known you five minutes."

"I tell you what. Let me start, then you can decide if you want to talk to me."

"OK."

She took a deep breath. "Do you ever watch *I Love Lucy*?" Ten minutes later she had told her story from the moment the show came on to the point where she found his blog posting.

"If you told that to anyone else, they'd think you're nuts."

"Maybe I am, but if so, I came by it honestly. Fifty-two other people saw the same thing and created blog postings about it."

"I didn't see that show. How did you connect with me?"

"I Googled the message I heard. Apparently you heard the same thing."

He stared into her eyes. "OK, I may live to regret this." He directed his eyes away from her. She followed his gaze. Two young men were looking back. He motioned to them, and one rose and approached. He held an electronic device in his hand.

"Everything OK, Ray?" He set the device on the table.

"Yeah, I think so." Ray opened the DVD player. "Give us a minute, Ted. This won't take long."

"Sure you don't want me to hang around? You might need a witness or something."

Ray waved him off. "No thanks." Ted returned to his table.

"Loyal friends."

"Yeah, for the most part." He pressed play then the pause button and turned the device. "This is why I'm so stressed about you being FBI. I took this while at the movie."

"You took a video camera to the theater?"

"Yes, but it's not what you think. I'm a college student in an expensive university. I get by on grant money and student loans. Sometimes I do odd jobs. I'm not exactly flush, if you know what I mean."

"So you tape movies and sell them or put them on the Internet? You know that is a crime."

"I don't do anything like that. I shoot the movie for references.

If I bought every DVD for every movie I watched, I would be living under a bridge. Movies are my life. I do this for reference material."

"Still…"

"Still nothing. If I were a pirate, that thing would be all over the net by now, but it's not. I believe in creative copyright. I don't want anyone stealing my stuff, but the way I figure it, I pay for the movie and I only use the copy for my personal benefit, no one else's."

"You're still breaking the law."

"You going to arrest me?"

"Nope. I think we're looking at something bigger here. Just don't go around telling folks you do this. What now?"

"Press play when you're ready. It's cued up. Wait." He reached into his backpack and removed a small pair of headphones. "Use these."

Katherine did. A few minutes later, she said, "Oh my."

EDDIE MOVED FROM RESTAURANT TO RESTAURANT asking the same questions. No one had seen a long-haired man in blue jeans and flannel shirt. Oak Grove might be a small town, but it seemed like a megacity to Eddie who did his work alone.

He encouraged his flagging spirit with reminders that Henick would be on foot and couldn't travel very far, but the pessimist that resided in his head reminded him that Henick could have caught a ride with someone, just as he did with Jake and Eleanor. The same noisy pessimist also reminded him that a man on foot, especially a man with several hours head start, could easily disappear in a community of twenty-five thousand. The ebony night that settled on the city only made things worse.

Eddie returned to his truck, leaving behind the Bob's Big Boy eatery, slipped behind the wheel, and slammed the door. The Chevy rocked with the force of it. The anger that had been Eddie's companion since childhood roiled in him like a potion in a witch's cauldron. He squeezed the wheel until his knuckles blanched.

"Think. Think. Think."

His eyes drifted open, and he gazed over the hood into the streetlamp-washed night. "Where are you?"

Eddie had been quizzing restaurant hostesses because he had first seen Henick in a steak house. Not bulletproof logic, but he had to start somewhere. He had nothing else to go on. He thought for a moment. Where else had he seen Henick? Jail.

He exited the truck and walked to a payphone at the front

of the Bob's Big Boy. He felt fortunate—the directory still hung from its metal support. He tilted the holder up, pushed back the hard, black plastic covers, and turned to the front of the phonebook and found the government listings. Three minutes later he had the address for the deputy substation. Fortunately, the streets perpendicular to Main Street were numbered. He had only to find Twelfth Avenue.

Ten minutes later, he stood at the counter of the local sheriff's substation. Five minutes after that, he again sat in his truck. Henick had not been arrested for vagrancy or anything else.

Eddie pulled from the lot, returned to Main Street, and cruised its length several times, his eyes scanning both sides of the road. Maybe he could catch sight of the man by chance; lousy odds, but he had no other ideas.

Real estate offices, boutiques, dentist offices, fast-food joints came one after another, and Eddie studied each one. Disappointment followed every moment of hope.

At the east end of Main Street was the community hospital. Eddie pulled in as he had done several times before to turn his truck around for another pass down the thoroughfare. The lot held cars of all types. Expensive BMWs sat next to battered and weary Ford Pintos. He made his turn and started back to the street when his peripheral vision caught something familiar. A tall man in jeans and a flannel shirt walked through the main entrance and into the hospital.

Eddie hit the brakes and rolled his window down as fast as he could. "Hey! Henick! Hey!"

Too late. The automatic doors of the hospital foyer closed.

Eddie swore, rolled up the window, and began searching for an empty parking spot. Cars filled most of the stalls. Eddie pulled into the closest slot. A metal pole with a sign that read Chaplain stood at the front. He felt a moment of guilt, but only a moment. Seconds later, Eddie sprinted across the lot.

Before the automatic doors had slid fully open, Eddie turned sideways and plunged into the lobby. Naugahyde-upholstered seats dotted a pale yellow vinyl floor. Most of the seats were empty. An elderly couple sat in one corner, gazing at things only they could see. Each wore a deep frown. A middle-aged man sat alone on another seat, his head propped up by a hand. He seemed to be asleep. An information counter occupied the center of the room. No one manned the station.

He scanned the area for Henick—nothing. He moved to the elderly couple. "Excuse me?"

"Are you the doctor? Is Helen all right?"

"What? No, I'm not a doctor." Eddie wondered how they could confuse him with a physician. "Did you see a man with long hair and wearing a flannel shirt come in here?"

"No," the old man said.

"What about you, ma'am? Did you see him?"

"I haven't seen anyone."

Eddie struggled to keep calm. "How is that possible? He just walked in."

The old man shrugged.

Eddie turned and started for the other man, then dismissed the idea. He looked sound asleep.

Eddie saw two sets of elevator doors on the far wall and one steel door with a wire glass window that he assumed led to the stairwell. Having driven through the parking lot several times tonight, he knew the hospital had just three floors. He'd search all of them if he had to. He started for the elevators and noticed a short corridor leading to another wide hall forming a T-intersection. He moved to the large corridor, but both sides were empty. Doors lined each side of the hall.

For no reason in particular, Eddie turned right and walked slowly down the corridor, looking in each room. The passageway widened at the end to accommodate a nurse's station. He approached. Three nurses sat behind a counter looking at charts. A man in a white smock sat at a desk by himself, writing in a notebook.

"Excuse me, have you seen a man—"

"One moment please." A severe-looking woman in her fifties raised a finger but not her eyes. When she had finished reading the chart, she looked up and forced a smile. "May I help you?"

Eddie repeated Henick's description.

She shook her head. "I'm sorry, sir, but I haven't seen anyone like that. Is there a problem?"

"Um, no. No problem. I'm just trying to find him."

"Is he here to see a patient? If you know the patient's name, then I can direct you to the right floor."

"That's OK. I'll just keep looking."

"All right." The woman lowered her head again, and Eddie started to the other end of the corridor. He had no better luck there. He repeated his actions on the second floor, looking in each open door and quizzing the nurses. As he got in the elevator and started toward the third floor, Eddie began to wonder if Henick might be moving down through the stairwell. "Just my luck if he is."

The doors to the elevator opened; he stepped out and collided with Henick.

20

EDDIE STEPPED BACK. "HEY, I'VE BEEN LOOKING ALL OVER for you."

"I am here."

"Well, yeah, I can see that. What are you doing here?"

Henick smiled. "Talking to you."

"You know what I mean. I've been searching all over Oak Grove trying to find you. Are you sick or something?"

Henick shook his head. "I am well."

"Then why are you in a hospital?"

Henick's smile dropped, and for a moment Eddie thought the corners of his mouth would touch his shoulders. He didn't answer. Instead, he turned and moved from the elevator lobby to the corridor. He showed no hesitancy when turning left. He did, however, pause outside room 312.

"Hey, man, talk to me. What are you doing here?"

Henick looked at him. "Come and see."

Eddie grabbed Henick's arm. "Do you know the people in this room?"

Henick pulled his arm free and stepped into the room. Eddie followed.

The room sported pale green paint, gray vinyl flooring, and two beds. Only one bed was occupied. A boy Eddie judged to be ten lay beneath a sheet, his eyes directed at a television mounted on the wall. LA played San Antonio in basketball. The Spurs led by fifteen. The boy had light hair, what Eddie's mother used to call towheaded.

Next to the bed sat a dark-haired woman whom Eddie guessed had yet to see thirty. She sat with her eyes closed as if in prayer. Although still young, the woman looked as if she had been down some rough roads.

The boy looked at Henick. "Hi."

"Hello."

Eddie raised a hand and said, "Hey."

The woman opened her eyes. "Oh, I'm sorry. I didn't see you come in. Are you—" She straightened then rose from the chair. "You're not with the hospital."

Henick smiled. "No." He turned his eyes on the boy. "Hello, Rory."

"How do you know my name?" The boy's voice struggled across the five feet that separated him from Henick.

"My name is Henick. I came to talk to you."

"Talk about what?" The mother's brow furrowed and her eyes narrowed. "If you're not with the hospital, then what are you doing here?" She looked at Eddie, who, if asked, would swear in court he *felt* her gaze. "Um, my name is Eddie. Eddie Feely."

"What do you want?"

Eddie could tell she was a woman who didn't tolerate much nonsense. "Nothing. We're just here to…" He turned to Henick. "Just why are we here?"

Henick stepped to the side of the bed, ignoring Eddie's question. He took Rory's hand.

"Look, mister," the mother said, "I think you should leave."

Henick lifted his gaze to her. "Jennifer, you and Rory are in no danger from me."

"How do you know our names?"

He shrugged and returned his attention to Rory. Eddie stepped to Henick's side. "Listen, maybe we should come back later."

Henick shook his head. "I must be here now."

Eddie lowered his voice. "Are you going to...you know, like what you did to me?" He touched the hand that had been a mess of broken bones.

Henick made eye contact. In the dim light of the television Eddie saw the thick layer of moisture in his eyes. He had his answer.

"Your prayers have been heard and answered, Jennifer—yours too, Rory."

Eddie saw the air leave the mother's lungs. "You mean..." she began but couldn't finish. She gulped air. "You mean he's going to be all right?"

Henick pressed his lips together. "No, not as you mean."

"But you said our prayers were heard and answered. Why are you playing with our emotions?"

"The answer does not match your expectations."

She raised a tremulous hand to her mouth.

"Hey, man," Eddie said. "You can't fix things?"

"No."

"Then why did you come here? If you can't fix the boy like you fixed my hand, then why are we standing here?"

"I do not know why you are here. I only know why I am here."

"Man, this is cold. I can't believe you're yanking the people around like this. Definitely not cool."

The boy gazed at Henick's face. "Am I going to die?"

"No, of course not, sweetheart," Jennifer said. "The doctors will make you well. You'll see. Soon. It will be all over soon." Tears raced down her face. She stepped to the side of the bed opposite Henick. "I want you to go. Leave or I'll call security."

"Do you want me to leave, Rory?"

"It's all right, Mom. I think he's OK."

"I don't care. I want him to leave."

"Come on," Eddie said. "We'd better get going." He laid a hand on Henick's arm and pulled gently. The arm didn't move. That's when he saw a tear drop from the man's cheek.

"Rory, you are going where I've been," Henick said.

"Will I like it?"

"Yes. You will like it very much. Someday I will show you my favorite places."

Rory looked puzzled. "Are you dying too, mister?"

"In a way, son. In a way."

"I'm afraid." Tears flooded his eyes.

"I know. That is why I am here. Don't be afraid. Sometimes a difficult path means a better destination. One day you will close your eyes, and when you open them, things will be more wonderful than you can imagine. You will see amazing things, hear indescribable sounds and music, and feel things none of us can feel now. There is so much to see, so much to experience. You will not miss this place."

"But what about my mom? I'll miss her."

The words snatched sobs from the woman, who shuddered as if her legs would fail any moment. Henick held out his free hand and the woman reached for it. Eddie stood waist deep in confusion. The woman who had moments before looked ready to claw Henick's eyes from their sockets now held the man's hand as if she had known him for a decade.

"And she will miss you, but only for a time. Then you can show her your new favorite places."

"But why doesn't God heal me? Have I been that bad?"

"No, Rory, you have not been bad."

"Then why doesn't He make the leukemia go away?"

Henick cocked his head to the side for a moment. "I do not know."

The welling tears breached Rory's eyes and streamed down his cheeks and onto his pillow. Henick released the boy's hand and touched the rivulets coursing down the lad's cheeks. "I want to show you something. Close your eyes."

"How can I see if my eyes are closed?"

"Some of the most beautiful things we see, we see with closed eyes. Your mind can see more than you think."

Rory closed his eyes as Henick laid his palm to the boy's forehead. The boy's breathing escalated. "Wow. Oh, wow." A few moments later his breathing slowed.

"He is asleep," Henick said and moved to the door, Eddie a step behind.

"Wait," Jennifer said.

Henick turned. She approached slowly as if uncertain of her steps. "Who are you?"

"My name is Henick. God sent me."

"What…what did my son see?"

Henick raised his hand to the side of Jennifer's head. "Close your eyes."

She did.

She stiffened, arching her spine. Her head rolled back as if she were looking at the ceiling.

"It's so…beautiful. So very beautiful."

When Henick lowered his hand, Jennifer relaxed and slowly opened her eyes. He ran the back of his fingers across her cheek.

"Will the pain go away?" she asked just above a whisper.

"No," Henick said, "but it will become…" He trailed off as if grasping for the right word. "…manageable. You will know happiness again, and your son's memory will be with you until you see him again."

"How long before…I mean, how long until…"

"Not long."

Henick stepped from the room. Eddie chased after him. They moved in silence through the hospital. Words burned in Eddie's mind, but he held them back until he found a better place to say them.

A short elevator ride later, they stepped from the lobby and onto the parking lot. Eddie led Henick to the truck and motioned for him to get in. Once inside, Eddie turned to the mysterious man. "You OK?"

Henick wiped at his eyes. "I am well."

"Yeah, bet me." He turned the key, and the old V-8 cranked to life. "I gotta ask. Why didn't you just heal the kid like you healed my hand? I mean, he's just a kid."

"I couldn't."

"What do you mean, you couldn't? You did all right by me."

"You were meant to be healed. Rory is not."

"What gives you the right to make that kind of decision? Who died and made you God?" The heat in Eddie's words surprised him.

"I am not God. God is God. I am just me."

"Don't go cryptic on me, longhair. I've spent most of the day and half the night looking for you."

"Why?"

"Because."

"Is 'because' an answer?"

Eddie fingered the steering wheel. "No, but it's all I got." He gazed into the dark. "It's not right, man. It just ain't right. My hand got busted because I was liquored up and angry. I did it to myself, but that kid, he ain't done nobody any harm, yet he's going to die. That's wrong, just plain wrong."

"I don't choose who lives and who dies."

"Who does?"

Henick closed his eyes. To Eddie he looked like a man at the end of a hundred-mile hike. "Usually, life decides on death. Things happen. Death happens. Sometimes God decides."

"And the Man upstairs has decided little Rory ain't good enough for this world, so He's going to kill the boy."

"The disease will kill the boy, not God."

"Can God stop it?"

"Yes."

"Well, to my way of thinking, not saving the kid is the same as killing him."

"Your thinking is wrong."

"I'm not a smart man, Henick, but I got enough brain cells to figure this one out." He put the truck in reverse and backed out of the parking space. Once clear of the cars on the side, he turned the wheel and pulled down the aisle of vehicles. Moments later he slowed to a stop.

"Why did you stop?"

"I don't know where I'm going."

"Perhaps you are right," Henick said.

"You mean about God?"

"No. About you not being a smart man."

Eddie stared at Henick and blinked several times. "What? Is that a joke? It's a joke, isn't it? You're having fun at my expense."

Henick smiled.

Eddie laughed. "I've met some crazy people in my time, but you take the cake." He paused. "When did you eat last?"

"This morning."

"Let's get a bite. I know where all the restaurants are."

21

THE RINGING PHONE ON HIS NIGHTSTAND JARRED GEOFF Barry from a dreamless sleep.

It rang again, and Geoff responded with several sharp-edged curses. He looked at his alarm clock—8:10 in the morning. He had only been asleep for a few hours. He snatched the remote handset and placed it to his ear. "Someone had better be dying."

"Geoff?"

At least it wasn't a wrong number. Working the graveyard shift at the *New York Times* meant sleeping when most people where just starting their day. "Who is this and why are you calling at such a hideous hour?"

"It's Bryce. Sorry to bother you at home."

Bryce Sandburg, the assistant editor. Geoff rolled on to his back and stared at a ceiling he couldn't see. Heavy curtains kept daylight at bay. "Can't it wait until this afternoon? I'm beat beyond words."

"No can do, pal. The big guy is about to pop a hernia."

"Then he needs a doctor, not me."

"He wants to know about the full-page ad in Section A."

"What full-page ad?"

"It's on page A3, Geoff. Pull back the front page and the thing is staring you in the face."

"Um, Bryce?"

"Yeah?"

"I love my job and I'm as dedicated as the next guy, but I don't sleep with the paper."

"Oh, you're still in bed."

"That's where we denizens of the night sleep during the day."

"Can you get a copy?"

"Bryce, I set the paper; that's my job. Now what's the problem?"

"I told you; it's the full-page ad on A3."

"There is no full-page advertisement on A3."

The assistant editor sighed. "Geoff, I'm looking right at it."

"Then someone is having a good laugh at your expense."

"If it's a joke, then the jokester managed to play it on 1.6 million Sunday subscribers."

Geoff slung his legs over the side of the bed. "You're telling me that this ad appears in every copy?"

"It's in every one I've seen. I even made calls to our other print stations, and they show the same thing."

"I'm telling you, Bryce, when I put the thing to bed there was no full-page ad on A3 or any other page in the front section."

Geoff pulled the cord on his bedside lamp. The light stabbed his eyes. "Hang on." He padded into the living room, squinting against the sunlight pushing through the thin drapes over the front window of his loft.

It sat just where he expected it. It looked untouched. His wife must not have had time to read the issue before leaving for work. She liked to read the paper "hot off the press." After twenty years of marriage, the joke had grown old, but he never said so. He sat on the sofa, thankful that his eighth-floor loft prohibited neighbors from peering in through the gossamer drapes and seeing a middle-aged man in boxer shorts and a white T-shirt.

"Got it." The front page looked the same as he set it. He peeled it back. There it was: a full-page spread of an indistinct man walking a two-lane road. A beam of light shone from the top of the picture to the man, silhouetting him. Geoff could make out no features.

"Do you see it?"

"Yeah, I see it all right, and I'm telling you it wasn't there last night when I sent the files off to the printer."

"I spoke to the printers. They checked the digital files and films, and the ad is there as big as life."

"I don't know what to tell you."

"You can tell me how to tell the old man how the paper didn't lose several fistfuls of cash running an ad no one paid for."

"You checked with display advertising?"

"Of course, Geoff. They were my first call. They know nothing about it. They're not real happy over there. The mystery ad knocked out several paying clients. People want answers."

"I don't have any to offer. This isn't what I set."

"Yet there it is."

"I can see why they made you assistant editor, Bryce. Your grasp of the obvious is stunning."

"Don't get mouthy with me, Geoff. I don't need any more grief."

"What do you want from me? I'm telling you that I did not set this page. Someone else did."

"Who?"

He swore. "How should I know? I did what I do with every issue I set. When I was done, I sent the digital files to the printers. Maybe someone sent an alternate file."

"They have only the files you sent."

"Then they're lying. Someone is lying. The only thing I know is it's not me." He gazed at the large display ad. "I don't even know what this means. What does 'Look for the one I AM sending' mean?"

"You tell me."

"I can't— Whoa!" Geoff shot to his feet and stepped away from the paper.

"What? Did you find something?"

Geoff couldn't speak, nor could he move his eyes from the image on A3. The man on the road was walking.

"It—it's moving."

MARY-MARTHA SIPPED COFFEE AND REVIEWED HER notes. Willie watched her. For the last ten years it had been the same every Sunday. Mary would rise early and take a long shower. "It helps me think," she often said. Willie learned not to complain. Sundays made his wife edgy, and more than once he had become the target of her anxiety. She could be short-tempered any day, but Sundays with the stress of the service on her mind made her especially volatile. Perhaps the thought of twelve thousand people waiting for her to channel her spirit guide put her on edge. He knew it would unsettle him.

While she showered he would make coffee and bring it to her in a large mug. He would then take his turn in the shower, hoping enough hot water remained for him to do the job before the tank emptied.

He would dress quickly, then move to the kitchen to make breakfast. He'd have bacon and eggs, but she seldom ate more than two pieces of rye toast. Very few words would be exchanged between them until the service was over. The roles were clearly defined, and Willie had learned to accept them.

"You look especially lovely this morning," he offered after fifteen minutes of silence at the breakfast table.

"What? Oh, thanks."

"I like that outfit. It brings out the blue in your eyes."

She didn't look up from the note page in front of her. "That's nice."

"Can I get you more coffee?"

"What you can get me is a little silence. You know I have to memorize all this."

"Sorry." He rose, retrieved her cup and entered the kitchen, and poured a fresh cup from the high-tech coffeemaker. The two-thousand-dollar device ground the beans, filtered the water, and came equipped with more dials and switches than the space shuttle. In the end, however, it could only produce a decent cup of coffee. *Now if it would only clean itself, then that would be something.*

He opened the new refrigerator and retrieved a container of hazelnut-flavored creamer. He set the cup on the new black marble countertops. Everything in the luxury kitchen was new— $125,000 new. Every time Willie stepped on the russet-colored granite tiles, he wondered about the need for such opulence. Did a middle-aged couple need two sizes of microwaves, a top-end double oven, and a commercial stove that could heat the house should the HVAC system fail?

What he wondered didn't matter. Mary-Martha wanted it, so she got it. Never mind that she never did more in the room than retrieve a snack from the fridge.

Willie prided himself on being a simple man. Mary-Martha often treated him like a simpleton. He returned to the table and set the coffee down. She didn't acknowledge him. He watched her read a line or two, close her eyes, and mouth the words just as she did every Sunday.

Although she spoke twice a week at the Church of New Revelation, Sunday drew the crowds. A crew of technicians videotaped each utterance to be broadcast across the nation on scores of television stations. She did the midweek message in studio. On Sundays, she worked before the large congregation, and that, she often said, was a very different dynamic.

Willie sipped his coffee again. Cold. He didn't care. He wasn't getting up again. He opened the *New York Times*. On most days, Mary-Martha scoured the news looking for tidbits to use in the message. Several newspapers and a score of magazines arrived at the house. The digital age had made the East Coast newspaper available in their area—even in New Mexico.

The front page held little of interest for Willie. He had grown tired of reading about military conflicts, politicians in some kind of sex scandal, and the most recent financial crisis. He did find an interesting article on another state rejecting the death penalty. Page A2 held four columns of news summary. He also saw ads for a Chanel handbag, Tourneau wristwatch, Gucci shoes, Louis Vuitton luggage, and Macy's department store.

His eyes drifted to A3, where he saw a full-page, color ad for… He couldn't figure out the product. A photo of a silhouetted man walking a two-lane country road dominated the display. At the top were the words, "Look for the one I AM sending." What did that mean?

The man in the photo took three steps.

"What!" He dropped the paper to the table and slid back his chair as if the print had caught fire.

"Willie, I told you I need quiet."

"It moved."

"What moved?"

"The picture…the man in the picture—I saw him move."

She reached across the table and snatched the paper. "The one with the man walking in the road?"

"Yes. Scared me to death."

"I can see that. Well, he's not moving now. Maybe it's just your imagination."

"Maybe it's not. I know what I saw." He rose and stood behind her chair. "He took two, maybe three, steps."

Mary-Martha tilted the page and brought it close to her face. "It's just ink on paper. I don't see anything different."

"Digital ink? I read somewhere that they're making something called digital ink."

She shook her head. "That's something else. There's no such thing as ink that simulates motion."

"I'm telling you what I saw."

She set the paper down. "And I'm telling you what I see. It was just a trick of the eyes. Perhaps you dozed off. Did you sleep well last night?"

"Pretty good."

"Well, there it is. You're just overtired." She returned her gaze to the ad. "What's this thing selling?"

"Beats me, but they sure got my attention."

She studied the paper more. "I don't see a product, just the photo and the one line of text. Who spends that kind of money and not mention their business or product? Ads this size take major corporation dollars. You'd have to be Verizon or Sprint to have this kind of advertising budget..." She hesitated, then read, "'Look for the one I AM sending.' Did you read that?"

"I saw it."

"Did you notice the capitals?"

"Capitals?"

"The words 'I AM' are in caps. Why would anyone do that? Unless..."

"Unless what?"

"I need a Bible." She moved from the table and strode to her home office, a wide, comfortable room with painted panel walls and thick, dark blue carpet. Floor-to-ceiling bookshelves lined one wall. She pulled a leather-bound Bible from one of the shelves. "It's been a long time...where is that verse?"

While Willie watched, his wife turned to the back of the book, stopped at a page, and ran her finger down one of the columns. "The concordance has it. Exodus 3:14. That's one of the books of Moses." She fanned the first pages. "Here it is. Exodus." She licked the tip of her finger and began flipping page by page.

Willie waited, knowing that any comment he made would only distract her, and she hated distraction. "Got it. God is speaking to

Moses. 'I AM WHO I AM. Thus you shall say to the sons of Israel, I AM has sent you.'"

"OK, what's it mean?"

She closed the Bible and returned it to the shelf. "It's been a long time since I've been in a Christian church. Not since childhood, but if I remember, the I AM becomes a name for God, a name so holy that no one dared pronounce it. The people began using 'Adonai' instead of the four letters for God's name."

"You think the 'I AM' in the newspaper is a reference to God?"

"Perhaps, perhaps."

She smiled, and Willie grew nervous. Mary-Martha kissed him on the cheek. "Thanks for showing it to me. It's given me an idea."

"Like what?"

"You'll see. You'll see."

THE CONGREGATION MILLED AND MINGLED IN THE AISLES and seats of the massive sanctuary, creating a white noise of friendly laughter and conversation. Mary-Martha found it intoxicating. Every Sunday morning she arose skewered through the gut with anxiety. She seldom slept well on Saturday nights; bizarre dreams haunted the corridors of her mind, oozing through closed doors that even her conscience couldn't unlock. Every Saturday night became a journey through murky lands. When the alarm sounded, she would roll over and wish for a different day.

She kept the morning stroll through purgatory her secret. She could think of no reason for Willie to know. Loving and attentive, he would want to help, and that would be a slippery slope to disaster. It was important to keep Willie at just the right distance from her work. His unwavering devotion made him the ideal spouse for a woman with her kind of influence. A more assertive man might want to run the business side of things, be her "manager." There would be nothing but disaster in that. She knew herself well enough to know that her headstrong ambition and quick temper would lead to an earthshaking battle, leaving her church and career in rubble.

The fitful nights didn't matter anyway. By the time she arrived at the set of buildings known as the Church of New Revelation, her anxiety had morphed into excitement. The sight and sound of twelve thousand people working their way into the cavernous, glass-walled sanctuary always drove away the mental gloom.

Twelve thousand was a large number, but she knew of evangelical churches that ran two and a half times that. And there were at least two Asian churches that drew five times her attendance. Of course, they had centuries of Christian doctrine and history behind them. She was making up her doctrine and history as she went along.

Thirteen musicians filled the stage. Drums began to beat, electric guitars began to wail, and vocalists sang. High-end projectors shone on tall screens so those in the spacious auditorium could see every action. The congregation sang the words of spiritual songs similar to those they sang growing up in church but with different words. Someone unfamiliar with church life might assume they had entered a Protestant megachurch; those familiar with Christian doctrine would be appalled. Every Sunday a few walked out of the service, but Mary-Martha never complained. She didn't want Christians in her church. They asked too many questions. To her, each one that left was one less problem to deal with. There were always two to take their place.

Willie stepped to her side. "You've come a long way."

"*We've* come a long way, dear."

He chortled, but Mary-Martha heard no humor in it. "You've done a lot in the last ten years. This is a long way from reading palms and conducting séances. A decade ago you said this was your destiny. I doubted you then. I shouldn't have."

"This is just the beginning."

"Beginning? What else can there be? Maybe we can add a few thousand more, but why bother? You have wealth and fame."

"That kind of thinking is what separates us, Willie. I didn't build this church by being satisfied. Satisfaction is a poison that kills ambition."

Willie nodded. "If you say so."

"I say so. Now let me focus on the service."

Willie slunk away.

"What's up, Howie?" Gabriel Hoagland stood over a uniformed guard who sat at a counter with three large computer monitors. Each monitor showed four video feeds from one of the many security cameras.

"We have a little trouble in B-2. Looks like someone is casing the cars." Howie turned from the monitor to face Hoagland. "You want me to... What happened to your face?"

"Did a little boxing yesterday. My opponent got lucky."

"Against you?"

"His luck didn't last long. He looks worse than me."

"That's the boss we've come to know and love. Anyway, Robbie and Tom are walking the other lot. I can radio them. They can get there pretty quick, or I can pull one of our plainclothes men out of the service."

"No need. I can take care of it."

"There's three of them. Look college age. Two are wearing gang colors."

"Is that your way of asking if you can come along?"

"You know me too well, boss. I can get someone to take my post here for a few minutes."

"Nah, just leave it. We may not want anyone watching anyway." Howie smiled.

Hoagland and Howie walked from the upper floor at the back of the worship center, down the stairs, through the wide, marble floor lobby, and out of the building. Parking lot B-2 was on the south side of the twenty-five-acre campus. A white golf cart was parked to the side of the foyer. The two men entered, and Hoagland pressed the accelerator. The near-silent electric motor cart carried them over the concrete plaza and onto the asphalt.

"See 'em?" Howie asked.

"Yup. Let's split up and see if we can't catch them in the act."

"Sure. How do you want to play this? Up and up, or do you want to be creative?"

"I'm feeling creative. Besides, this is the second time these guys have come by."

Hoagland stopped the cart, and Howie slipped from his seat. Hoagland continued forward, then turned away from the trio just in case they spotted him. He stopped a short distance away and walked to the area he had last seen the men.

He moved in a crouch, slipping between cars and sprinting across driving lanes. He peered around the back end of a Humvee. He could hide a squad of men behind the massive vehicle.

Howie had been right. The three appeared college age, but Hoagland doubted they had ever set foot on a university campus. From the looks of them, he doubted they saw the end of high school.

The city had several street gangs, most centered on race and neighborhoods they felt they owned. Recently a new group had arisen: an ethnically mixed gang living in middle-income neighborhoods. Before him were two Hispanics and one tall white young man. He took the tall one to be the leader.

Hoagland stepped from his hiding place and started for them. They had stopped by a Jaguar convertible. Hoagland couldn't decide if they were looking to burgle a car or steal one. Many of the people who came to the Church of New Revelation walked the paths of the wealthy. Every fourth car in the lot topped fifty-grand as a base price.

"Can I help you gentlemen?"

The three jumped at the sound of Hoagland's voice. They stared at him, no doubt judging what level of danger he presented. Since he wore a blue pinstripe suit, he assumed they thought him to be a small threat.

"We ain't doing nothing," the tall one said.

"That a fact? Well, I think you are."

"You can't prove nothing."

Hoagland nodded. "That's true, but then again, I don't care about proving anything."

One of the hoods turned and fled. It was a mistake. While Hoagland had kept their attention, Howie had come up from behind. The kid never knew what hit him, but Hoagland did: Howie's fist to the young man's throat. The kid crumpled to the warm asphalt as if all the joints in his body had come loose. Howie didn't bother to see if his victim was going to get up. That's what Hoagland liked about Howie: he was so efficient; something he learned during his ten years in a California prison for manslaughter.

The last member of the trio, a five-foot-ten bundle of gymnasium muscle stepped toward Hoagland, moving his arms in some martial arts fashion and making cooing noises. He charged and threw a vicious kick at Hoagland's midsection—a kick he caught. Hoagland pinned the man's extended leg against his body and drove his elbow deep into the man's thigh. He then yanked the leg up and pushed. The man landed hard on the macadam. His head bounced twice.

That left the tall man. He looked at his two unconscious pals, then turned white. A second later he pulled a switchblade from his back pocket. "I'm gonna cut you, man."

"Really?" Hoagland reached beneath his coat and produced a 9mm pistol. "You think your knife can move faster than my bullet?"

He dropped the knife.

"Smart boy. Now here's the deal. Listen carefully. Are you listening?"

"Yeah."

"What?"

"Yes, sir. I'm listening."

"You see this, Howie? They say guys like him can't learn, but he seems to be catching on just fine."

Howie laughed. "Must be the teacher."

Hoagland returned the weapon to its shoulder holster. He

looked around and, feeling comfortable that no eyes were directed their way, took two long strides forward and delivered a punch to the belly that dropped the man to his knees. He waited for his victim to regain his breath.

"I've grown weary," he began, "with half-baked hoods like you coming around here thinking you can take what you want. If I see you or anyone of your gang on this property again, I will hunt you down and gut you like a fish. It will be slow. It will be painful. You will beg to die. Do you understand?"

The man nodded.

"Say it."

He had just enough air to whisper, "Yes, sir. I understand."

MARY-MARTHA STOOD IN THE GLARE OF STAGE LIGHTS. A spotlight shone from the lighting rack near the ceiling, bathing her in a golden hue. The floor-length regal blue robe she wore sparkled in the beam. Over the last ten minutes she had talked about the ministry and upcoming events. She also thanked those who had demonstrated their belief by their faithful giving.

"Don't forget. Next week we will be having our question-and-answer session where you get to ask the spirit guides whatever you have on your mind. Now, I want to thank some very special people." The microphone and sound system projected her voice to every seat. "Mr. and Mrs. Williams...well, where are they. Are you present?"

An elderly couple stood. They held hands. The man waved. Mary-Martha smiled and waved back.

"They didn't ask me to do this. In fact, I may get in trouble for it, but I believe good work should be praised, don't you?"'

Applause rolled through the sanctuary.

"Jim and Judy Williams have invested in the ministry of this church. Of course, I can't give the details, but let me say their gift came with a whole bunch of zeroes."

More applause. Jim looked embarrassed, but to Mary-Martha it was clear he enjoyed the spotlight. Mary-Martha joined the applause. A moment later, twelve thousand people stood applauding. Someone behind Jim patted him on the back.

She let the ovation continue for several minutes before raising her hands to quiet the congregation. "It's people like the Williamses who make sure our message goes out to the world. But don't think that we only appreciate large gifts. Small gifts make a difference in the lives of thousands. When you support the Church of New Revelation with your monetary gifts, you cast a vote saying you believe in our work and our mission. Thank you."

She paused then said, "Let's see what our spirit guides have for us today."

As she said the final word, the curtains at the back of the stage parted just enough for the high-back white and gold throne to slide into view. It moved on a stage device designed to make the throne appear as if it floated above the hardwood deck.

Mary-Martha stepped to the large chair but hesitated before sitting. She took several deep breaths as if the next few moments would tax her physically and mentally. She pulled her gown up a few inches and stepped on the throne's platform. As she did, wisps of stage smoke wafted from beneath the structure and rolled toward the audience. She had made certain the stage crew calculated the release of the smoke to add a sense of eeriness but not so much as to look overly staged.

Stepping in front of the throne, she turned and faced the congregation, folded her hands in front of her, bowed her head as if in prayer, and stood as unmoving as the marble statues that decorated the ornate walk leading to the lobby.

A minute passed, then another. Finally, she lowered herself to the gold cushion. She let out a long breath, a sigh faithfully carried by the sound system.

She set a hand on each armrest as if expecting the throne to begin flying around the room.

"Blessings, my brothers and sisters." Her voice emerged an octave lower.

"Greetings," Mary-Martha said in her own voice. "Is this Lustar?"

"Yes, child. I bring you greetings from the upper dimension."

"And we greet you in love and respect. May your name be blessed through the ages."

Mary-Martha spoke slowly. Carrying on a dialogue with one's self demanded concentration. Using the wrong voice would break the moment and destroy the illusion.

"I have been blessed and am blessed. I bring news of great joy to you and the faithful. The council of elders agreed that your planet is to be honored with great peace and prosperity. Your repeated request will soon be answered. The world will know peace for the first time."

She paused to give the crowd time to respond, which they did with robust applause. Mary-Martha fought down a smile.

"This peace will take time, but it will come to pass as surely as your sun rises over the horizon."

"This is wonderful news, Lustar. We have longed for world peace."

"There shall be more than peace, brothers and sisters. There will be great prosperity. Poverty will soon be a thing of the past. All of this will come about through you and your faithful followers. The world will rise and call all of you blessed for the good you will bring."

"But Lustar, how can we bring about so great a change? We are small in number and in resources."

"You are wealthier than you realize, wealth in belief. In a world filled with false churches, yours shines like the brightest star in the night sky. In your midst are those who can meet every financial need. All you need is faith and love."

"We have faith, Lustar. We have love..."

The room began to spin. Mary-Martha blinked and tried to force the sudden dizziness from her mind.

"We have love. We are willing to sacrifice—"

Her stomach burned as if she had swallowed lye. Fire raced through her arms and legs. Arctic-like cold touched the back of her neck. She felt cold and hot at the same time.

She tried to focus, to push aside the sudden illness. Concentration was her strength. It always served her well. If she could just force her mind to dwell on the words of the message—

Something pressed her back and down in the seat until she felt the hard wood surface beneath the cushion. Her head snapped back, banging the solid wood behind her. Sparks flashed in her closed eyes.

Focus. Think.

The acid in her stomach boiled. Something was wrong. Very wrong.

She clamped her jaw shut and tried to hide any signs of distress. The congregation had grown used to long pauses when she "channeled" a spirit guide. If she could continue, they would never know that she felt like hurling her morning toast.

"Lustar, we are honored. What must…we…do?"

"Find the one I am sending." Bringing up the strange ad had been part of her intent. She hadn't had time to plan everything. All she wanted to do this morning was mention the unknown messenger. She would figure out how to get mileage from the strange ad later.

The pressure on her chest increased, and she struggled for breath. She wondered if her heart were about to give out. Then the pressure stopped.

"The messenger speaks for you: Mary-Martha Celestine, prophetess of the new humanity."

The voice sounded wrong. She had changed pitch and tempo, the one thing she worked so hard never to do.

She shook her head, trying to dislodge the thoughts.

"Lustar, I am not worth—"

"You are the one they will seek. You are lord of the messenger. You are the anointed one. The world awaits you."

The spotlight dimmed. No, she realized, not the spotlight.

All the lights grew dark. The pressure pinning her to the throne disappeared, and she drew in a long, wheezing breath.

Her stomach settled; the fire in her limbs disappeared. She stood on tremulous legs. She opened her mouth to speak.

Everything went dark.

"That was a great touch," Willie said.

"What?" Mary-Martha sat in a folding chair just off stage.

"The whole thing. The voice change. Dropping the staccato cadence. Altering the subject matter. You had me going there. Then passing out. Brilliant."

One of the stagehands brought her a cup of water. Why did people think a cup of water fixed everything? She took it and drained the cup.

"How did I get here?"

"We carried you offstage. You should have told us you were going to do that. We weren't ready."

"I didn't tell you because I didn't know."

"Well, you are the queen of improvisation."

"No, you moron, I really passed out. I don't remember anything."

He paled. "You really…I thought—We need to get you to a doctor."

"I'm fine. Tell me what happened."

"You really don't remember?"

"I remember feeling ill, then…nothing."

"You changed voices; used one I haven't heard before. You began talking about being lord of the messenger. I assume you got that from the paper this morning."

She nodded. "I intended to use it…" She stood, and Willie held her arm.

"Maybe you should sit a little longer."

She pulled her arm away. "I want to see the video."

"Sure, just take a few minutes."

"I want to see it now."

Willie assured the stage crew and staff members that his wife was fine; then he led her to the video room. One of the techs ran the last part of the service. Mary-Martha watched from the angle of each of the four cameras that recorded the service. Second time through, her memories returned.

"I've been thinking about how to edit out the fainting part—"

"You'll leave it in," she said.

"You want to broadcast the whole thing?"

She nodded. "Absolutely." She turned to Willie. "I want to see Gabriel Hoagland right away."

THE MONDAY MORNING WASHINGTON TRAFFIC SHUFFLED
along in starts and stops. Still, Gene Manford arrived at the
FCC building fifteen minutes before his workday was due to
begin. When he entered his office he found the FCC director
Alec Casey waiting for him. He was leaning against Manford's
desk reading a newspaper.

"Hey, Alec. I see you made better time than I did."

"I got lucky." Alec was a thick man. Thick at the waist; thick at
the neck. Even the horn-rimmed glasses he wore were thick. The
only thing thin and agile about the man was his intelligence.

"I suppose you're wondering what I've learned about the radio
broadcast."

"I am, then I have something else for you." Casey took a seat
opposite Manford's government-issue desk.

"Sure you don't want to go first?" Manford set his briefcase on the
floor, removed his gray suit coat, and then sat in his office chair.

"Everything in its proper order." Manford's boss pulled a pipe
from his suit coat pocket and put the stem in his mouth. Manford
held no worries that his boss would light up. Smoking wasn't allowed
in the building, but that didn't matter. The man had quit smoking
twelve years before. He gave up the tobacco but kept the pipe.

"I worked over the weekend but came up with zilch. I talked
with several station managers and even visited a few local radio
stations. No one knows how the message was transmitted. and
everyone I spoke to swore they had nothing to do with it."

"A pirate station?"

"Perhaps. We've had our share of offshore and onshore illegal broadcasters, but this *feels* different."

"How so?"

"Well, for one thing, the length of the broadcast was short. As you know, many pirate stations operate from international waters or across our borders. Most have an agenda or are trying to work outside U.S. laws. This broadcast was short. Not only that, it went out over legal frequencies assigned to legitimate stations."

"So they stepped on several frequencies."

"Yes. AM and FM. I'm not saying it can't be done, but what would a pirate station get out of such an effort?"

"So you think it's a prank." Casey frowned.

"That's possible, I suppose, but why bother?"

Casey shrugged. "Who knows why anyone does anything. Got anything more?"

Manford shook his head. "I interviewed as many radio engineers as I could reach over the weekend. Bottom line: no one knows anything. Unless this thing repeats, we'll never get a handle on it."

Casey stood, unfolded the paper he held, and spread it on Manford's desk. "I brought you a paper."

"The *New York Times*? I'm a *Washington Post* man."

"This may change your mind." He peeled back the first page. A full-page image captured Manford's attention. His eyes fell on the only text present: Look for the one I AM sending you.

"It's the same message."

"I thought you'd catch that."

"Who's the person in the photo?"

"I have no idea." Casey sat again. "If your chair had a seat belt, I'd suggest you fasten it. We've received several calls about that photo. Print media isn't under our purview, but since the message is the same as what went over the airwaves, I think we have reasonable cause to investigate."

"You bet we do. I'll get on it."

"There's more. The calls we've been getting say the image moves, or moved."

"What do you mean, moved?"

"They say the shadowy man walked."

Manford laughed. "That's ridiculous. This is nothing but ink on paper." He looked at the paper again as if needing confirmation of his remark.

"You can't make this stuff up, Gene. It's not just one starved-for-attention nutcase, either. The guy at the *Times* said they've been getting calls all day."

"You can't believe the photo moved, Alec."

"I never said *I* believed it, only that other people said it did."

"Well, they're nuts. Our country has its share of paranoids and conspiracy theorists. It's one reason there are so many radio talk shows."

"Be that as it may, we're still left with a mystery broadcast and that ad in the paper with the same message. All you have to do is figure it all out."

"Is that all?"

"Sure. I'll bet you're done by lunch." Alec stood and started for the door.

"You'll lose that bet, you know."

"I didn't say I'd put money on it." As he reached the door, he turned to Manford. "I want this to be your priority. As soon as the *Times* learn of the break-in broadcast with the same message as their print ad, we'll be front-page news. I don't want to read an editorial about how the FCC has been dragging its feet."

Over the next two and a half hours, Manford cleared his workload, reassigned cases to other personnel, and briefed them on what he had done. He then turned his attention to his remaining assignment. A call to the editor of the *New York Times* earned him nothing but a sore ear. He did learn more about how a newspaper is published. Unfortunately, the new education took him nowhere. He reviewed the file of complaints received from listeners whose music or news broadcast had been interrupted by the bizarre message.

The art deco clock on his desk read 10:32. He blew a stream of air through his lips. He had nothing.

The phone on his desk sounded, and he snapped up the handset.

"Gene Manford."

"Good morning, Agent Manford. My name is Katherine Rooney. I'm an agent with the FBI, Los Angeles office."

"FBI? To what do I owe the honor of a call from the Los Angeles...wait, it's what? Seven-thirty there?"

"I'm an early riser. Besides, in LA if you don't leave early, you arrive late, if you know what I mean."

"Yeah, DC isn't much better. What can I do for you?"

"I want to tell you a story, and I don't want you to think my mind has come unhinged."

"Today is good day for that."

"Why?"

"Never mind. You wouldn't believe me."

"You might be surprised." He heard her take a deep breath. "First things first, it's important that you know I am who I say I am. I assume you have more than one line on your phone?"

He said he did.

"OK. I assume you have a government directory there. I want you to put me on hold, call the Los Angeles FBI office and ask for Special Agent Ted Baker. He's in the next cubicle."

"Why would I do that?"

"So you know this isn't a prank. It's important that you know that I'm the person I say I am. Put me on hold. I'll wait."

"If you say so." Manford did as instructed.

"FBI. May I help you?"

"Good morning, this is Agent Gene Manford, FCC, Washington. Is Agent Ted Baker available?"

"One moment please."

Over the handset he heard the phone begin to ring. "Special Agent Baker."

Manford identified himself. "This is going to sound strange, but do you work with an agent named Katherine Rooney?"

"I do. Why?"

"First, let me ask another dumb question. Is she on the phone?"

"Hang on."

Manford could imagine him peeking over a short cubicle wall.

"She is. She said she's on hold with you. What's going on?"

"I'll let her explain. Thank you." Manford hung up and punched the button on the phone reconnecting him to Katherine. "Your buddy must think I'm an idiot."

"He thinks everyone is an idiot. I wanted to make sure there was no doubt in your mind that I'm legit."

"OK, you're an agent with the FBI; now what can I do for you?"

"I'm going to tell you a story you're not going to believe. I want you to let me tell the whole thing."

"OK, but why me?"

"Because you're the head of the enforcement division of the FCC, that's why. This is more your bailiwick than mine. This is going to take about five minutes, so sit back."

Manford did and tried to imagine what the caller looked like. Her voice was pleasant, and she seemed confident. He took notes as he listened, a task that became more difficult when he heard about Lucille Ball talking about the need to look for a messenger.

"Wait a sec—"

"No. The deal is that you listen to the whole thing before you decide to call the padded wagon. I'm holding you to it."

"Fine. You got my attention."

She continued. Over the next two minutes he learned of her Internet search, of a young film student with a pirated video of a Thom Blake movie, and of the actor delivering the same message to the theatergoers.

When she finished, she sighed and said, "OK, there it is."

"That's quite a story, Agent Rooney. Let me ask you something. Would you have called if you hadn't run across…" He looked at his notes. "…Ray Tickner and his pirated video?"

She didn't hesitate. "No. Would you if you were in my place?"

"I doubt it. OK, it's your turn to listen. I'll give you the *Reader's Digest* version." He relayed the account of the illegal broadcast and the reports about the moving full-page ad in the *New York Times*. He ended with, "Still feel crazy?"

"Yes, but not alone. What's going on?"

"I wish I knew. The radio broadcast is no biggie. Anyone with a little money and a hatred for rules can cobble together a broadcast station. What you saw on television is a little harder to explain, as is the movie."

"Just a *little* harder to explain?"

"I'm sure there's a reasonable answer. We just have to find it."

"What about the newspaper?"

Manford reached for the copy Alec had left on his desk and opened it. "I'm looking at it now, and I don't see how the image can move. If it were an electronic device—"

Manford released the paper and bolted to his feet.

The handset fell and landed hard on the desk. A distant voice poured from the receiver. "Hello? Agent Manford? You there? Hello?"

Manford didn't care about the phone; his eyes were fixed on the image of the man in the ad—a man who seemed to be walking.

YOU SNORE." EDDIE DIDN'T MOVE HIS EYES FROM INTERstate 10. They had traveled Interstate 20 to the junction of the two freeways. Henick wanted to continue west. Behind them the late morning sun shone from a cerulean sky. Traffic traveled at seventy-five with some vehicles stretching the speed limit even more. Eddie took the right lane and drove just faster than the eighteen-wheelers but slower than most other cars coursing the asphalt river.

"So do you," Henick replied.

"No I don't. You, on the other hand, rock the rafters, and that cheap hotel didn't look strong enough to withstand much ceiling shaking."

"I shall try to sleep more quietly."

"I'm just yanking your chain, longhair. You haven't said a word in the last fifty miles."

"I have been thinking."

"About what?"

"The land. There is a beauty to the land."

Eddie laughed. "Most people don't use that word for West Texas. East Texas, sure. It has tons of trees and green. Here, we got miles and miles of nothing."

"But people live here, built homes and cities."

"It's good ranching land. Of course, some areas have black gold beneath the surface. A man can live in some pretty harsh conditions if he's pumping money out of the ground."

"Black gold?"

"Oil. You know, the stuff that makes the world go around."

"Oil does not make the earth go around."

"It's a figure of speech."

"An inaccurate figure of speech."

Eddie frowned. "Well thank you, Dr. Carl Sagan."

"My name is not—"

"Never mind. I know your name." He chuckled. "You are one odd duck, Henick. I can't figure you."

"I am as God made me."

"Now you sound like my mother."

Henick looked at him. "Your mother was wise. You should heed her words."

"Yeah, well maybe." Eddie changed subjects. "Where are we headed?"

They whizzed by a sign: VAN HORN 40 MILES.

"Farther."

"Um, could you be more specific? Got a town in mind, or do you just want to drive west until we hit the Pacific Ocean?"

"I will know."

"Know what?"

"When we arrive."

"Arrive where…never mind. Just give me a heads up *before* we get there."

Henick said nothing. Eddie stole a glance at him, and the strange man's mood seemed to change. His face was mostly a frown, and his eyes seemed to have an extra layer of moisture than usual.

"Hey, you OK, man?"

"No."

"You're not carsick, are you?"

"My body is well."

"Then what?"

He shook his head. "Pull to the side."

"Whoa. If you're going to upchuck, at least wait till I stop."

Eddie hit the turn indicator and pulled to the shoulder, slowing as he did. Thirty seconds later, the truck crunched to a stop on the sand-laced asphalt edge of the freeway. He slowed to a stop.

"OK."

Henick craned his neck, taking in the surroundings. "Back up."

"What? No, if you gotta puke, then pop the door and do your business. This place is as good as any."

"Do not argue, Eddie. Back up. Back up now."

Eddie swore under his breath, put the truck in reverse, and eased backward along the shoulder.

"More," Henick said.

Eddie started to speak but decided against it. Henick looked like a man unwilling to listen to anyone but the voice in his own head. Eddie estimated he had backed up close to a hundred yards before Henick told him to stop.

"You know, I can get a ticket for backing up like this on the freeway."

"Wait."

"For what?"

"Wait."

"Fine," Eddie snapped. He punched the emergency flasher button, and the click-click-click filled the truck's cab. "So you're not sick."

"I told you my body is well."

"Yeah, but I just thought you were trying to be tough or something." He looked at Henick again. "Ain't none of my business, but you don't look so good. What's eating you?"

Henick nodded forward, and Eddie followed his gaze. Traffic zipped by: cars, SUVs, pickup trucks, vans, motorcycles, and the ever-present tractor-trailers.

As one big rig passed, Eddie heard an explosion. He jerked at the sound of it. Smoke and rubber filled the air a short distance in front of them. A large strip of tread flew into the air and struck a black SUV on the windshield. The driver of the car jerked the wheel to the right, trying to avoid the flying rubber, but it was too late. The power of the expelled tire section coupled with the speed of the SUV shattered the windshield. The vehicle lost control and skidded to the right—impacting the left rear of a school bus.

The bus turned sideways and began to roll. It flipped three times before coming to a stop in the middle of the freeway. The SUV also rolled, sliding off the road and over the shoulder—the area of shoulder Eddie had stopped in a few moments before.

Screeches like those of a tortured animal filled the air. One car collided with another. Some spun like tops. Just as Eddie thought the carnage had ended, he heard the deep roar of large tires scratching at the road surface. He snapped his head around to look in the side mirror. A fuel delivery truck had locked its wheels in a desperate effort to avoid adding to the mash up of metal and flesh.

It plowed through three cars, glanced off the school bus, and impacted the jackknifed big rig that had started it all with a blown front tire.

The massive stainless steel containers of the tanker truck split. A second later Eddie saw flames. He couldn't tell what started the fire, but he knew there were plenty of sparks from metal and electricity from batteries to do the job. How it started didn't matter. If they didn't move, they would be dead.

"We gotta get out of here, man." He threw the transmission into reverse but stopped when Henick opened his door. "Hey, what are you doing? Don't be a fool."

Henick slipped from his seat. Eddie began swearing, using every obscene word he knew, then moved the gear lever from REVERSE to PARK and against every instinct exited the pickup.

A short distance away more tires screamed against the freeway surface, but Eddie heard no more metal crumbling metal. He did, however, hear chugging engine sounds, noises from radiator fans chewing into their housings. Above it all, he heard the screams of children and injured adults. Scores of them filled the air with terror-laced pleas for help.

"Henick. Henick! What are you doing?" Flames from the fuel truck reached for the sky. Eddie could hear it sucking air, could feel it growing hotter by the second. He sprinted to Henick and stood in his way. "We gotta go, man. That truck's a bomb waiting to go off."

Henick stepped around him. Eddie grabbed his arm, but Henick pulled free. Again, Eddie stepped in front of him. "You've lost your mind. I'm not letting you lose your life. You can't help the guy in the truck. He's a goner for sure." Eddie grabbed Henick by the shoulders and tried to turn him. He refused to budge.

"Go back to your truck. I will need you soon."

"You're going with me."

Eddie could not have imagined what happened next. Before he had time to utter another word, Eddie was on the ground looking up at the sky. Somehow, Henick had freed himself from Eddie's grasp and spun him to the ground.

Eddie sprang to his feet, but he was too late.

Henick ran into the orange, churning flames of the gasoline-fed hell.

NO!"

Eddie couldn't see Henick, who had disappeared behind a curtain of flame. The inferno grew hotter and seemed alive, more beast than simple combustion.

"Friend of yours?"

Eddie turned to see a middle-aged man at his side.

"Yeah."

"I can't tell if he's brave or nuts."

Eddie took no time to mourn the loss. He stood in the middle of death and turmoil. A school bus lay on its side. Two big rigs were entwined and burning. A half dozen cars held unconscious passengers. What Eddie saw next froze him to the marrow. Burning fuel raced toward the school bus.

"The kids. We got to get the kids out of the bus. Come on."

"Not me, pal. One step in that thing, and you're a dead man.

Eddie didn't argue. The man was right, but Eddie couldn't stand by and watch it happen. He ran to the back of the bus and tugged on the emergency exit door. It took four hard pulls before he got the door to release from the bent frame. A chorus of cries, sobs, and howls of pain greeted him. Heat from the approaching fire baked the side of his face and his arm.

Mayhem waited inside for him. There were no seatbelts on the school bus. Children lay piled on top of children, crushing those at the bottom. Blood splattered seats and faces. Fire began to lick at the exposed undercarriage.

Something in his mind reminded him that moving an injured person could make things worse. A tongue of flame shot up like a solar flare. Eddie decided he couldn't make things worse.

He took one step into the bus, lifted the first child he saw, and exited.

"My arm! My arm!"

"I know, buddy, but I gotta do this."

He ran from the bus and set the child down by his truck, then sprinted back to the bus. This time he entered without hesitation, without thought. Thinking would only make him hesitate. The next child looked to be about ten years old. Blood poured from her nose and stained a yellow, flower dress. She didn't cry, but she did wrap her arms around Eddie's neck.

He made two steps out of the bus when a man stepped in front of him. "I'll take her." It was the middle-aged guy. In a moment, a silvered-haired man wearing a dress shirt and silk tie followed Eddie into the bus. The temperature in the bus continued to grow. The smell of burning fuel choked Eddie, and the thick, black smoke that billowed from the burning truck covered the bus, cutting off most of the light.

"We can't do this much longer," the silver-haired man said.

"No one gets left behind," Eddie snapped. "No one!"

Eddie picked up two children. He no longer noticed if they were boys or girls. It didn't matter. This time as he stepped from the bus he found a line of people, men and women each waiting for someone to hand them a broken child. Eddie wished he had time to feel proud of his fellow Texans.

A movement to his right caught his eyes. Henick walked from the raging fire with a body in his arms. The body was too burned to recognize gender. Why Henick bothered carrying a corpse made no sense to Eddie, but he didn't have time to think it through. He stepped into the bus that now felt like an oven. The businessman stayed with him, coughing and wheezing. Sweat soaked every inch of his body.

They made two more trips out of the bus before it happened. The fuel truck rumbled and blew out the side of one of the large fuel tanks. Gasoline poured from the storage container and flooded toward the bus in a tsunami of fire.

The line of helpers ran, and Eddie, who stood closest to the truck, was blown off his feet. He struggled to rise. The fuel spread beneath the upended bus, running between its thin metal sides and the pavement. It was the side the child lay on.

"No. Oh, God, no!"

Henick walked past him. His clothing hung on him in smoldering shreds. The skin of his arms, neck, and hands was blistered and charred.

Henick walked into the burning bus. Someone yelled, "Stop him!" No one tried.

Henick returned with the burned corpses of two children. Eddie did the one thing he didn't want to do, the one thing he couldn't—he took one of the corpses and carried it to the side of the road. Charred flesh hung in clumps on the girl's arms and legs. The smell gagged him.

He began to weep.

Henick returned to the bus again and again. The last fragment of his clothing had burned off. His skin was a mass of blisters and scorched tissue. Still he walked into the inferno over and over until the bus driver, a large woman, was freed from the burning tomb. Eddie helped Henick carry the heavy form. They laid her next to the children who had been her charges.

Those children who had survived wept from the depths of their souls. Several men and women were attending the wounds the best they could and trying to comfort them.

So did Eddie.

So much life changed to so much death in minutes.

He looked at Henick, who swayed. The fire left him a mass of second- and third-degree burns; most of his hair had been singed from his head. Eddie knew he was looking at a dead man.

"Oh, man; O God; oh…" Eddie stepped closer but the smell of charred skin stopped him after only two steps. "You…maybe you should lie down. I'm sure ambulances are on the way."

"Not anytime soon," the middle-aged man said. "The nearest town with medical facilities is thirty minutes away—"

Eddie gave him a cutting glance.

"Right. Of course. Sorry."

"Your friend is right," silver-hair said. "You shouldn't be standing." Then he did what Eddie thought was beyond human effort: he touched the blistered, blackened Henick.

"No." Henick's voice sounded like a rusty hinge. Superheated air must have damaged his throat. Eddie, shamed by the stranger's ability to touch the hideous, stepped closer. When in grade school, he had been taught that of all the human senses, smell was the weakest and the first to fail. He had never been so glad of a fact. The odor of burning fuel, rubber, and skin had come close to forcing him to his knees. He reached for his naked friend, but Henick pulled away and raised his hands, revealing hundreds of putrid white blisters. "No."

"OK, man. But I'm staying with you. I'm…" Tears crested his lids and poured down his face. Eddie tried to speak again but couldn't. Too much to see; too much to experience. He felt faint.

He turned his face away. Several men were helping the passengers in the overturned SUV. Eddie's emotion coagulated in his brain, bringing his ability to reason to a halt.

The wails of broken children mixed with the roar of the burning tanker truck and bus. They cried for their mommies; they pleaded for their daddies. His eyes took in the lifeless forms of the unlucky ones. Soon mothers, fathers, grandparents, brothers, and sisters would receive the horrible news shattering their lives forever.

It was wrong in so many ways. For a moment, Eddie knew what it meant to stand at ground zero of a bomb blast. There were no words to describe the scene. *Tragedy, disaster, calamity,* and *catastrophe* were words too weak, too insipid to begin telling the story.

"What? That can't…this can't be." The voice of the silver-haired man cut through the morass of Eddie's thoughts.

He looked at Henick—and stopped breathing.

Henick had not moved. He stood as still as a tree rooted to the asphalt. His eyes were closed as much as the swollen tissue would allow. A moment later he began to sway slightly like a sunflower in a light breeze. But his hands…his hands.

The blackened and blistered palms had changed. Pink skin had replaced fried tissue. As Eddie and others watched, scabby charred tissue dropped to the ground, pushed from the body by new epidermis and underlying tissue.

Eddie's knees shook, but he could not take his eyes from the metamorphosis. A woman gasped. A man uttered profanities.

What hair remained on Henick's head fell to his shoulders, then to the ground. Swollen tissue returned to normal. Eddie had no idea how much time passed. He didn't care. He wasn't even sure he was conscious anymore. Perhaps he had died in the bus trying to rescue children. Maybe this is what death was: standing around the place of one's demise.

Finally, Henick lowered his arms, opened his eyes, and looked around. Before Eddie stood a naked man with skin as fresh as a newborn's.

"It's a miracle," a woman said. Several others repeated the statement. The crowd moved toward Henick, but he turned his back on them and walked to the corpses of the children that had been laid side by side. Eddie followed.

Henick stepped next to a young boy. The child's bloodied Dallas Cowboy's cap had been fire-fused to his scalp. Vacant eyes faced a cloudless blue sky marred by billows of black smoke roiling over-head. Henick bent and touched the boy's arm. "Awake."

The lifeless eyes blinked, and Eddie jumped back two feet. If the child felt pain, he didn't show it. As with Henick, blisters faded and blackened flesh fell away. A moment later, he sat up. "He will be cold. He needs to be covered."

"What? Oh, right. Yeah." Eddie turned to the crowd and asked for coats, blankets, anything to cover the child. When he turned around, Henick had moved to the next child in line: a girl in expensive jeans and sneakers.

"Awake."

Henick moved from child to child repeating the word. The crowd went from weeping to cheering. Eddie felt lost in a dream. He took what blankets, sweaters, and coats the people provided and covered the shivering children. The air was warm, and Eddie assumed the shivering came from the shock of the accident, or death, or being brought back to life.

Soon fifteen children huddled together, several crying. It was music, a symphony of life reborn, of losses regained.

Henick moved to the injured children. Eddie followed. Ten chil-dren suffered from broken bones, lacerations, and a dozen other injuries. The first child Henick approached was a lethargic boy with blood running from his nose and ears. Henick crouched next to him and touched the side of his head; he then rose and moved to the next child, a girl struggling to breathe. Blood marred the right side of her shirt. Henick placed two fingers to her sternum then moved on.

Broken bones mended themselves; blood stopped flowing; damaged ribs became whole again. Finally he knelt by the dead trucker. Eddie stopped trying to believe his eyes. He just accepted it. Maybe later he could sort through it all and make sense of it. For now, he chose to drown in the joy of the miraculous.

Every child on the bus stood whole and healthy. One of the girls giggled.

"A child's laughter is a father's wealth."

"I think she's laughing at you," Eddie said.

"What do you mean?"

"I hate to be the one to bring it up, friend, but around these parts we'd say you're buck naked."

Henick looked at himself. "Oh."

"Here," a man said. He held a white T-shirt, a pair of jeans, boxer shorts, white socks, and a pair of Nike jogging shoes. "Me and the wife are traveling cross-country on vacation. I brought plenty of clothes. We're about the same size."

Henick took the garments and thanked the man. From overhead came a pounding, rhythmic thumping. Eddie looked up. Two helicopters circled overhead. In the distance, a score of sirens cut through the Texas air. "The cavalry is starting to arrive."

CAN'T MAKE OUT THE CHOPPERS. MY GUESS IS ONE IS Texas Highway Patrol or country sheriff. The other looks like an air ambulance. Here comes a third. Maybe a news chopper."

"We should leave." Henick slipped on the boxers, jeans, shirt, socks, and shoes.

"Why? We didn't do anything wrong." Eddie looked back at the helicopters.

"Questions will be asked."

"Ya think? Of course they're gonna to have questions. Who wouldn't?"

"We should leave."

"So you said. What's the deal? What aren't you telling me?"

"Many things. Questions would be awkward. Too much is already known. We should leave." He started to the truck, then stopped and returned to Eddie and the man. "Listen for the message. Please tell the others. Listen for the message." He turned and walked to the truck.

"Hey," the silver-haired man asked, "where are you going? Emergency personnel will be here soon. The cops will want to talk to everyone."

"You a cop?" Eddie asked.

"I didn't say that."

"You didn't answer my question either."

"I'm a fed. Homeland Security." He pulled an ID wallet from

his pocket. Eddie saw the name: Timothy Gardner. "I can't let you go."

"Great. Look, man, I don't have any answers. I'm not sure I believe what I saw; I know I wouldn't believe it if someone told me the story. You know what I mean?"

"Who's your friend?"

"Honestly, I don't know. We spent some time together in—I met him at a restaurant. He's—how do I put this—weird."

"What's his name?"

"Sorry, officer, or special agent, or whatever you are. He did me a huge favor. I owe him." Eddie glanced at the kids. Several women stood with them. "Look around you, Gardner. Have you ever seen anything like it? Ever see burns disappear and the dead come back to life?"

"No."

"If we stay here, we will be swamped with reporters, police, and who knows what else. For all I know, you government types might hold him and run some kinda sci-fi tests on him."

"Maybe, but you get the point."

Eddie softened his tone. "Look, we need your help. What if one of those kids had been yours? A whole bunch of parents have been saved a lifetime of nightmares. The man very nearly died saving the truck driver and others. For the love of… His clothing was burned from his body, but he kept going. How many people do you know who would do that? Miracle worker or not."

"Not many."

"I know this goes against everything you guys are taught, but he wants to leave, and I'm going to help him. The only way you're going to stop me is by cuffing me right now—or shooting me."

The man chuckled. "I don't carry handcuffs or a gun. I'm a paper pusher."

Eddie smiled. "For a paper pusher you showed a lot of guts helping me get those kids out. If you ask me, there are several heroes around here."

"Thanks. You did pretty good yourself." He inhaled deeply. "Be safe."

"We will."

Gardner turned to the crowd. "Folks. Folks! Can I have your attention for a moment? Gather around."

Eddie jogged to his truck and slipped behind the wheel. "Are you sure about this? You really want to leave?"

"Yes."

Eddie looked at Henick. "Well, I guess I can't call you longhair anymore."

Henick ran a hand over his bald head.

"You look great. It's all the fashion now." He started the truck, dropped it in gear, and slowly pulled forward, driving around the burning bus.

"Henick?"

"Yes."

"You and me gotta have a heart-to-heart talk, and I'm not going to take no for an answer."

Henick sighed.

GABRIEL HOAGLAND TURNED OFF THE SHOWER AND covered his head with a large towel. Steam filled the room and the shower enclosure. The towel trapped the moist air near his face, and he inhaled deeply. Truth was, there was very little for him to do at the Church of New Revelation during the week. Sometimes he trained new security guards, other times he checked security systems, but most of the time he served as Mary-Martha's bodyguard.

He had spent forty-five minutes in the shower, his mind churning over the new orders he received. Yesterday, Mary-Martha had called him to her office and showed him the *New York Times* ad. "I want to know who this person is."

Hoagland studied the full-page ad. "Too indistinct. I can't even be certain if it's a man or a woman. I'd guess a man. Not much in the hips."

"How do we find him?"

He tilted his head. "We're going to need more than this ad. For all we know, the person in the picture is a model hired to do a little posing."

"There must be a way." She leaned back in her chair. "I depend on you for so much, Gabriel. I'm helpless without you. You know I need you. You're smarter than any man I know. Please find him."

Despite her soft, needy tone, it wasn't a plea. He knew an order when he heard one, even if it came with a sugary coating.

"I'll do what I can."

"Don't be concerned about expenses."

He now knew how serious her desire had become.

Unfortunately, he had no idea how to carry out the order. He had thought of little else that night or this morning. Shortly after slipping from bed, he placed a long-distance call to New York. Pretending to be a reporter for *Advertising Weekly*, he asked to speak to the person in charge of display ads. The receptionist transferred him to some guy who refused to talk about the ad. The man sounded angry.

Drying himself off, Hoagland stepped from the shower. True to years of habit, he turned on the television in his bedroom. It was already set to CNN. A commercial for Shell Oil played. He pulled a pair of black jeans and a black polo shirt from the closet, underwear and white socks from the dresser, and threw them on his unmade bed and began to dress.

"If you've been with us throughout the morning, then you know we've been following a story that can only be called bizarre." The anchor was a pretty woman just this side of forty. Her reddish-brown hair bounced slightly with each head movement. Hoagland always thought she'd be a good date.

As he sat on the bed he heard her lilting voice continue. "In West Texas a fifteen-car pileup looked to be a monumental tragedy, but according to eyewitnesses, something miraculous happened. In a moment we will show you some video. I need to warn you that what you are about to see may disturb some viewers and children. Please use discretion."

Disturbing videos? The anchorwoman's word caught Hoagland's attention. "The accident occurred on Interstate 10, forty miles east of the small town of Van Horn. As can be seen in this aerial video taken by one of our affiliates in El Paso, the accident involved several big rigs and a dozen cars. One of the big rigs involved was a tanker truck carrying gasoline. Witnesses say the vehicle began to burn within moments after impacting another truck."

The announcer disappeared behind a full-screen roll of the carnage. Thick, black smoke churned in the air; yellow-orange flames leapt from the tanker. A short distance away a yellow school bus lay on its side. Fire followed spilt fuel and engulfed the vehicle. Hoagland turned up the volume.

"The news copter, which was on assignment a short distance away, arrived a few minutes after reports began to flood the Highway Patrol division of the Texas Department of Public Safety. By the time the helicopter arrived, the bus was already ablaze. We are told the bus was transporting twenty-five elementary school–age children. As yet we don't have specific ages, but emergency personnel now on scene tell us ages range between eight and ten."

The voice-over continued. "What you're seeing now is a live shot. As you can see, people are milling about, well away from the blaze. If you look closely, you can see children huddled next to adults as fire crews examine them for injuries. Now…" She faded. "Excuse me, this is so hard to believe."

Hoagland heard her take a deep breath.

"We are going to roll footage taken by the news copter when it first arrived. Again, these images may be disturbing."

The live feed disappeared, replaced by one of the anchor looking at her monitor. "Do we have that?" she asked someone off camera. "OK, here we go."

Another aerial stream of video flashed on the screen. Hoagland ceased dressing and stood in front of the flat screen with his arms crossed.

"As you can see…" She cleared her throat. "As you can see, the tanker truck is fully involved in flame and the bus is beginning to burn. Several men are attempting to remove children through the back emergency door, and…there you can see one man charges into the burning bus and begins passing children to others, who carry them a safe distance away. The first few to be rescued are clearly alive but then..."

Hoagland watched as a man passed unmoving bodies to other men. Despite the helicopter's altitude, he could see that many of the children had been severely burned. The camera shifted its angle, and Hoagland saw something unbelievable. Another man stepped from the fire that surrounded the tanker truck. He carried a man, presumably the driver. The body in the man's arms was a charred corpse, and what little clothing remained on the hero continued to burn as he walked away from the roaring flames. The man's hair smoldered on his head. All that remained of his clothing was a pair of smoking sport shoes.

"As a reporter I have seen—well, everything, but never could I imagine this. I...you know, the video speaks for itself. Just watch."

Hoagland did, and what he saw iced over his spine. The camera tightened on the naked man. Burns covered him from head to foot, yet he had the strength to hold onto the corpse then set it on the ground. He then did what Hoagland knew no man would do: he turned to the burning bus, approached, and stepped through the emergency exit door. He carried child after child from fury and finally carried another adult from the flames. Several people gathered around him, blocking the camera.

"C'mon, get out of the way," Hoagland said to the television. Although bystanders blocked some of his vision, he could see enough to know that something was happening to the man. A few moments later he walked to the dead children. Hoagland couldn't see a burn on the man's body. He touched one of the dead children.

For a moment, Hoagland thought the channel had changed to some science-fiction movie. He looked at the bottom of the screen. It said: CNN BREAKING NEWS. Even then he fought what his eyes told him to be true.

The dead girl came to life. Her burns disappeared. The man

repeated the act again and again. Something tickled Hoagland's brain. He slipped into the living room and returned a moment later with the copy of the *New York Times* Mary-Martha had given him. He studied it again. "The terrain could be West Texas." He looked back at the video. "It certainly could."

He set the paper down. "So there you are."

He picked up the remote and pressed the record button.

HOW MANY TIMES ARE YOU GOING TO WATCH THAT?"
Willie glanced at his wife. She sat at her desk in her home office, and he stood at the door. Her eyes remained fixed on the computer monitor.

"What does it matter?"

"It's your day off." Willie stepped into the room and stood behind her chair. "I thought we might go out for brunch, maybe catch a matinee."

"Thanks, but I'm not interested."

"You work too hard. It can't be good for you."

"I'm fine. I'm just trying to figure this out."

Willie tried to keep the disappointment from his voice. Brunch and an early matinee had been a mainstay of their relationship during the early years of their marriage, but it, like so many other things, had been tossed away. "Can I help?"

"I doubt it. Besides, you wouldn't believe me."

"I've always believed you." *Even when I knew better.* "That's yesterday's service, right?"

"Of course."

"I thought you delivered one of your better messages."

"That's just it…"

"Just what? Come on; include your husband for a change. I've been known to have an insight or two. You used to consult me about everything."

She pressed her lips then said, "All right. You just said that this sermon was one of my better ones. Well, that's the thing. I don't remember most of it."

"Don't remember? How can you not remember what you said yesterday?"

She shook her head and frowned. "I didn't say that. I remember everything but a few minutes of my sermon." She clicked on the rewind icon on the computer screen, backed up a few seconds, then clicked on pause.

"OK," she said. "I got a copy of the sermon burned to CD so I could study it today."

"And most of yesterday."

"Whatever. I made some last-minute changes to the sermon. I wanted to bring up the message we read in the *New York Times*. I was just going to mention the sent one, judge the congregation's reaction, and go from there. In short, I was winging it, but I figured if we saw the ad, then others had as well. We have some well-educated people in church, the kind who like to read the *Times* and tell people about it. You know what I mean."

"I know."

"Now watch." She ran the video and turned up the sound.

"The messenger speaks for you: Mary-Martha Celestine, prophetess of the new humanity."

She paused the video. "Notice anything?"

"The voice is different."

"Exactly. You know how hard I work to be consistent. When I'm channeling Lustar, it's important that he sound the same every time."

"So you were off a little."

Again she shook her head. "Listen."

"Lustar, I am not worth—"

"You are the one they will seek. You are lord of the messenger. You are the anointed one. The world awaits you."

Willie listened carefully. "You're using the same voice as before, but not Lustar's."

"Here's the thing: I don't remember saying that. I felt ill, dizzy, and heavy even though I was seated. I have no recollection of saying anything about me being the messenger."

"You passed out for a few moments right after that. Maybe you were already out."

"Then how did I utter the words?"

Willie had no idea. "What are you saying? Are you telling me that you really channeled someone or some—thing?"

The phone rang before Mary-Martha could speak. She snapped up the receiver. Willie took a seat on the small, contemporary sofa.

"Texas? Why Texas?" A second later his wife grabbed the remote control for the small flat-screen television mounted to the wall opposite her desk and tuned to CNN.

She watched for a moment and said, "Oh my. Keep me posted, Gabriel."

Hoagland had finished dressing and began packing a bag. As soon as he hung up from his brief conversation with Mary-Martha, he placed two more calls, all during the commercial breaks. CNN's special report continued to play. One call was to the travel agency used by the church. "I need two tickets to El Paso today, first class if you can get it. I need two hours to get ready and drive to the airport. See how close you can get to that time." They promised they would.

He dialed another number. It rang twice before a familiar voice said, "Talk."

"Howie, it's Gabe. We're taking a trip; pack for three or four days. We're flying, so no hardware."

"What's the world coming to when a man can't fly with a gun?"

"We'll pick up whatever we need when we get there."

"Where we going?"

"Texas. El Paso."

"Texas? Why? What did I do?"

"Some people like Texas, Howie."

"Well, I ain't one of them."

"You want me to get someone else?"

Howie laughed. "Of course not, Boss. I'm just yanking your chain."

"Stop yanking and start packing. As soon as I hear back from the travel agency, I'll let you know when and where to meet. Got it?"

"Got it."

Hoagland hung up and rewound the DVR to catch the few minutes of the report he missed while on the phone. The anchor was talking by phone to a trooper.

"But there were witnesses, right?" the reporter asked.

"Quite a few, but they don't seem to know what happened."

"I don't understand," she said. "How can that be?"

There was a pause. "No one seems to remember a man saving a trucker, or one rescuing children from the bus."

"Excuse me, officer, but the nation has seen them on video."

"We will be analyzing the video as soon as possible. We hope to have a lead on them soon."

The anchor was incredulous. "Are you saying none of the witnesses can remember this man?"

He cleared his throat again. "That's what they say."

"And you believe them."

"Well, at this point, it's not my place to believe or disbelieve their testimony."

"Forgive me, officer, but I'm trying to read between the lines here. I'm sure that in your experience you've questioned many people."

"That's true."

"You don't believe them, do you?"

A long pause.

"Officer."

"I should be returning to my duties. We have quite a mess here."

"A mess with no injuries."

"It seems so."

"One last thing, officer. We're getting reports from those on scene that the mystery man said, 'Listen for the message,' or something like that. Are you hearing the same thing?"

"Yes. He seems to have told one person, who spread the word."

"The people can remember that but not the man who said it," the reporter pressed. "Is that person reputable?"

"I would say so. Now, I really must go."

"Thank you, officer. That was..."

Hoagland stopped listening. Why would anyone lie about what they saw? If they had committed a crime, then lying made sense. He and falsehood were old buddies, but he learned to lie only when absolutely necessary. Experience had taught him that lies were the weakest link in the chain.

So why protect this guy, this healer? How does a man get a bunch of strangers to agree to a cover-up? Hoagland didn't believe in conspiracy theories. Conspiracies were only as strong as their weakest member. And people who conspired together are held together by some bond: fear, wealth, power, or morality.

Was that it? Were they protecting Mr. Hero? Had he asked them to do so?

Hoagland rewound the DVR until he found the earlier recording, the one with obviously dead children coming back to life. He watched it closely. Something nibbled at the back of his brain. At the end of video he saw a truck parked to the side, a truck on the shoulder of the freeway not far from the children. The cameraman had chosen that moment to aim his camera back at the burning truck before immediately returning it to the children. But Hoagland had seen enough—a Chevy pickup, black, maybe from the early to mid-1980s. He wished he had more, but it was more than he woke up with. He had a place to start, a vehicle to search for, and a mystery man to track.

The day just got better and better.

HENICK LOOKED ILL, NOT SICK, BUT WEARY BEYOND words. He sat in the passenger seat of the truck with his now bald head resting against the side window. Eddie shifted his eyes from the road to Henick and back to the road a dozen times. Every glance made Eddie worry more. Although all evidence of severe burns had disappeared, leaving not a single scar, Henick appeared an empty shell. His open eyes were fixed on the dashboard as if reading something of great interest on the blank surface.

"Are you sleeping with your eyes open?" Eddie chuckled. Henick gave no sign he had heard him. "C'mon, man, we've been driving for thirty minutes and you haven't said a thing."

"I have no words."

Eddie huffed. "I've got plenty for both of us."

Henick didn't respond.

"Are you hurt? Sick? Depressed? What?"

"My body is well."

Eddie tapped his teeth together, making a clicking noise. "What about the rest of you? 'Cause at best you look like warmed-over death...sorry, bad word choice. I mean for a man who just worked a dozen miracles, you look like your best dog died."

"Dog?"

"Never mind. Come on, man. Sit up. Talk to me."

Henick shifted in the seat, straightened, but kept his eyes forward.

"That's better. My mother used to tell me that if I acted happy,

I'd be happy. I always thought that was a crock." He paused. "Sometimes I think she was right about that—and about so many other things."

"She was a wise woman."

Eddie frowned. He hated it when Henick spoke of his mother like they had been longtime friends.

"If she were so smart, how did we end up living in a trailer?"

"Wisdom and wealth do not always travel together."

"Whatever. What I can't figure out is why you're so bummed. We just saved a bunch of kids and you healed their wounds and brought some back from the dead. That's a good piece of work for one day." Eddie watched the road course by. He checked his rearview mirror as he had done a hundred times in the last half hour. He saw no cars. More importantly, he saw no troopers. The road would be blocked for hours. Had they not been on the side of the road and close to the front of the accident, they would never have been able to drive around the carnage.

Eddie leaned over the steering wheel and stretched his back, then leaned back again. "It's time we talked, Henick. I know you didn't ask for a sidekick, but after what just happened I think we may be bound by some cosmic something-or-another."

"Sidekick?"

"Sure, like in the movies or in books. A sidekick is the guy who travels with the hero and helps out, like Robin to Batman."

Henick furrowed his brow, and Eddie started to explain when Henick said, "You need to go home when we reach the next town."

"What? You can't send me home."

"Your life may be in danger. I made a mistake."

"A mistake? What, in letting me drive you around? Gee, thanks."

"I appreciate your help, but—"

"And what do you mean, my life is in danger?"

"You don't understand."

"You got that right. I don't understand. That's why I've been nagging you to open up to me." He sighed. "Man, now I sound like a woman. You know what I mean. I knew you were different when you healed my busted hand, but back there...I mean..." His eyes began to burn as he recalled pulling dead children from the burning bus. "I saw everything with my own eyes, but I still don't believe it."

"If you do not believe your eyes, can you believe your nose?"

"What's that supposed to mean?"

"You stink of smoke." Henick's mouth turned up at the corners.

Eddie sniffed. "Of course I stink. I'm covered in soot from burning fuel, tires, upholstery...OK, fine, laugh it up, Chuckles."

Henick turned somber again. "I am sorry I let you get involved."

"I'm not. You may be the best thing to happen to me. God knows I've had enough bad things happen."

"Yes."

"Yes what?"

"Yes, God knows."

"OK, I've been around you enough to know you're some kinda spiritual guy, but I can't pin you down."

"I'm just a man."

"I doubt that. Spill the beans. Where do you come from?"

"A long way away."

"Can you stop being cryptic? You mean you're from another country? Is that why your speech is so...stiff? English isn't your first language, right?"

"No. I am still learning."

"And where is 'a long way away'? England? No, I'd recognize an English accent. France? No. The Middle East?"

"In that area. My home has not existed for a long time."

"OK, so you're...I don't follow the news. Just tell me the name of your country."

"It had no name. It didn't need one."

Eddie scratched his eyebrow. "That makes no sense. What do I have to do to get a straight answer out of you?"

"It is better if you do not know."

"I don't buy that. You need me. I know you do. I feel it. You're stuck with me."

"No, you should go home."

"Forget it. If I go back, I'm taking you with me."

Henick looked out the side window. "I've already made too many mistakes. I have taken my eye off the course."

"What course?"

"My course."

Eddie yanked the wheel to the side, steering the truck onto the dirt shoulder, then slammed his right foot on the brake. The Chevy shuddered to a stop, sending plumes of dust and dirt into the air. The sound of rubber tires biting into the gravel-laced soil filled the cab.

He turned the truck off and faced Henick. "No more games, man. No more. Two people don't go through what we just did back there and not learn to trust each other. I got questions, I want some answers." His words came hot and fast.

"I will not answer all your questions. I've already endangered you."

"Enough of the danger talk. I'm a big boy. I can take care of myself. I'm not afraid of what's ahead. I'm going with you. I have to. I don't know why, but I know I'm supposed to go with you."

"My work must be done alone."

"No it doesn't. I don't believe that. Why are you so doom and gloom?"

"Because it wasn't supposed to happen this way."

Eddie paused. "What wasn't?"

"The children. I was there for the man in the truck, not the children."

Eddie blinked several times. "You mean you were supposed to save the truck driver but not the kids?"

Henick broke eye contact.

"You knew the accident was going to happen. That's why you

had me pull over. You even knew where it was going to occur, so you had me back up so I wouldn't be killed in the truck when that SUV went plowing through where I first parked."

"I knew some."

"What's that mean?"

"I knew there would be an accident and death. I did not know the details."

"You knew enough to have me back up."

"Yes, but not until we stopped."

"So…so you're making this up as you go? You're winging it?"

"I must move forward to events I do not fully understand. Being here is confusing."

"Being where?" Eddie asked.

Henick frowned. "I have not told you where I'm from because it no longer exists."

"So you've said. What happened? Another country take over yours?"

Henick shook his head. "No, Eddie. My home place ceased to exist long ago."

"How long?"

"It is too much for you to believe."

Eddie laughed. "I just saw you walk out of a blazing gasoline fire carrying the charred remains of the driver, bring him and a dozen dead kids back to life. What on earth can you tell me that I won't believe now?"

"I lived thousands of years ago."

"Yeah, right. I don't believe it."

Henick shifted his eyes back to Eddie and raised an eyebrow.

Eddie raised his hands. "OK, OK. It's not that I don't believe you; it's just that I don't know how that can be true. Are you saying that you died and somehow came back to life?"

"No, I've never died."

Sitting back in his seat, Eddie rubbed his eyes. "Everyone dies, man, and you don't look like you've been walking this world for centuries."

"I have not been on Earth—"

"Now just stop there. If you're going to tell me you're some kinda space alien, then my brain is going to turn into pudding." He waited for Henick to continue. When he didn't, he said, "Well? Are you going to tell me you're an alien?"

"I don't want your brain to turn into—"

"So help me, man, if I don't get a straight answer from you—"

"An alien, yes, but not from space. I'm as human as you except I'm older—six or seven thousand years older."

Eddie opened his mouth and worked his jaw, but no words came. He shifted in his seat, started the truck, and pulled back onto the road. "We should keep moving."

"Yes. That would be wise."

"I believe you," Eddie said softly.

"No, you do not."

"I will. Just give me a few minutes. I don't hear stuff like this every day. It's a good thing too."

"I'm sorry."

"Stop saying that. Stop apologizing."

"Sorry."

Eddie ground his teeth. "I like you, Henick. I really do, and that's saying something. There aren't many people I like, fewer still that I'd tell about it. You, I like, but you are the most frustrating person I've ever met. And don't apologize."

"OK."

Eddie's mind spun like a child's top. He couldn't decide who was more confused, he or Henick.

He pressed the accelerator and pointed the hood of the Chevy down the straight empty road.

MARY-MARTHA STEPPED INTO THE SHOWER FOR THE second time that day. When she arose in the morning, she followed her usual routine, which included a long hot shower and thirty minutes of makeup and hair work. This day she avoided the makeup, but the rest of the ritual remained the same. After a light breakfast, she sequestered herself in her office and watched yesterday's sermon again and again, wondering what it all meant. Her memory seemed intact for everything else except for a few moments during the message and her subsequent blackout.

During those hours and with each viewing of the video she felt awkward, confused, and a little frightened, not that she would let Willie know. He'd dote on her as if she were a toddler.

She felt something else: dirty. With each viewing it seemed a thin layer of dust covered her skin. Not just on her bare arms but on parts of her body covered with clothing. The soiling sat upon the skin of her legs despite the casual pants she wore. And although she wore a yellow long-sleeve tee and beige capris, the feeling of filth touched her entire body.

Willie had left to golf with friends, leaving her the joy of solitude.

She trod across plush carpet on bare feet until she stood once again in her spacious master bath. She had paid a designer handsomely to make the room feel like a Roman bath—dark marble tile on the floor, light Mediterranean marble on the counters, and scenic vistas painted on one of the walls. When most stressed, this was her refuge.

She turned on the shower, and hot water sprayed from eight heads on the walls. A turn of a bronze handle and the shower's ceiling-mounted rain showerheads dropped water into the large stall. Mary-Martha stripped, tossing her clothing on the bed, and slipped into the multiple streams of warm water. Within moments she was soaked from head to foot.

With eyes closed, she stood and let the rush of water run over her head and shoulders and down her body. The heat made her skin sting slightly, a sensation she enjoyed.

For several minutes she thought of nothing, embracing a blank mind like an artist before an empty canvas. The warmth, the caressing water, the sound covered her.

Hers was a taxing job, something she reminded her husband of frequently. This bathroom was a necessity, not a luxury. She doubted he understood.

The newspaper ad and the words she heard herself say on the video came to her mind again. Who was the messenger? If she believed her own voice, then the messenger was to be her servant.

"The messenger speaks for you: Mary-Martha Celestine, prophetess of the new humanity. You are the one they will seek. You are lord of the messenger. You are the anointed one. The world awaits you."

She had viewed the video so many times the words had become engraved in her mind.

What should she do? She had uttered the words and then passed out. The congregation would want an explanation. She couldn't pretend nothing had happened. That was an easy realization. Deciding what to do next was far more difficult.

Through the years, she had taken such care never to say anything that would destroy the image. Sure she stretched that rule from time to time, but she never broke it. People in her line of work rose slowly but fell at meteoric speeds. As one who loved praise so much, she couldn't tolerate the thought of disgrace.

She had come a long way from serving breakfasts and burgers in one of the small towns of New Mexico. The thought of returning to an old trailer in the seamy part of town chilled her more than the shower's hot streams could warm her. Her mother had died in that trailer; her father too. No, there was no going back. She would see to that.

Mary-Martha reached for the soap bar and rubbed the silky surface over her arms and torso. The many jets immediately flooded away the bubbles.

She still felt dirty. Nothing was visible on her hands, arms, or anywhere else on her body, but she could feel it—clinging. She washed again, but the film of filth clung to her skin. Replacing the bar of soap with shampoo, she washed her hair, scrubbing her scalp with fingernails then let the rain showerheads gently rinse the suds away.

Her hair still felt contaminated.

"What is this?"

She opened her eyes and…

…screamed.

Something was in the shower with her, its face just inches away from her own.

She screamed again and took a rapid step back, intent on fleeing the shower. Instead she slipped.

She felt her head bounce off the back wall.

EDDIE PULLED FROM THE FREEWAY AND SLOWED AS HE drove along the off ramp.

"This is wrong. We should go further." Henick looked puzzled.

"I'll tell you what's wrong. Being hungry is wrong. All that fear and adrenaline needs to be paid for with solid food in the belly."

Henick's brow furrowed. "This is the wrong town."

"I know. We'll get right back on the road just as soon as we grab a little grub. Don't tell me you're not hungry after all you did."

"I'm not hungry."

"Well, I am. I could eat a horse."

"I don't eat meat."

Eddie started to explain, then gave up the idea. "OK, no meat." As he drove through the small town he found a small fast-food restaurant. "Look, a Taco Jack. That'll do."

A few minutes later, Eddie and Henick were back on the highway. Eddie steered with one hand and held one of three tacos in the other. Henick studied the paper-wrapped bean and rice burrito. It took several minutes, but he figured out how to strip away half the paper. He took a small bite.

"I like this."

"I thought you might. Nothing better than Mexican fast food." He hesitated. "Well, maybe a Tex-Mex barbeque."

After Eddie downed the last bite of taco and crumpled up the wrapper, he turned to Henick, who devoured the burrito. "Feel better?"

"Yes. Thank you."

"Don't mention it. Now I'm going to ask a question, and I'd like a straightforward answer. Can you do that?"

"What is your question?"

"You said you made a mistake with the kids. What did you mean?"

"I was there for the man in the truck."

Eddie nodded. "You said that before. What's that mean?"

"It means I was there for the man in the truck."

Instead of snapping at him, Eddie tried a gentler approach. "I got that part. You knew an accident was about to happen. You even knew where it would happen. So you knew the tanker truck would crash and burn."

"Yes."

"Did you know about the children in the bus?"

He tipped his head to the side. "No."

"Did you know that other cars and trucks would be busted up in the accident?"

"Yes."

"But not the children?"

"No."

Eddie gazed down the road. He had gained a few more pieces of the puzzle, but he still had no idea how they went together. He drew a long breath through his nose. "Are you saying you shouldn't have healed those dead kids?"

Henick lowered his head and stared at the burrito wrapper. "I was not there for them."

For reasons he couldn't articulate, Eddie felt ill. His next sentence floated from his lips in a barely perceptible whisper. "They would be dead if not for you. How can that be a mistake?"

"I did not have permission."

"Permission? From God?"

"Yes."

A fist balled up in Eddie's stomach. "Are you telling me God was fine with letting those kids burn to death? How can that be? No, I'm not buying that. I can't believe anyone, especially God, would want those children to be dead."

"That's because you see death as a bad thing."

"It is."

"How do you know?"

Eddie tightened his hands on the wheel. "That's a stupid question. How do you know it's not bad?"

"I know."

"I thought you said you never died."

"True, but I know many who have." Henick raised his head. "I may have put you in danger, and now I may have endangered the children."

"What kinda danger?"

"I am not alone."

"Meaning what?"

He shook his head. "I do not yet know fully, but I am not alone."

Eddie wasn't satisfied with the answers Henick was giving, but he asked no more questions. He had seen the man's face in the restaurant when he threatened to pound him until he was no more than a grease spot and saw no fear; he saw him confined in jail but detected no worry; and a short time ago he had watched the strange man walk through a wall of flame, emerge barely able to stand, and holding a fried corpse, but still he saw no fear...

...until now.

Adam Liptak had been restless all his life. It was what had drawn him to trucking. Although he traveled the same roads daily, every day proved a new adventure. The world always provided something new to see.

Twenty-two years he had been on the road. The money was lousy, and the constant vibration and bouncing in the cab had left his lower back a chiropractor's dream. Still he never once thought of changing careers. The open road and his personality fit like lock and key. Until now. Sitting on the back of one of several ambulances that crowded the closed highway gave him time to think and to study the burned wreckage of his 2006 Peterbilt. White foam from the fire department trucks covered the bright red cab and blackened stainless steel tank. He had bought the nearly new rig for $120,000. Insurance would take care of that as well as the tanker trailer and the cargo. Still, he would be off the road for weeks.

He pulled the blanket tight around his shoulders to fight a chill he couldn't shake. His back, arms, and legs hurt from the constant trembling. Being naked beneath the blanket didn't help, but it wasn't modesty that made him shiver; it was the constant replaying of the bus and other big rig that crashed in front of him.

His mind struggled to take in the chaotic movements of those around him. Paramedics treated some people; troopers interviewed others; children, some in burned and tattered clothing, huddled around teachers, the bus driver, and sympathetic adults; firemen washed the unburned fuel from the highway. For the last fifteen minutes, panicked parents arrived, pushing through the crowd and screaming the names of their children. Tears flowed everywhere.

"Mr. Liptak?"

"Yes?" He looked up into the lined face of a trooper. Gray hair peeked from beneath his hat. Liptak knew he had been one of first on the scene; he also knew that the last hour had deducted ten years from the man's life. The officer removed his wide-brimmed hat and drew a sleeve across his sweaty brow. His drawn face was familiar, as were many faces of the troopers. Truckers and troopers often ate at the same truck stop cafés.

"You still doing OK?"

Liptak gave a nod. "I feel fine for the most part, but I do feel a little exposed."

"I don't doubt it. I wish I could give you something to wear, but I hadn't planned on needing extra clothing. I'm afraid the blanket will have to do for now."

"Considering everything, I don't have much right to complain."

The trooper chewed his lower lip and glanced around the scene. "There should be a lot of dead people here, but there aren't. Not one." He looked at Liptak. "I know you've gone over all this with one of the other troopers, but I'm gonna be the one to fill out the report and answer to the higher ups, so I have to ask. Were you really driving the tanker?"

"Yes. And yes, I was in it when it…blew." Liptak looked away. It had taken him thirty minutes to calm his nerves enough to tell the story the first time. He had no desire to relive it again, although he held no doubts that he would see the scene unfold in his dreams for years to come.

"I've talked to a dozen witnesses, and they each tell the same story. They tell me a man walked into the flames, pulled you out, then carried you to safety. Do you remember any of that?"

"No. I was already… No, I don't remember anything after my rig went on its side."

"So you didn't see anyone come to your rescue."

"No. I was out cold, or…"

"Dead?"

"Some have told me that. All I remember is waking up naked as a blue jay and looking up at a group of people, including some guy who wasn't wearing any more than me. Then I saw him walk over to some children lying on the ground. A few looked burned real bad. Next thing I knew, the kids were up and walking around. I know that sounds crazy, and maybe I hit my head or something, but that's what I remember." He mustered the courage to look at the trooper. "It must have been my imagination, right? I mean, the accident must have knocked something loose in my head. Because if it really happened, then some of those kids would be dead. Right? Not only that, someone else would have seen it all happen."

The trooper's eyes misted. "If the witnesses are to be believed, then what you saw wasn't a dream."

"You mean some guy fished me out of the burning wreckage and kept me from burning to death?"

The trooper leaned against the ambulance and gazed at something only he could see. "Yes and no. Everyone I talked to says the same thing. You were..."

"Just say it."

"They say you were dead. Burned beyond all hope. The man who pulled you from the burning truck touched you and... well, you see how you are now."

"That's impossible. You mean I did see dead kids come back to life?"

"That's what they tell me."

"And you believe them?"

"I don't know what to believe, Mr. Liptak."

"I was dead?"

The trooper rose. "We're taking everyone who was injured to the hospital for a better exam."

"But I feel fine."

"I'm glad to hear that. You're going anyway."

COLD.

She shivered.

Her head hurt.

A voice. Indistinct.

Mary-Martha ran her hand down her bare arms, then raised it to her head. Something soft and warm settled across her chest.

"Shirley. Don't move, sweetheart. Help is on the way."

Mary-Martha's lids opened slowly. Light stabbed her eyes, and she slammed them shut. She groaned then shivered. Why did her head hurt?

She touched the cold hard surface that surrounded her. Something wet dripped on her face. Another drop fell on her feet.

Slowly she opened her eyes again, holding a hand up to cast a shadow over her face.

"Is the light bothering you?"

The room dimmed.

"Is that better?" The voice sounded familiar.

"Y-yes."

The fog that swirled in her mind evaporated, replaced by memories. Odd shapes around her sharpened as her eyes adjusted. She lay on the floor of her shower. Why?

The Face flashed in her mind. She sucked air like a drowning woman and pushed back against the shower wall. The Face. So close. So evil. So nearly human.

"What is it? What's wrong?"

She turned her head expecting to see the narrow eyes; the flat, nearly nonexistent nose; the thin mouth; the green-gray skin. Instead she saw a face she knew. "Willie?"

"It's me. Try not to move. You hit your head. Paramedics are on the way."

She sat up and snapped her head around looking for the Face. It was gone.

"What happened?"

"I saw…I must have slipped and fell. Why am I so cold?"

"You must have been unconscious for some time. I came home and found you lying here with cold water running. I guess you drained the water heater. I covered you with towels and was about to get the bedspread. You were shivering."

"Help me up."

"You shouldn't move, dear. The paramedics will be here in a few minutes."

"Nonsense." She reached for the grab bar with her right hand. Her elbow complained with several sharp pains. "Ouch. I think I bruised my arm."

"You may have done worse. Please stay still."

"I'm not going to let a bunch of strangers look at my naked body lying in the shower. I'm OK. Just a little bruised. Now, are you going to help me up, or do I have risk another fall?"

"OK, but let me do the lifting." He stepped into the wide shower and placed his hands under her arms. "Let me do all the work." A second later, Mary-Martha stood and swayed. The shower stall seemed to orbit her head. "Easy. Let the blood get back to your head."

"I'm OK. Really. Just a little woozy. Help me out."

He did, almost holding her off the ground like a puppeteer working a marionette.

"Robe."

"I have to let go—"

"Just hand me my robe."

Willie pulled the ankle-length, pink terrycloth from a bronze hook on one of the walls that defined the shower and helped his wife slip it on.

"OK, now help me to the bed. I want to sit down for a minute."

"Can you make it that far?"

"Yes. My head is clearing." Mary-Martha felt her husband's hand take her arm. It trembled. His grasp touched her a few inches above her complaining elbow. "Easy on the arm."

He moved his hand higher. "Is that better?"

"Yes. Still hurts like a—"

Someone was pounding on the door. Willie eased her down on the edge of the bed. The soft surface felt good. "Underwear."

"I have to let the paramedics in."

"Not until I have at least some underwear on. This is embarrassing enough."

"Sweetheart—"

"Just do it."

More pounding rolled up the stairs. Willie raced to the antique dresser drawers and removed a pair of white panties and handed them to her.

"Your bra is on the bed beside you."

"I need your help. My arm is too sore to—"

"Sure."

A few moments later, Willie bolted through the bedroom door. She could hear him lumbering down the stairs and then the door opening. This was going to be embarrassing.

The paramedic worked quickly and with minimal discussion, something Mary-Martha appreciated. He flashed a penlight beam in her eyes to see if her pupils were equal and responsive.

They asked her silly questions, which she assumed were meant to test how rattled her brain was. The worst part was the poking. They poked her ribs and ran probing hands down her arms and legs. They even peeked in her ears. When she asked why, they said something about cerebral spinal fluid.

"Everything looks good, Ms. Celestine, but we should transport you to the hospital." The paramedic looked young enough to be her son. The other paramedic was a pretty blonde with light blue eyes. The sight of her made Mary-Martha wish for her youth again.

"That's not necessary. Really, I'm fine. Just sore and cold."

The young man shook his head. "We need you to cooperate with us. You have a pretty nasty lump on your head. We need to rule out a concussion or worse. Head and neck injuries can be tricky. That arm needs to be x-rayed. I don't think anything is broken, but it's best to let the doctors make the final call on that."

"I said I'm not going."

Willie took a step forward, his panicked expression replaced by determination. "For once you're going to do as you're told."

Anger ran through every fiber of her, but she said nothing—not with the two unwanted guests in her bedroom. "OK, but only if I can get dressed first."

"Deal," the man said. "I want your husband to help you. We'll be right outside the door."

"No need. Willie can drive me to the emergency room."

The male paramedic glanced at his partner. A sweet, daughterly grin crossed her face. "If you go in on your own, you may have to spend hours in the waiting room. You know how ERs are. But if you let us take you, we can get you in through the ambulance entrance. That should save you some time."

"You can guarantee that?" Mary-Martha asked.

Both paramedics laughed. "Nothing is a guarantee at the ER," the man said. "But if it were me, I'd go the ambulance route."

They helped her stand. "Can you walk? We can get the gurney."

"I'm not going to be rolled out of my house while I can still stand. I'll be fine. I'm not even dizzy anymore."

"Very well."

The paramedics left, and Willie helped her dress. She said nothing. She couldn't fault him for doing what he did. It was the right thing to do. Still, it was all so irritating. "We will keep this little incident to ourselves. Got it?"

"Yes. Let's just get you to the hospital."

"I don't want the congregation finding out. It was bad enough I fainted right in front of them. If this leaks out, the rumor mill will have me a stroke victim or something."

"I'm more worried about you than your image," Willie said.

She sighed. "Please leave the worrying to me."

"Thanks. I feel better already."

Dressed in loose-fitting sportswear, Mary-Martha walked from the bedroom and down the steps. As she entered the home's foyer, she passed by an antique walnut high-back hall bench, the kind with hooks for coats, a mirror, and a seat lid that could be lifted to store shoes and other items. The piece of furniture had belonged to her grandmother. As a child she used to hid her toys in the space below the seat and play dress up in front of the mirror.

She paused and ran her fingers through her damp hair. "I look like a mop with arms and legs."

"You look fine," Willie said.

"I could frighten children and small dogs—" She stopped breathing and her jaw swiveled open.

"What?" Willie asked. "What's wrong?"

The paramedics stepped to her side, each taking an arm.

Mary-Martha tried to tear her eyes away, to look somewhere else, anywhere else, but the Face in the mirror wouldn't let her.

The hospital staff was kind and efficient. The ambulance crew, as promised, brought Mary-Martha into the ER through the ambulance entrance at the back. This time they insisted that she ride the gurney in. She refused at first but had no heart for arguing. The image in the mirror leapt forward in her mind every few seconds. She chose to keep that symptom to herself.

Another bit of luck—the ER had few patients. That's where her good fortune ended—Dr. Harry Moskos and his wife attended the Church of New Revelation. More accurately, his wife attended regularly and participated in the women's outreach. Dr. Moskos came on occasion but Millie made him watch the broadcasts.

He stepped to her bedside, introduced himself, then stopped mid sentence. She could see the confusion on his face. "Reverend Celestine?"

"Yes, although I imagine I look a little different than you're used to."

"That doesn't matter." His brow wrinkled as he looked at the chart. "You were admitted under the name Shirley Lennox. There must be some kind of error."

Willie stood by her side. "No, that's right. Our medical insurance—"

"Mary-Martha Celestine is a family name. It comes from my mother's side of the family. Scotch-Irish ancestry. I'm trying to honor several of my ancestors. I use Mary-Martha for most things. Legal matters like insurance I use my birth name."

"Oh, that makes sense." The doctor set the chart and metal clipboard to the side. He slipped a sphygmomanometer cuff over her left arm. "This isn't the arm you injured, is it?"

"No. A nurse checked that a few moments ago."

"I know, but she used digital device. I like the old pump-up-the-cuff-and-listen method. Believe it or not, it's more accurate."

Moments later he removed the cuff and jotted down a number. "BP is a little high, but that's to be expected. Pulse is also high."

"White-coat hypertension." Mary-Martha forced a smile.

"Ah, afraid of doctors, eh? You're not alone. My BP goes up every time I have a physical. It's pretty bad when physicians have doctor phobia."

He repeated many of the paramedics' actions, peeking in her eyes and ears, palpitating her sore arm, listening to her heart, feeling the back of her neck, and asking question after question. Finally he said, "I don't see anything to be overly concerned about, but I do want to get a few images of your head, neck, and arm."

"Is that really necessary? I don't feel that bad."

"It is, Reverend. A fall in the shower can be serious business. You'd be surprised how many injuries I've seen come out of a bathroom. Besides, I don't want you telling the congregation I cut corners. Worse, I don't want you telling my wife. If I don't give you the best attention, then my wife will send me back to the ER—as a patient." He chuckled at his joke. "Don't worry, we will take good care of you." He jotted a few more notes in the chart. "After I see your X-rays, I'll prescribe some pain meds."

It took two hours for X-rays. An hour-forty-five of that she spent waiting and watching Willie worry. When she couldn't stand his fidgeting any longer, she closed her eyes and tried to make sense of what she had seen. She failed.

Weary of staring at the ceiling or the inside of her eyelids, she turned her head to the side and gazed at a white plastic electronic device with a small LCD screen. A small metal placard glued to the surface read CardiDig EKG. Her gaze traveled to the small screen. For a moment she could imagine a pulsating line streaming across the display.

There was something about the monitor, something soothing. The dark monitor beckoned her like a serene lake in a verdant forest. She longed for a place to relax, a place to set aside her pains and burdens for a few moments.

A bubble appeared in the center of the screen, and for a second Mary-Martha thought the display had developed the technical equivalent to a blemish.

The bubble widened until its curved edges touched the perimeter of the screen. She narrowed her eyes. Maybe it was a type of screen saver. The idea didn't fit, and she dismissed it. Her gaze followed the device's power cord. It was unplugged.

She squeezed her eyelids shut then opened them, forcing them to focus.

The bubble was gone.

The Face replaced it—and it was smiling.

"MAN, THAT SMELLS GOOD." EDDIE STEPPED FROM THE hotel room's small bathroom, rubbing his hair with a towel.

"A man brought it a short time ago." Henick stood at the dirty window and peered into the parking lot.

"Yeah, that's the beauty of pizza. They bring it right to the door. You gave him the money I left, didn't you?"

"Yes."

Eddie tossed the towel into the bathroom and slipped into the "new" jeans and shirt he had purchased at a nearby thrift store. His smoke-laced clothing soaked in the tub.

"What's so interesting out the window? Ain't nuthin' there but a half-empty parking lot. Don't get much of a view in a thirty-dollar-a-night motel."

"I'm looking at the darkness."

"Darkness is what you get when the sun knocks off for the day. Come on, let's eat."

"I'm looking at the other darkness."

Eddie opened the pizza box and inhaled the rich aroma of melted cheese, spicy tomato sauce, and pepperoni. Life was looking up. He lifted a slice and bit off a mouthful. Grease ran down his chin.

"What other kinda darkness is there?"

"Many kinds." Henick turned and joined Eddie at the small battered, cigarette-burned table. "What are the round things?"

"Pepperoni. It's a spicy meat…oh man, I'm sorry. I forgot you don't do the meat thing."

Henick picked off the red circles and stacked them in the corner of the box. He looked at Eddie, who took another bite. "What is the rest of it?"

"Cheese, bread, and tomato sauce. You can eat cheese, can't you? I mean, it comes from an animal, but it's not the same as eating an animal."

Henick raised a piece of pizza to his mouth and took a small bite. He nodded then took another bite.

Eddie grinned. "Not half bad, is it? I don't believe I've ever met a man that hasn't tasted pizza."

Taking the remote from the nightstand that separated the room's two single beds, Eddie turned on the small television. "Not much of a TV, but at least we have cable." He began flipping through channels. Henick stepped to his side and watched as if analyzing it.

Eddie stopped on MSNBC. "Let's see if they have any news about the accident." He sat on the foot of one of the beds. It didn't take long before the newscaster said, "Returning to the unusual events on Interstate 10 in West Texas, we can now report that traffic is once again moving. The accident may be clear, but the mystery isn't."

The hunger that had plagued Eddie for the last hour dissipated, not because of the pizza but because of the aerial footage of the burning tanker truck and bus. Although the helicopter's distance and the cameraman's desire to keep as much action in frame as possible kept faces indistinct, Eddie knew he was seeing himself carrying bodies from the bus. He also saw Henick walk from the furnacelike flames.

The voice of the male newscaster droned on, becoming mere background noise to Eddie. His heart tripped when he and Henick drove off in the truck. The camera followed them for a short time then came back around to the accident.

"Wow." It was all Eddie could think to say.

"Your truck is known."

Eddie looked at Henick. "So? We didn't do anything wrong."

Henick didn't reply.

Henick's comment roused Eddie's attention enough for him to hear the news anchor again. "Witnesses describe a man who walked into and out of the fire surrounding the truck, healed himself of burns, and then brought the dead back to life."

"It looks like we're famous," Eddie said.

"It would seem so." Henick finished his slice of pizza.

"For more strange goings on," the announcer said, "we turn to Susan Dove."

"Thank you, Sean. We at MSNBC have been receiving reports about some unusual messages delivered in even more unusual ways."

Eddie stopped mid-chew as he heard about the *New York Times* ad, the unusual radio broadcast in Washington DC, and the Internet buzz about a movie with an actor who steps out of character. The reporter rounded up the report with a broad smile and a quip. During the commercial break, Eddie watched a similar ongoing report on CNN.

"This is all about you, isn't it? The moving newspaper ad, the radio announcement, the movie; it's all centered on you."

Henick said, "Yes. For now." He returned to the window.

"Are you the Messenger?" Eddie asked.

A pair of headlights flashed past the window.

"Did you hear me?"

"I heard you," Henick said. He walked to the door, opened it, and stepped outside.

"Where do you think you're going?" Eddie joined him just outside their room. A late model Beemer sat in the parking stall near the door of a room.

"You see that car?" Eddie said. "That's a BMW M6 coupe. You can't buy that with pocket change. You need a hundred grand to think about taking one of those home. I couldn't afford insurance on that baby."

Three young men in hoodies stood smoking cigarettes near the driveway. One pulled from the group, eyed Eddie and Henick, and apparently decided they were harmless and jogged down the walkway of the motel wing opposite theirs. He looked nervous. He knocked on the door.

Eddie watched the other two. They split up. One stayed near the street; the other moved halfway down the walk and stopped. Eddie grew up and lived in a small town, but he knew when he saw something about to go down. The young man at the street was the lookout. One signal from him, and the second man would sprint to the hotel room to warn his friend.

"We should go back inside. This ain't the greatest neighborhood."

Henick didn't move. A blue tinted light held back some of the darkness covering the motel and parking lot.

"Seriously, man, we should pull back here. Trust me, I know trouble when I see it."

A second later, the hooded man emerged from the room and walked to his companion; both met the third at the street. A minute later, they walked off.

"Drug dealers," Eddie said. "I bet this part of El Paso is crawling with them. Blink, Texas, might be little more than a wide place in the road, but at least we don't have pushers hanging out in front of our motels. Most of our drugs come out of liquor bottles."

"Is that better?"

"Maybe not, but you can bet it ain't worse. Now let's go in. The pizza is gettin' cold." Eddie stepped over the threshold

Henick started across the asphalt lot.

It took Eddie a moment to realize what Henick had in mind. "Are you nuts?" He shot out the door and caught Henick by the arm. Henick jerked away and continued on course. "I can't let you do this," Eddie said.

"Wait in the room."

"Only if you come with me."

Henick frowned and continued on.

"Look, this is a bad idea. It ain't none of our business."

Henick reached for the doorknob and turned it.

"Hey," Eddie whispered. "You're supposed to knock first—"

Henick stepped in. Eddie stopped at the doorjamb and looked around the parking area. No one watched. Every alarm bell in Eddie's mind sounded at once. He ignored them and walked into the room, closing the door behind him.

The place matched theirs: same dingy curtains, same yellow-stained walls, and same cheap carpet. Only the cigarette burns were in different spots. A noticeable difference was the occupant: early thirties, expertly cut dark hair, thin frame, expensive shoes, pressed white shirt, blue silk tie, and a dark blue suit. The man had more money hanging on his body than Eddie had earned in three weeks. To Eddie, the man should be sitting behind a fancy desk in a corner office, not hunkered down on the edge of a bed with a hypodermic sticking out of his arm.

As soon as the man saw Eddie and Henick, he slammed the plunger down in the hypodermic as if fearful that they would take away his high. On the bed nightstand between the beds rested a spoon tinged with a white powder and a cigarette lighter.

Desperately the man released a section of surgical tubing from around his right bicep. Eddie knew the heroin was finding its way to the man's heart and brain.

"You're too late," the man said softly. "You can arrest me if you want, but you can't take the high out of me."

"Henick, we should go. A man should be allowed to do some things alone."

"Dying does not help."

"What?" A second later, Eddie realized Henick wasn't speaking to him.

"No sermons, officers. Sermons never take with me. Never

have. Never will." The man fell back on the bed.

"We're not cops," Eddie said.

"Then what are you doing here?"

"Yeah, what are we doing here?" Eddie asked Henick.

"Rory needs you." Henick sat on the opposite bed.

"Who?" The man sat up suddenly.

"Bryan, your son Rory needs you, but you haven't much time."

"You know my name."

"Yes, you are Bryan Stover."

Stover swayed, and even from a half-dozen feet away Eddie could see the man's pupils had constricted to pinpoints. He blinked several times. "You said, 'Rory.'"

It took several seconds before Eddie attached the name to the situation. "You mean that kid in the hospital. The one you wouldn't heal?"

"He is the same Rory." Henick never took his gaze off Stover.

"How do you know my son?" He licked his lips and tried to swallow. It seemed a struggle.

"He is very ill and needs his father. You need your Father."

Stover rubbed his face. "My dad is dead. Died a long time ago. Never knew him. Didn't care then. Don't care now."

Henick's tone never changed. "I meant your heavenly Father."

"Oh, no. What are you guys? Go away. It's too late to save my soul, and it's certainly too late to save my body." He doubled over. "Oh, my stomach."

Eddie glanced again at the powder-encrusted spoon. Three small plastic bags, all of them empty. "Hey, Henick, I think this guy is trying to do himself in. I'm no expert, but shooting up three bags can mean only one thing. I'll call an ambulance."

Bryan fell back on the bed again. He seemed to be struggling for breath. "No job. No money. No future. No love."

"Your son will love you. Your heavenly Father loves you."

"Too...late."

Eddie snapped up the phone and punched in 911. "I'd like to

report a drug overdose at the Roadway Motel, room 22. Never mind my name. Just send help." He dropped the phone into the cradle. His ear felt dirty. "Help me lay him out."

Together they straightened Stover on the bed so that his feet no longer hung off the edge.

"Why do people do such things?" Henick said as he stood over the unconscious man. "He carries so much regret and pain, yet he seeks out more regret and pain. Men were not created to live this way."

"People deal with pain in different ways, I guess." Eddie studied the man. The ends of his fingers and his lips were turning blue. "This doesn't look good, man. I saw this once before. A kid in high school overdosed and died on the track field during PE."

Henick looked at him.

"Oh, don't give me the look. I said we didn't have pushers on street corners in Blink, I didn't say no one used drugs." Eddie saw the man's keys and wallet on the top of the television set. He picked up the wallet. "Yup, you're right. Bryan with a y Stover. He's got a couple hundred in cash. His driver's license says he's thirty. That'd be about right to be married to Rory's mom." He looked through the rest of the wallet: debit cards, an American Express Platinum, and a business ID. "Wow. The guy's a VP at an investment firm. No wonder he's driving a high-end Beemer." He returned the wallet and turned back to Henick.

Henick stood over the body, his arms stretched over the unconscious man, palms turned down. In the dim light of the room, Eddie saw a blue mist fall from Henick's palms and cover Stover like a fog. Although Stover's breathing had slowed to just a few respirations, Eddie could see the vague haze flow into the man's body with every weak inhalation.

Eddie had seen enough over the last few days to not be surprised; nonetheless, he was. "I don't know what you're doing, but do it quick. I don't think we should be here when the emergency personnel arrive. There's bound to be cops, and where there are cops, there will be questions."

Henick lowered his arms. "Can you write?"

"Of course I can write. I may be stupid, but I'm not ignorant. Why?"

"Please write the name of the hospital where his boy is. Write the room number too."

"We don't have time for that. I can hear sirens."

"Then I will stay until the police arrive and tell them."

A curse dropped from Eddie's lips. "How much do you want to bet that every kinda cop is out looking for the guy who heals people on the freeway? You want to keep heading west. Well, that little journey might be held up while one agency after another takes turns asking you questions."

"After you write the message, then we will leave."

Eddie had no choice. He had given up hoping to win an argument with Henick. He found a small notepad in one of the dresser drawers, wrote the name and city of the hospital and the room number where little Rory lay dying, then stuffed it into the man's wallet.

The sound of approaching sirens crawled through the night. Eddie and Henick left the room. Eddie once again scanned the area and saw no one. They walked slowly back to their room.

HAVE YOU BEEN TO DC BEFORE?" GENE MANFORD PULLED his red Dodge Charger from the Ronald Reagan National Airport parking lot and onto the George Washington Memorial Parkway.

"A few times. All business related." Katherine Rooney shifted in her seat.

"By business, you mean FBI business."

"What else is there?"

"We at the FCC have our own ideas about that." He gave a polite but still professional smile, then did his best to tear his eyes from her and focus them on the road where they belonged. Something about her red-tinted brown hair and blue eyes was magnetic. But there was more. She had a confidence about her that proved just as attractive.

"So how do we do this?" she asked.

"Do what?"

"Inter-agency cooperation works best when we know who gets to call the shots."

"I see. I assumed we'd work together. My task is to find out who's messing with radio and television. Since some of this crosses state lines and may involve more criminal activity than it first appeared, we need the FBI muscle."

She chuckled. "Muscle, huh? That's me—muscle."

"You know what I mean. My saying, 'Hi, I'm field agent Gene

Manford of the FCC' doesn't carry the same weight as someone like you saying, 'FBI.'"

"It works great with my dates," Katherine said. "If they get fresh, I just break out my little badge."

"Nothing like intimidation to make one feel powerful."

"Where am I staying?"

"I got you a suite at the Hyatt, but you won't be there very long."

She looked at him. "Texas?"

"I see you heard."

"Had a two-hour layover in Denver. Found a television with a cable news broadcast. It helped pass the time."

"Do you believe what they're saying about the accident?"

She shook her head. "What? You mean about the healing of dead children and a man who walks through fire? No."

"The video didn't convince you?"

She laid her head back on the seat and closed her eyes. Manford knew how tired air travel made him. Flying from the West Coast to the East Coast was the worst, and Special Agent Rooney had just winged her way in from Los Angeles. "I don't know what to think about that. It looked real, but it couldn't be, could it? Dead children suddenly coming back to life just because some stranger touched them? That takes a big leap of faith."

"It happened in the Bible." He pulled off the GWMP and started down a side street.

"Really? The Bible has a tale of dead kids brought back to life? I know there were a few resurrections, but nothing like this."

"Maybe. I'm no expert." He stopped at a red light. "I can take you straight to the hotel if you would like, or if you're ready to get down to business, I can drive us straight to the FCC building."

"When do we leave for Texas?"

"Tomorrow morning. We've chartered a jet. Should save on time, and I won't have to be battered by the goody cart driven by a nearsighted stewardess."

"In that case, I say we hit the office. I can check into the hotel later."

"Your wish is my command. I'm dying to see the video your contact gave you."

"And I'm interested in hearing the radio broadcast."

The light turned green, and Manford pressed the accelerator.

Manford ran a hand through his hair and watched the pirated video of Thom Blake turning to the camera and saying, "Time grows short. Look for the one I send you. He walks among you."

"So what do you think?" Katherine stood with Manford behind a balding man in a polo shirt. The painfully thin man looked pale in the dim light that poured from the flat-screen monitor.

The bald man answered. His nasal resonance made him sound like he was talking through a garden hose. "It's seamless."

"Do you think it's CG, Tom?" In Manford's mind Thomas Brem was the best tech jockey in the FCC.

Tom wagged his head a few times, then shrugged. "I suppose. I'm not looking at the original film or tape. Some directors have gone all digital, you know. Easier to edit and manipulate. Film is dying a rapid death."

"What if we were to get a copy of the film? Would that help?"

"It might," Tom said. "Of course, it's almost impossible to prove something is computer generated. Still, the eyes, the mouth, and the facial expressions are what we'd expect from a real person. Of course, I'm looking at a pirated video of a projected image. I can't get all the detail I would like. The I Love Lucy tape was much better."

Manford looked at Katherine. "So we make a call and see if the production company will volunteer a copy. If not, then we get a court order."

"I spoke to the director, producer, and distributor before flying out here," Katherine said. "They've received several complaints and checked the master from which the prints were made and sent to theaters. They tell me the master has no such scene. They offered to show it to us and seemed eager to cooperate."

"Do you believe them?" Manford asked.

"I do. What do they have to gain by pulling this kind of prank? They're pretty unhappy with everything. I don't think they like someone playing with their creative property."

"Can't blame them for that." Manford laid a hand on Tom's shoulder. "You feel like taking a trip?"

"Sure. I don't get many field assignments."

"Good," Manford said. "I want you to interview anyone who had access to the film. Take a look at the master and see if you can't find something interesting."

"Will do, boss."

For the next two hours, Manford and Katherine reviewed the radio broadcast, the *New York Times* ad, and the news video of the crash site in Texas. In the end, Manford felt no closer to an answer than when he started the day.

"It doesn't make sense," he said. "If we were looking at just one anomaly, then we could conclude that someone is playing a game."

"Like a pirate radio station broadcasting over radio frequencies they have no right to." Katherine sat in the chair opposite Manford's desk.

"Yes, or the movie company doing something creative to build buzz about the film, or some high school kid taking liberties with an episode of *I Love Lucy* and getting a local station to play it, but—"

"But several stations played *Lucy*, several theaters played the film, several radio stations broadcast the same message at the same time but over different frequencies—"

"And the *New York Times* ad appeared in too many places to count, including here."

"You really saw the ad move?"

"I wouldn't lie about something like that. Just about scared the pants off me."

Katherine smiled. "Let's hear it for belts."

"You don't believe me, do you?" He reached for the newspaper and unfolded it on the desk.

"I didn't say I don't believe you. I don't want to believe you, but I'm in no position to cast judgments. After all, Lucille Ball speaks to me."

Manford gazed at the ad. "I've opened to this page a hundred times and nothing happens. I saw the figure move, but just the once."

"What do you suppose the message means?"

Manford scratched his head. "That's the only consistent thing in this whole mess. Newspapers, television, movies, radio, all different mediums but only one message: there's a messenger coming."

"And he walks among us," Katherine added.

"Right, but is it real?" He shook his head. "No, someone is messing with us, and I'm going to find out who it is."

"*The Next Voice You Hear*." Kathleen turned her head and gazed out the window.

"What?"

She returned her attention to Manford. "Something from my childhood; actually from my father's childhood. It was a movie."

"I don't follow."

"I don't mean to be mysterious; I was just recalling a movie I saw with my father. I remember him being excited about it playing on television. He was ten when it first ran on television. He watched it with his father, so naturally he wanted me to watch it with him. The title was *The Next Voice You Hear*. My father died that year, so I guess that hour and half took on a special meaning."

"Your dad died when you were a child?"

"I was twelve. It crushed me. Cancer."

"I'm sorry." He could see her eyes glisten.

"That part doesn't matter right now. The movie came to

theaters in 1950. After that it ran on television several times. It was a low-budget affair starring James Whitmore and Nancy Davis."

"The future Mrs. Ronald Reagan?"

"The very same. Anyway, the movie is about a blue-collar worker and his family who hear a voice over the radio. A voice that identifies itself as God. Of course, they're not the only ones to hear it. Over six days, God speaks to the world, leading up to a reminder that we should all love our neighbors."

"I wonder who played God."

"No one. The audience never hears God's voice; they just see the response."

"And you think that God is sending these messages."

"I never said that. I merely mentioned that the situation reminded me of a movie."

"I wonder...I wonder how God would speak to the world today? There are six and a half billion of us on the planet. Using the media might be a reasonable way to communicate."

"Logical but not practical."

"Then who is this messenger?"

"I don't know," she admitted. "Maybe we'll find out more in Texas."

GABRIEL HOAGLAND KNOCKED ON THE ROUGH DOOR
that needed a touch of paint ten years ago. Hoagland wore a
gray blazer over a collarless shirt and gray slacks. Howie wore a
white shirt, black pants, and black suit coat. They stood on the
porch of the Van Horn, Texas, Craftsman-style home he assumed
was built in the early sixties.

Hoagland knocked again. Harder.

"Who is it?"

"Mr. Liptak?"

"Who wants to know?" The voice was saturated with anger.

"My name is Gabriel Hoagland. I'm—"

"No more press. I've had my fill of reporters."

Hoagland looked at Howie and saw angry impatience. Howie
reached for the doorknob, but Hoagland stopped him.

"I don't blame you. Reporters are bunch of maggots who like to
squirm all over a man's life."

"You're not a reporter?"

Hoagland tinted his voice with amusement. "No, sir. As I said,
my name is Gabriel Hoagland. My partner and I are contract
investigators for the National Transportation Safety Board." He
heard the door unlock and watched it swing open. On the other
side of the screen door stood a man in an old pair of slacks and
white T-shirt. He held a cigarette in his right hand. Hoagland
thought the man would have had enough of fire and smoke.
Hoagland suppressed a frown. He hated cigarette smoke.

"What's a contract investigator?"

Hoagland chuckled. "I get asked that a lot. I work for a company that provides different investigators to large corporations and government agencies. Just like the military uses civilian contractors for certain work they don't want to tie soldiers up with, the government hires us to do certain types of leg work."

"What's that got to do with me?"

"This is my associate, Howie. We've been sent to ask a few questions. I promise it won't take long and you're in no trouble. You're a professional truck driver, so you know that the NTSB oversees highway safety among other things."

"Yeah. I know that."

"May we come in, sir? I promise not to take too much of your time."

Liptak pushed open the screen door. "Sure. Sorry about the attitude. I've had my fill of reporters."

"I imagine you have." Hoagland was thankful for the pesky press. It was how he learned Liptak's name and address.

As Hoagland entered the small house, he took a good look at the man he had come to see. His skin looked smooth and pink. He saw no scars—and no hair. If he didn't know what happened, he would have assumed the man spent too much time indoors.

"Have a seat," Liptak said, motioning to a rocker, a sofa, and a love seat. "Sit wherever you like. I'm taking my usual spot in the easy chair." He sat in a brown leather La-Z-Boy. Howie took a spot on the love seat, and Hoagland lowered his large frame on the sofa. The house appeared meticulously neat.

"Is Mrs. Liptak home?"

Liptak shrugged. "Beats me. She left me five years ago and changed her name. I don't know where she calls home."

"Sorry to hear that."

"Don't be. She's an evil woman, mean as they come. Pit bulls avoided her."

Hoagland laughed. "I almost married a woman like that." A

photo on the fireplace mantle caught his eye, and he rose to look at it. The color picture rested in a silver frame and showed Liptak, with hair, in front of a white and red Volvo truck. "Is this your rig?"

"That was my first rig. I bought my current truck in 2006. Nothing left of it now but twisted metal."

Returning to the sofa, Hoagland lowered himself and placed his elbows on his knees. "Well, I promised not to take too much of your time. Since the accident involved a school bus, the NTSB wants me to ask a few questions."

"OK, I'll tell you what I know."

Hoagland remind himself to be careful. Ask a few related questions before getting down to business. "As I understand it, you were hauling fuel."

"That's right. I service the independent stations along I-10. I had a full load of gasoline."

"Tell us what happened."

He shrugged. I don't have much to tell. I was…out of it soon after it all happened." He closed his eyes for a moment, then opened them again. "I was doing maybe sixty in the right lane when I saw something flying through the air. It looked like a big rig had blown a tire, so I let up on the gas. That's when it all fell apart. There was a good bit o' traffic. The cars in my lane hit the brakes, and I started to do the same, but I knew there weren't no way I was going to stop in time. I veered to the left. Of course, the cars in the next lane had to do the same. I saw an SUV steer right and flip. I also saw the school bus go over on its side then roll…" He closed his eyes again. "I never want to see anything like that again." He rubbed his neck. When he opened his eyes again, they were brimming with moisture.

"Take your time, Mr. Liptak. I know this is difficult."

"Like I said, the bus tipped over; so did the SUV. I think the rig in front of me hit something. Maybe the bus. I know he was trying to avoid something because he crossed lanes in a way no trucker would do unless he was sure he was about to kill somebody. The rig tipped. Cars in front of me locked up their brakes. I'm carting eight thousand pounds of fuel. A truck like that doesn't stop on a dime. So...I hit the brakes, but I still plowed through two or three cars and hit the big rig in front of me."

He looked at Hoagland, but Hoagland knew he was seeing something else.

"The impact must have knocked me out. I don't remember the next few moments. When I came to..." He turned his face away. "The flames. Fire was everywhere. I saw my windshield melt. The heat...couldn't breathe...I screamed for help. I begged for help, then the flames came in. The pain. God. Dear God. The pain." He rubbed his arms and face as if the flames were still there. "I was on fire." A moment later he began to sob, and Hoagland let him.

After a few minutes, Hoagland said, "Did you see the man who rescued you coming through the flames?

He nodded. "But just for a moment. He was just a shape in the flames. For a moment I thought it was the devil himself walking through hell. I don't remember much else until I woke up on the pavement, looking at the strangest thing I've ever seen: a naked man standing over me. He was burned. I mean horribly burned. The fire had scorched his flesh black."

"Then how could he be standing?" Howie broke his silence.

Liptak shook his head. "How should I know? None of it makes sense to me. I was dead, yet here I sit. How do you explain that?"

"Maybe you weren't dead."

"Howie, that's enough."

"Yes, sir."

"Go on, Mr. Liptak."

Liptak eyed Howie, then turned his attention to Hoagland. "Look, you guys asked me to tell the story. If you don't believe me, then fine. You know where the door is."

Hoagland had to think quickly. "It's not a matter of belief, Mr. Liptak. Skepticism is part of our job. We have to look at things from every side. Speaking off the record here, I believe you."

"OK, not that I care if you do. I know what I saw."

"What did you see?"

"Like I said, I don't know how I got out of the truck. The next thing I know I'm looking up at this guy who looks like he just stepped from some cheap horror movie, but I know it ain't no movie, because I'm in as bad a shape as he is. You ever been burned?"

Hoagland shook his head and Howie said, "No, not bad; a cigarette burn now and again."

"I've experienced some pain in my life," Liptak said. "Broken both arms. Took some shrapnel in the first Gulf War. But what I felt there on that road was the worst. I didn't know a man could hurt so much. The fire had exposed all my nerve endings. I would have screamed if I had enough air in my lungs and my throat weren't swollen nearly shut."

"It must have been excruciating." Hoagland tried to manufacture some sympathy with his words.

"Excruciating was just the start. When I think that some of them kids went through the same thing—" The words died in his mouth.

Hoagland let the man have some time but wished he'd get on with it.

"Anyway…" He sniffed. "Anyway, I began to pray. I'm not much of a praying man. Never have been. Me and God, well, we just never bothered each other, but I felt He might listen since I was so bad off." Again he looked away. "But I didn't pray like you probably think I did. I prayed that He would let me die and let me do it quick. Why live? Even if they got me to a hospital and they kept me alive, I'd be nothing but scarred, useless flesh. Not much sense living like that. You know, the strange thing is…"

"Is what, Mr. Liptak?" Hoagland leaned forward.

"I think I may have already been dead. I know that sounds stupid. How can a dead man see what's happening around him, hear the voices of people talking, and feel pain? I've been over those questions a thousand times since the accident and haven't come up with a single idea. Maybe I was in hell. I don't know."

"What about the guy who rescued you?" Howie said. Hoagland stopped any future questions with a glance.

"Yeah, right, OK. I tend to get distracted by my own situation." He looked back at Hoagland. "I stared at the guy. Truth is, I couldn't move, so staring that direction was all I could do. He began to sway then...then his skin began to change. The charred flesh fell off him, but instead of leaving holes or showing what lay beneath the skin, new flesh appeared, all pink and clean. Of course, I thought the pain had driven me insane, that I was hallucinating or something.

"Then he bent over me and touched me. A new fire raced through me, but not like the heat that burned me. This felt— good, right. The pain stopped the moment his hand touched my burned flesh. I thought, 'At last I'm dying. It's over.' But I didn't die. Next thing I knew I was sitting up, naked as the day I was born, just like the guy who rescued me.

"I struggled to my feet and watched the same guy move to the dead children. Even from where I stood I could tell they were dead. He touched them and they began to move." He raised his hands to his face and sobbed.

"Can you describe the man?" Hoagland leaned an inch forward.

"Not much...not much to describe." He passed a hand under his eyes, then wiped them on his pants. "He looked to be in his late forties maybe. Bald because, like me, all his hair had been burned away."

"What was he wearing?"

"I told you he was naked."

"He left the scene naked?"

"No, I see what you're getting at. After all the children were made well, some white-haired guy gave him some clothes. He was traveling in some kind of Jeep Cherokee. It looked packed to the hilt like vacationers do. Said he and the wife were traveling cross-country. He gave me a pair of dress pants, some flip-flops for my feet, and a beige golf shirt. Oh, and he gave me a pair of boxer shorts." He chuckled. "Never wore another man's skivvies before. Can't say I want to again, but given the situation…" He shrugged.

"Where did the man go?"

"The guy who gave me the clothes? He hung around until the troopers arrived."

"I meant the guy who pulled you from the fire."

"I don't know. Some kid was hanging out with him, and they got in a pickup and left."

"Tell me about the kid."

Liptak leaned back in the chair. "I suppose I shouldn't call him a kid. He's a grown man but hadn't been one for long, if you know what I mean."

"I know. He was older than a teenager."

"Yeah, I guess he might be twenty-two or twenty-three. Short brown hair, bulky but not fat, maybe six-one, a hundred and eighty pounds. Something like that. I heard someone tell the cops he and someone else pulled the kids from the burning bus. I guess that makes him a hero."

"Did you talk to the man or his young friend?"

"Nah. I wanted to, but he was busy with the kids and I was a little confused, if you know what I mean. The man that gave me clothes did the same for the guy who rescued me. Before you ask: tennis shoes, Nike I think, jeans and a white T-shirt."

"And they went west."

"Yeah, west. At least best I could tell. They were on the west-bound side of the freeway. I suppose they could pull a U-turn somewhere, but why? I don't know where they went."

Hoagland stood. "Thank you for your time. You've been very helpful." Liptak started to rise, but Hoagland raised a hand. "Don't get up. We'll see our way out." He led Howie out the front door and to their rental sedan.

"So what do you think?" Howie asked.

"I think we need to find this guy and do it quick."

THE SUN TOOK ITS TIME SLIDING TO THE MOUNTAINS, casting late, golden rays on the Manzano to the east of Mary-Martha's home. To the west, the New Mexico desert absorbed the last of the day's warmth. Soon the night creatures ventured out of hidey-holes and dens to search for food or be food. Overhead a hawk rode easy on thermals rising from paved streets, tile rooftops, and parking lots of Albuquerque.

Mary-Martha and Willie reclined in lounge chairs near their pool and listened to the late business of their neighborhood. In the distance the laughter of children rose in the cooling air. The neighbor's air conditioning rumbled to life. Soon, the smells of a hundred kitchens would blend in the air. Shortly after that, the cool night would become home to the aromatic smoke of blazes in fireplaces.

It all gave Mary-Martha a sense of peace. Yesterday had been rough. Her elbow still showed swelling from the indignity of being slammed against the hard tile of the shower, and her neck and head ached from being bounced off the same hard surface. Pain meds kept the bruises and bumps from aching too much.

She hated taking another day off from the church, but Willie showed signs of growing a spine when he insisted that she stay home. She appreciated his wisdom even though she despised his pathetic attempt at manhood. He had never been able to carry such theatrics off in her presence. Rather than argue the point, she complained a few times and then acquiesced. It kept peace

ENOCH

for the day. Besides, the pain meds unsettled her stomach and made her sleepy. She doubted that she would get much done at the office, not with the other staff and her assistant checking on her every fifteen minutes.

"How are you feeling?" Willie asked. "Chilly yet?"

"I'm fine for now."

"I can get you a blanket, and we could spend a little more time out here."

"Maybe later. And please stop fussing over me. You heard the doctors say I'm fine. The tests came back negative."

"I wonder why they say it that way." He put his hands behind his head and gazed at the darkening skies.

"What way?" She rubbed her neck and then touched the lump on the back of her head. It felt about two-thirds the size it had been a few hours before. Who said hardheadedness wasn't a virtue?

"When they say, 'All the tests are negative.' Doesn't sound right. Every time I hear that, it makes me think something is wrong. Wouldn't it be better if they said, 'The tests are all positive, we found nothing wrong'?"

The neighbor's dog, which had been in the house, ran to the fence that separated the two properties and barked once.

"I suppose it's a point-of-view thing. Doctors make their living from what's wrong, not what's right. A negative means nothing bad was found."

"I understand the principle, but it still sounds wrong to me."

The dog barked again and pawed at the redwood fence. The vertical fence slats were spaced about an inch apart, and Mary-Martha could see the black Lab through the narrow openings.

"I don't think they're going to change for you, Willie. You'll have to learn to adjust."

The dog began running up and down the length of the fence, alternating between barking, growling, and whining.

"I think I can manage that. I don't care how they say it as long as it means you're all right."

The black Lab howled.

"What is wrong with Tuffy?"

"The dog?" Willie said. "Probably still mad about his name."

"The dog is two years old, Willie. I think he's adjusted." Mary-Martha pushed herself up and turned on the lounge chair so she faced the dog.

Tuffy stopped and stared at her through the gaps in the fence planking.

"What are you doing?" Willie asked.

"I'm going to see what's wrong with Tuffy."

"I'll do it. You take it easy."

"Stop babying me. There's nothing wrong with me."

"OK, but I'm going with you. Maybe he sees some critter. You wouldn't want to step on a snake, would you?"

"Depends who the snake is."

Mary-Martha strolled across the wide backyard. Willie moved in step with her. She had no fear of the dog. Black Labs were known for their social personalities. Loving someone to death was the greatest danger they posed.

A flower bed ran along the fence on their side. Gardening was the only physical effort Mary-Martha enjoyed. She had a professional gardening service take care of the rest of the yard, but this one strip she kept for herself, and even that took too much time from her schedule. Even so, every week she spent a few hours tending her agapanthus and daylilies.

During those times, Mary-Martha and Tuffy had learned to get along. She often brought a snack of cheese for Tuffy. A ritual was established. She'd feed the dog a few pieces of cheese, and the Lab would keep her company by lying near where she worked, moving when she did. She enjoyed the company and Tuffy enjoyed the cheese.

As she and Willie neared the fence, she noticed Tuffy didn't move. She could only see part of the dog through the fence planks, but she could tell the dog was tense. From her position she could only see one of the dog's eyes—an eye that didn't blink.

"Hey, boy," Mary-Martha said. "What's got you so uptight?" She looked along the flower bed and saw no snakes, cats, or anything that would agitate such a gentle and well-behaved dog. She extended her hand as she always did to scratch Tuffy on the nose.

Her fingers were an inch from the fence when the dog exploded into a snarling fury, hitting the fence with his head. White teeth flashed, and for a moment she thought she saw its eyes blaze yellow.

Mary-Martha snapped her hand back, then lost sight of the animal as Willie imposed himself between Mary-Martha and the dog. Tuffy slammed into the fence again, and it shook along its length.

She stumbled back and peered around his shoulder. The third time Tuffy slammed into the fence a board came loose. Mary-Martha could see blood running from the dog's head.

"The dog's gone crazy." Willie turned, spun Mary-Martha around, and marched her to the house, keeping his body between her and the fence. She heard the dog hit the fence again.

Seconds later, Mary-Martha sat at her dining table watching her hands shake. Willie marched the length of the room, fuming. "The animal is vicious. It should be put down. How could any thinking person harbor such a beast?"

"The dog has always been so friendly. I don't understand."

"I don't either. Maybe it's rabid or something."

"Don't you think Ben and Wendy would notice something like that? A rabid dog would be as much a danger to them as to us."

"I'm going over there and tell them what I think."

"No, you're not."

"Why not? Someone needs to talk some sense into their head."

"Let it go, Willie. Ben and Wendy are good neighbors. If something is wrong with Tuffy, they'll know soon enough." She rose from the chair, rounded the dining room table, and peered out the French doors that lead to the backyard. Tuffy had not moved. Even at this distance she could tell the dog was staring at her. Her heart stuttered with fear and her head pounded from tension.

A sharp laugh from behind her startled her back to the moment. She turned from the door and turned on her husband. "How dare you laugh about this?"

He was still pacing. "What? I didn't laugh."

"Yes, you did."

"No, I didn't. I'm far too ticked off to muster a smile, let alone laugh." The tension in his face softened. "Are you all right? You're not hearing things are you?"

The one thing Willie would never do is lie to her. As she thought about it, the laugh sounded different from his. "I'm fine. Just a little shook. I thought I heard you laughing. I'm sorry."

"I would never laugh about anything that endangered or upset you. You know that." He stepped to her and wrapped his arms around her.

She let him and rested her head on his shoulder.

A short distance away, over the dining room table and in an antique china hutch, rested her mother's silver platter, polished and shiny—with a face full of yellow teeth gazing back.

It was laughing.

And she could hear it.

A tear rolled from her eye.

The flight, Katherine's second in two days, was cramped, bouncy, and delayed for two hours. They spent an extra hour on the runway, inhaling eye-watering perfume worn by a woman who must have bathed in it to save water. For the first time in her life she wished she could open a window in a 757.

When the flight touched down in El Paso, she and Gene Manford took a chartered flight to Van Horn and were met by Lieutenant Michael Flannigan of the Texas Highway Patrol.

Flannigan stood tall, straight, and too young to hold the position he did. He wore plain clothes and led them to a rental Lincoln. He helped them with their luggage.

"Flannigan," Manford said. "Sounds Irish."

"You noticed that, did you? Yes, sir, my mother and father immigrated two years before I was born. I tell you what, it sure confused the guests when they'd hear my parent's brogue and my Texas drawl. Made for interesting gatherings."

"That might be worth paying money to see," Manford said.

Flannigan looked in the rearview mirror to make eye contact with Katherine. "Unless I miss my guess, ma'am, with a name like Rooney you have some of the noble blood in you."

"I don't know how noble it is, but my grandfather on my father's side grew up in County Cork."

"So you know your way around stewed cabbage then?"

"I do. I'm also pretty good at detecting blarney when I hear it."

Flannigan laughed. "A definite plus in our business." He drove from the small airport and onto the side streets of Van Horn. "I gotta admit I've worked with the FBI a few times, the DEA even more, but never the FCC and FBI together. That's kind of an odd pairing, isn't it?"

"We're all just one big brotherhood," Gene said.

Flannigan said, "There are several hotels. I can take you to the better ones if you want to get a place."

"No need," Katherine said. "We can do that later if necessary. I understand you're the lead investigator."

"For this region, yes, ma'am. I've seen some strange things in my day, but this beats them all. How much do ya'll know?"

Katherine filled him in about the video they had studied.

"I've seen that video. I didn't arrive on scene until five minutes after all that happened. Many of the emergency vehicles got there about the same time. The fires were still burning, but everyone was fine. Well, there were quite a few bumps and bruises, but no deaths."

"Do you believe the video?" Gene asked.

"What's not to believe? I spoke to the deputy in the helicopter. He saw it all, and he told me the video is dead-on."

"Is it worth seeing the accident site?" Katherine asked.

Flannigan shrugged. "I'll be happy to take you out there, but the road has been cleared and the vehicles towed. All that's there now is skid marks, broken taillights, and one very charred section of road. Road crews have one lane closed until they can make sure the road is safe at that point."

"What about people?" Katherine shifted beneath her seat belt.

"Yes, ma'am. I have names and addresses of everyone involved."

"Including the two in the pickup truck?" Gene said.

"No. I'm afraid not. You have to understand: it was bedlam. There were forty cars and trucks involved, some with little more than scrapes to their fenders. Others were in worse condition. My office will be sending out accident reports to insurance companies from now until doomsday."

"Forty vehicles, an overturned school bus, a burning tanker truck, and several rolled cars, yet the worst injuries are bumps and bruises." Gene shook his head. "It's a miracle—" he caught himself.

"That's what people in these parts are saying," Flannigan said. "I've heard the word *miracle* more times in this investigation that I have in lifetime of church attendance."

"You're a churchgoer?" Katherine said.

"This is Texas, ma'am; even the crooks go to church. There are still parts of Texas where church membership is required if you want to run for office."

Gene jerked his head around. "You mean there are laws—"

"No," Flannigan interjected. "I mean there are places where people won't vote for you if they think you have a problem with the local churches. It's amazing the number of politicians that get religion about a year before an election." He laughed. "I guess you don't see that in DC and California."

"No," Kathleen said. "We don't see that."

"What about you, ma'am? You a church person?"

"Used to be as a child. Haven't been since high school."

"Don't look at me," Manford said. "I go on Easter and that's about it. Sometimes not even then."

"Too bad," Flannigan said. "I'd feel like half a man if I couldn't go church to every week."

"You were saying something about miracles," Kathleen said.

"Some of the first words I heard when I rolled up on the scene. I was expecting some rescue situations; instead, I find people standing around talking about people coming back to life, including some children."

"You know that's impossible, don't you?" Manford said.

"No, sir, I don't know any such thing, and neither do the parents of some of those children."

"Can we talk to some of the kids?" Katherine asked.

"I'll see what I can do. When we talked on the phone, you said you wanted to talk to the driver of the tanker truck. He lives here in Van Horn. Why don't we start there?"

A bald man with fresh pink skin answered the door.

"Afternoon Mr. Liptak. I'm Lieutenant Flannigan with the Texas Highway Patrol; this is Special Agent Katherine Rooney of the FBI and Agent Gene Manford of the FCC—"

"You guys just don't let up, do you?" Liptak said.

"I know we should have called first—" Flannigan began.

"What do you mean 'guys'?" Katherine asked.

"You government types. How many times am I going to have to tell this story?"

"There were other agents here?" She felt her eyes narrow.

"Not more than four or five hours ago. Two men from the NTSB."

Katherine looked at Manford then back to Liptak. She pulled her badge and ID from the pocket of her pantsuit and flashed it. "Did they show you identification?"

"Sure...well, I don't remember a badge. Do NTSB people carry a badge?"

"What about a picture ID?"

"Come to think of it, I didn't see one of those either."

Katherine's jaw clinched. "May we come in, Mr. Liptak? I think we may have several things to discuss."

THE MEETING WITH ADAM LIPTAK LASTED OVER AN hour. Occasionally, the meeting ground to a stop as a cell phone rang. Katherine began the interview by pressing Liptak about the two men who had been in the home earlier. She learned several things. First, the men presented no identification, something a federal officer would always do. Second, they had accents—"Like yours," Liptak said. It took a moment for Katherine to realize that in Texas she was the one with the accent. And third, she got a physical description. Unfortunately Liptak didn't pay attention to their car. "I think it was a big sedan; black maybe."

Ten minutes later she pulled her cell phone from her pocket and made a call to her office. Flannigan made a call as well, and within minutes, every highway patrol officer in the area had a description of the men. Dispatch, he said, would also notify local sheriff and police agencies to keep an eye out for two men meeting the description. Katherine appreciated the effort but knew a four- or five-hour head start gave the imposters an advantage.

She learned one other thing in the Liptak interview: the two men were more interested in the mysterious man than in the details and causes of the accident.

Twenty minutes into the interview Katherine received a call from the agent in her office she called earlier. "NTSB is sending a team of investigators, but they're still on the ground and not expected to be on scene until tomorrow."

Liptak told his story again, and Katherine took the lead in

asking questions. Manford and Flannigan were professionals, and professionals didn't interrupt the lead investigator. Liptak already looked stressed, and enduring questions from three people might prove too much.

Back in Flannigan's car, the three pulled from the curb.

"Who do you think these guys are?" Manford asked.

"I have no idea," Katherine responded. "Impersonating a federal officer is serious. I'd love to put the cuffs on those two."

"Where to now?" Flannigan asked. "You want to interview more eyewitnesses?"

Katherine thought for a moment. "I think we're going to get the same info. What about the children? Could we talk to one of them?"

"Yes, ma'am. I have list of everyone there, including the children. The parents will have to be present, you know."

"I know. In fact, I want them there. A child is less likely to lie if mom and dad are around."

Manford asked, "Do you think a child will talk to us?"

"If we find the right child, yes. But let me do the talking. You guys are big and frightening."

Manford chuckled. "To you or to children?"

"I think I know just the child." Flannigan pulled over, pulled out his cell phone, and placed a call. A few minutes later they were headed down the main street of town.

"Who'd you call?" Katherine asked.

"Ken Newbaker. He goes to my church. One of the deacons. Parents are protective of their children. These parents are even more so, and who can blame them. Ken and his wife know me. Just go easy on the kid."

"I need to find a way to help her open up."

"No problem there. This girl will talk your ear off. When they invented the word *precocious* they had little Noel in mind."

The drive across town was short, and soon Flannigan pulled up to a Craftsman-style bungalow with a neat yard, trimmed grass, and a large cottonwood tree shading everything beneath. Clearly this house was well loved.

Flannigan took the lead and knocked on the door. A moment later a woman's voice pressed through the closed door. "Who is it?"

"It's Michael, Betty. I called Ken and he said to come on by."

Katherine heard a lock being unlatched. A woman with dark, curled hair that reminded Katherine of a hairstyle from the 1950s opened the door. Flannigan nodded and smiled. "Afternoon, Betty."

"Michael." She returned the nod and pushed the screen door open. "I had to make sure you weren't more reporters. They've been around like the plague. Ya'll come in. Ken is out back feeding the dogs. He'll be back in a second."

The house was small but meticulously clean. Katherine knew the woman didn't have time to do this nice a job in the few minutes it took for them to drive here. She must be a chronic cleaner.

The furnishings were simple but nice. A coffee table held copies of *Popular Science* and *Popular Mechanics* magazines. More interesting than the furnishings was the aroma wafting from the kitchen. Katherine became instantly hungry.

"It smells wonderful in here," Katherine said.

Betty smiled. "I've got a Crock-Pot of butter beans and ham. House has smelled like this all day."

"Betty here is one of the best cooks in the county. Anytime we have a potluck at the church, her food is the first to go. I learned to get in line early."

The sound of a solid screen door slamming rumbled through the house. The squeal of a little girl followed the harsh noise. A tall, thin man with two days' growth of beard on his face galloped into the room with a dark-haired girl on his back and hugging his neck. He barreled into the room. "I tried to feed Noel to the dogs, but they wouldn't eat her. They said she was too stinky…"

He stopped and straightened.

Again Flannigan took the lead. "Hey, Ken."

"Hey, Mike. You got here fast."

"We weren't far off. Is this still a good time?"

He laughed. "Sure, sure. Have a seat. Excuse me, I seem to have this ugly growth on my back."

"Daddy!"

"Sorry. I shouldn't have called you a growth."

The little girl pretended to choke him.

"OK, OK, you win." He moved to the sofa and sat, leaning forward so his daughter could slip from her perch. Ken looked at the others. "Have a seat folks." He stood. "We're a chair short. I'll get one from the dining room." A moment later he returned with a well-worn oak dining chair. He set it next to an easy chair. Katherine took a rocking chair that looked like a family heirloom, Manford sat in the easy chair, and Flannigan lowered himself onto the dining room chair. The family of three shared the sofa.

"I suppose I should make a few introductions," Flannigan said. "This is Special Agent Katherine Rooney of the FBI and her friend Agent Gene Manford of the FCC."

"What makes you a special agent?" Noel asked.

Everyone laughed.

"I've asked that question myself several times," Katherine answered. "It's how people who work for government law enforcement refer to each other. Sometimes the term 'field agent' is used."

"Oh." She thought for a moment. "You talk funny."

"I'm from California, so I sound like I have an accent to you. You, young lady, sound like you have a very pretty accent to me."

"Oh. Does my mommy have an accent?"

"Yes, to me she does."

"OK. Are you here because of the accident?"

Katherine leaned forward. "You know, Lieutenant Flannigan said you were a smart girl."

She looked puzzled. "I just call him Brother Mike."

"I understand you had a very scary thing happen yesterday." Katherine hoped she wasn't moving too fast.

"You mean the bus accident?"

"Yes. Does it bother you to talk about it?" Katherine saw the girl's parents tense.

"No. Not really. Maybe some." She looked at Manford and Flannigan, then back to Katherine. "Am I in trouble?"

"Oh, no, sweetheart. Not at all. Part of my job is to find out what happened. That's all. No one is in trouble."

She seemed to relax. "OK."

Katherine prodded. "What do you remember?"

"We were on a school trip and the bus crashed and fell over on its side."

"That had to be very scary."

"It was. Everybody was screaming and people fell on each other. Tommy Johnson fell on me and broke this." She pointed to her clavicle.

"He broke your collarbone?"

"He didn't mean to. He was in the other seat, and when the bus tipped over, he fell on me and it hurt real bad. I started to cry."

"I imagine so. I broke my collarbone once, and it really hurt."

"Really?"

Katherine shifted in her seat. "I don't usually tell people the story because I kinda feel stupid about it."

"Why? What happened?"

"Promise not to tell anyone? Not too far from where I live in California is a ski resort. I was trying to learn to snowboard. Do you know what snowboarding is?"

"I've seen it on the TV."

"OK then, you know snowboarding is like skiing but with

a board instead of skis." She leaned even closer as if telling her darkest secret. "On my first day, I lost control and crashed into a man. He was much bigger than me. We got tangled up, and the next thing I knew I was in the hospital with a broken collarbone and a whole bunch of bruises. I never went snowboarding again."

"I didn't go to the hospital."

"Really? Then how do you know your collarbone was broken?"

"Did you know before you got to the hospital?"

Katherine looked at Manford, who casually covered his mouth with his hand but not before she saw the grin.

"I guess I did. So Tommy fell on top of you. Then what?"

"I hit my head on the window." She pointed to the right side of her forehead. "The window was broken and it cut my head. I saw blood. The bus was still moving, and I could see the road moving under the window."

The visual gave Katherine the chills. She waited to see if Noel would continue on her own. She did.

"Tommy was screaming in my ear. All the kids were screaming…" Her eyes shifted to a scene only she could see, but she showed no fear. Her parents, however, looked ready to melt into the sofa. "Then the fire came. I could smell gasoline."

"A truck that carries gasoline to gas stations crashed nearby." Did Noel already know that?

"I couldn't breathe with Tommy on top of me. First there was fire, then there was smoke and everyone coughed. Those on my side of the bus got burned by the fire, then…"

"Take your time, sweetheart. I know this is hard."

"I felt the fire. It was burning me. It burned my hair. It burned my face. My lungs burned and my arms and my legs…" She stopped abruptly. "Everything became dark. I don't like the dark."

Katherine glanced at Betty and wondered how she could listen to this. A child's horror is a mother's horror.

"There was too much smoke to see?" Katherine said.

She shook her head so that her chin went from shoulder to shoulder and her hair flopped into her eyes. "I couldn't see the smoke no more."

"Anymore," her mother corrected, then drew a hand under her eyes to move away a tear.

"I couldn't see the smoke anymore. I couldn't see anything anymore. Not at first."

"Not at first?"

"When I opened my eyes, he was there."

Katherine looked at Manford, who shrugged. "Who was there?"

"The man."

"The man? You mean the man who pulled you from the bus?"

She shook her head with the same exaggeration as before. "I wasn't in the bus no more...anymore."

"I don't understand, sweetie. Where were you if you weren't on the bus?"

She shrugged. Someone with a broken clavicle didn't shrug, but then again, Noel showed no signs of burns or cuts or bruises.

"I don't know. It was nice. Kinda foggy."

Katherine leaned back, uncertain what to ask next.

Flannigan came to the rescue. "Tell Ms. Rooney about the man."

"Oh, he was real nice. He was tall like Daddy and strong. He picked me up and gave me hug. He hugged all the children."

"There were other children?"

"Yes. Tommy was there, and so were Susie Littleton and Ralph Moore and...almost everyone on the bus was there."

"What did this man do? Did he speak?"

"He was fun. He laughed a lot. He let us chase him. We caught him and wrestled him to the ground. He was ticklish."

All her life Katherine had forced her mind to see facts, to gather information and draw reasoned conclusions. Like a train that must travel on tracks, her thinking followed a course that allowed no room to wander from the path. That train just derailed.

"Did he tell you his name?" Katherine asked.

"He said his name was Joshua, but he pronounced it funny."

Flannigan asked the next question. "Did it sound like Yoshua?"

"Yeah. Like that."

Flannigan turned to Katherine. "Yoshua is the Hebrew pronunciation of Joshua. The New Testament was written in Greek. The Greek rendition of Joshua is Jesus."

Katherine blinked several times, then said the only thing her mind would allow: "Jesus is ticklish?"

"Big-time," Noel said.

It had to be a dream, Katherine reasoned. A death dream. The mind in such agony switches to something it can tolerate, a fabrication made to avoid a horrible reality. "You think you were in heaven?" She immediately regretted her phrasing.

"Not heaven. He said we weren't in heaven. It wasn't our time. We were just waiting for a few minutes."

"What was this place like?"

"Like I said, it was kinda foggy, but it was also beautiful, but I can't tell you why. I don't know how to tell you about it. Maybe the others can tell it better."

"Others?"

"The other kids. They all saw the same thing I did."

Katherine looked at Flannigan and sent her question with a raised eyebrow.

"I talked to them all, and the ones that were…the ones at the front of the bus all saw and say the same thing."

"He means the dead ones," Noel said.

"Did…I mean, what…" Words failed her.

"Do you want to know what happened next?"

"Yes," Katherine said. "Thank you."

"We played some more but then he asked us to sit in front of him. He sat down with us and told us the Messenger was coming and we should listen to him."

"The Messenger?"

"Yes," Noel said. "He's already here. He's the one who brought us back to life and made all our hurts go away."

"Several people helped take children from the bus," Katherine said.

"The one who walked through the fire. The one who was burned like me. He is the Messenger, and he's already here."

Katherine's mind raced with possibilities, reasons why none of this could be true, and searched for flaws in the little girl's story.

"Oh, I almost forgot. The man we tickled told me you'd be coming. He said to tell you, 'The Messenger needs your help.'"

BRYAN STOVER REFUSED TO LET GO OF THE SMALL PIECE of paper with a handwritten note about a hospital in Oak Grove and his son's name. The BMW moved along the freeway easily, but it took all of Bryan's strength to not excessively exceed the speed limit. He just got out of jail by paying a stiff bail and signing a paper promising to appear in court when summoned. He had lost several hours in an El Paso ER while they poked and prodded him to make sure he wouldn't die while in custody. The ER doc lectured him about heroin, which entered one ear, spent a three-second vacation in his mind, then exited through the other ear. He knew the dangers. He lived the dangers. Heroin addicts didn't keep up the addiction because it made them wonderful and admired people. They kept it up because they couldn't stop. What part of addition didn't the doctor understand?

Several more hours were spent in lockup until bail was set. He had no previous record, so the cops reluctantly let him leave through the front door. A cab ride back to the hotel allowed him to retrieve his car. Fortunately it hadn't been impounded, a very real possibility. Being an otherwise upstanding white-collar exec-utive bought him a few more favors than would be given most down-and-outers.

The note he held in his hand seemed to burn through his skin and crawl toward his mind. Seeing his son's name in connection with a hospital had driven away any drug-induced haze—but that was the mysterious part. There was no drug-induced haze, no inner urging for more "horse," no anxiety about where the next fix would come from; just an inner drive to get to his son.

The lights of El Paso were long behind him. He stopped only for gas, then got back on the road. Although he moved seven miles an hour over the speed limit—the most he'd press his luck—the mile markers crawled by.

He passed the time worrying about his boy, regretting his life and wondering who the two guys in his hotel room were. Most of those moments were too foggy to recall. He remembered a brief conversation with a bald man, another voice, and then darkness.

It had been the darkness he sought. He had used heroin for several years, and other drugs before that. He knew how much would kill him, and he injected twice that. Yet here he was, alive and driving to Oak Grove.

Bits of memory flashed strobelike on his mind. The darkness gave way to a foggy white and the sight of a tall, single figure indistinct but clearly there. Then the man was gone. The black returned, and then a new light, the dim glow inside the back of an ambulance.

The ambulance made sense, but his living did not. The ER docs found nothing wrong with him. When they examined his arms for needle marks, they found none. That made no sense. He had made a pincushion out of that arm. There were tracks there, but the doctors couldn't find them. And when they left him for a moment, he checked for himself. No marks.

Something wasn't right. Everything was right. Everything was wrong. He tightened his grip on the steering wheel and drove through the night.

What was wrong with Rory? What hadn't *she* told him?

He gave himself a mental slap. How could she tell him? When he left, he determined to never look back. But he did look back. In quiet moments, in the alone minutes, in the everlasting hours of guilt, he looked back and remembered and dreamed about what could have been.

The drugs robbed him of his joy and of his hope and were closing in on his career and life.

He gazed through the side window at the star-sequined sky and realized that had his plan worked, he would never have seen this sky. He would be dead from a planned drug overdose, and the universe would have continued without him.

And so would the wife he hadn't seen in years and the son who needed him.

Room 312 of the Oak Grove Community Hospital seemed twenty miles down the corridor. Every step made his feet heavier and his heart beat as if he had sprinted the distance from El Paso to Oak Grove. Everything hurt: his heart, his head, his muscles, but most of all his soul.

Bryan paused just outside the open door and took several deep breaths, re-tucked in his shirt, and straightened his suit coat. He had no idea how his hair looked, but he was pretty sure he looked like death warmed over. The last five minutes of the drive were spent creating the first words he would speak. After all, he was a well-respected businessman now, used to communicating with CEOs and corporate presidents. How hard could this be?

He checked his watch: twelve minutes past ten. It was late. Maybe he should wait until morning…no. No more waiting. No more excuses. No more avoiding his responsibility.

After one more breath, he straightened his spine and stepped into the dim room. A woman sat in a yellow vinyl chair, her head resting in her hand, eyes closed, and breathing in slow inhalations. The wall-mounted television silently bathed the room in gray light.

The bed by the window held a thin, small form. A boy rested beneath a white sheet and a goldenrod-colored blanket. He too slept. His left arm rested on top of the blanket. From it ran a clear plastic tube connected to an equally clear IV bag hung on a chrome stand. An IV pump worked tirelessly, offering a blinking light and a few digital readouts as proof of its diligence.

He stepped to the bed and gazed at a boy he hadn't seen since his second birthday, a boy who appeared perfect in every way— except he slept in a hospital.

Bryan felt tears sting his eyes. Lost years. Lost birthdays. Lost opportunities to play his first game of catch, to tease him about girls, to teach him to love Sunday afternoon football. Gone. Irretrievable.

They had not exchanged a word in eight years, yet Bryan would give his blood, organs, marrow, his very life to erase the words he had read on the note left in his pocket: Leukemia; Terminal.

He closed his eyes. *Dear God, take me. I've been useless, worthless, nothing but a leech on life, but my boy... he deserves better. Do what You want with me; just let Rory live.*

A stream of moisture lined his cheeks. He opened his eyes. Nothing had changed. A movement to his left caught his attention. Someone moved to his side and took hold of his arm and jerked it. A sharp pain ran from his elbow to his shoulder. Before he could speak, the person holding him led him from the bedside, through the room, and into the bright hall.

"Jennifer!" Her eyes looked hollow, her blonde hair hung in limp, unwashed strands, and her skin looked pale as soap. She looked ill.

"What are you doing here?" She pushed him back a step.

"Jennifer, stop."

She shoved him again. "You don't get to tell me what to do anymore." She raised her hands again. Bryan took her by the wrists and pulled her close, wrapping his arms around her in a firm hug. "Let me talk."

"Let go of me. I'll scream."

"If you do, you'll frighten Rory. Just listen to me for a moment."

Jennifer tried to pull away, but he refused to let her go. He lowered his voice to a whisper. "Just let me talk for a moment. That's all. I'm not here to cause trouble. I promise. Just let me talk, OK?"

She shivered in his arms. "Make it fast."

"I have no right to be here. I know that. Let me say what's on my mind, and if you still want me to leave, I will. All I ask is that you listen." He released her and saw tears brimming in her eyes. He felt his own tears on her cheek. "I wanted to see Rory."

"You haven't wanted to see him in years." She turned and leaned against the wall.

"I deserve that. I deserve a lot worse."

"You got that right."

He removed the note from his pocket and handed it to her.

"What's this?"

"When I woke up, I found this note."

She read it aloud. "Your son is ill. Leukemia. Terminal. Oak Grove Community Hospital. Room 312." She looked up from the note. "Someone snuck into your home to give you this note?"

He lowered his head. "I wasn't at home. I was in a motel."

"Lucky girl." He didn't miss the sarcasm.

"Nothing like that, Jennifer. I was alone." He rubbed his eyes. "Look, long story short, after I left you, I got a job in a bank. It turns out I've got a talent for it. I rose through the ranks and ended up being a VP. I made some good decisions in business, but I made some really bad ones with the rest of my life. Leaving you was the worst."

"That doesn't change anything."

"I know." He sighed. He had never given words to his story, and they came reluctantly. "When I left you, I was a drunk. It went downhill from there. I was in the motel to…"

"To do what?"

"To kill myself. With heroin."

"You're an addict."

He uttered the hardest word he ever said. "Yes. But I think that may have changed."

"How? People don't kick heroin."

"This is going to sound weird."

She gave a joyless laugh. "Yeah, it's been so believable to this point."

"Bear with me. It won't make sense, but you have a right to the story. I had just dumped a ton of heroin into my vein. Suicide by overdose, that was the plan. Before I went unconscious I see these two guys."

"Two guys?"

He saw something in her expression. "Yeah, two guys. I was pretty out of it, so I thought I was hallucinating. I'm lying on the bed, and one of the guys holds his hands over me. Blue mist began to fall from his hands. At least that's what it looked like to me. The other one was talking about the empty bags of heroin. I can't remember all that they said.

"Next thing I know, I'm in the back of an ambulance, but I feel great. The ER docs can't find anything wrong with me. The cops arrest me but can only charge me with possessing drug paraphernalia. I had used all the drugs, but the docs couldn't find any in my blood. While I waited to be released on bail I kept reading that note over and over. I knew I had to come."

"Why the sudden interest in Rory?"

"Not just Rory; you too, Jennifer. I don't know. Maybe you've remarried, but I had to see you and Rory before... Is it true?"

"About Rory?" She nodded and fresh tears appeared. "He's not responding to treatment."

Bryan raised tremulous hands to his face as if he could shield himself from the truth.

"What did they look like?"

"The two men? It's kinda foggy. The one talking about the drugs was young, maybe early twenties. The other guy looked older, maybe midforties. He was bald."

"I wonder…Two men came to Rory's room the other day. It sounds like the same guys, except the older man had long hair. He called himself Henick, and the younger guy said his name was Eddie."

"What did they want?"

"They came to see Rory." More tears. "Henick said Rory was going to a place Henick had been. I think he meant heaven."

"Mom?"

Jennifer spun on her heel and plunged into the dark room. Bryan followed. Rory lay staring at the ceiling.

"I'm here, son." Jennifer took his hand. Bryan moved to the other side of the bed.

"Who are you?" Rory asked. A red-hot sword stabbed Bryan's soul. He looked to Jennifer, who nodded.

"I'm your father, Rory. I'm sorry I've been gone so long."

"My dad?"

"Yes. You have grown up so much."

"Oh, hi." Rory looked at his mother. "I can see the place again— the place he showed us."

"What place?" Bryan asked.

Jennifer couldn't speak. She just shook her head and held Rory's hand.

"Wow. It's even more beautiful this time. It's so real." He lifted his free arm. "Hold my hand, Dad."

Bryan struggled to press down the emotion welling in him, but he would have had better luck stuffing down an erupting volcano. For the first time in eight years, Bryan Stover touched his son. A heartbeat later a scene of peace and light inundated his mind. Images of such exquisite beauty they defied words flashed in his mind.

He shook.

He gasped for air.

His heart tumbled and rattled.

A small voice said, "Thanks for coming, Dad."

"I love you, son."

"I know."

"I'm sorry."

"I know. It doesn't matter."

The air smelled sweet; the light in his mind gleamed like gold.

A tall and thin figure appeared and moved closer. He smiled, and for a moment everything in the universe was right. The figure extended a hand, and Bryan watched through closed eyes as his son walked away with the stranger.

The scene dissolved, replaced by the antiseptic smells of the dim hospital room.

On the bed lay Rory.

A smile graced his face.

He wasn't breathing.

Bryan collapsed by the bed and wept from places so deep in his being he didn't know they existed. Once again, he wished for death.

A pair of arms surrounded him, familiar arms from years ago. Jennifer's tears joined his.

41

THE NIGHT SEEMED TO HAVE SUBSTANCE, A WEIGHT THAT grew heavier with each passing moment. Mary-Martha lay in her bed watching the LED display on her alarm clock tick off the minutes. Next to her, Willie snored in soft rhythm. He could fall asleep in any situation and usually left the land of the wakeful within minutes of his head touching the pillow.

Mary-Martha often stared at the ceiling, her mind planning, scheming, or occupied with what could be. She did most of her planning lying beneath thick covers and on silk sheets. Here she could let her guard down and consider the unthinkable secrets.

Secrets made up her life and always had. As a child she kept secrets from her friends and parents. As an adult she kept secrets from her employees. Most of all, she kept secrets from her husband.

He was a good man and loved her deeply, although she knew she never gave him reason to do so. Being married was part of her image. Willie was window dressing, an accessory to the persona. Fortunately he had always been and still remained henpecked. Occasionally he would stand up to her, but the heat of her anger could melt him within minutes.

Secrets. She had kept the business side of the Church of New Revelation from him. He knew that it provided a six-figure salary to her, but he didn't know about other monies she channeled to other accounts. Of course, neither did the IRS. He did know that her spirit guides were fiction, but she had convinced him that they were merely a communication technique to help parishioners remember the message and they spoke to her in the privacy of her office.

Lies and secrets. Secrets and lies.

The biggest secret, however, she kept underground a few hundred miles away, a place deep beneath New Mexico soil. He would learn of it when the time came. Sanctuary was ready and waiting should the house of cards begin to wobble. Willie would go with her because she demanded it. He would also go because she had forged his name to several accounts in offshore banks.

Misrepresentations and misconduct. All of it necessary.

Mary-Martha rolled onto her back. She was paranoid and knew it. Not the friendly, amusing kind of paranoia that saw the occasional government conspiracy. No, her mistrust of others and the government raged within her. A psychiatrist would prescribe medication, but she couldn't have that. People didn't follow crazy people if they knew they were crazy. Many would follow someone they thought was sane even if there existed plenty of proof that the mental elevator didn't go all the way to the top.

Secrets from self. Self-delusion.

If self-deception were a martial art, then she would have a black belt. For years she knew that something in her skull was wrong, but she kept such self-revelation private.

The Face had to be a new manifestation of an old condition. She'd adjust. Maybe it would even go away. It didn't matter. She wasn't going to change a thing. She'd learn to live with it. After all, she had seen it a dozen times now, and it made no move to harm her. It wasn't real. It must be nothing but synaptic misfiring; perception overload; stress. Whatever it was, it wasn't real.

The bedspread moved. Willie always hogged the covers. She started to pull the spread back over her when she realized Willie had not moved. He still lay on his side snoring.

The covers slipped down.

Dreaming, she decided. *I must be having a waking dream, or dreaming that I'm awake, or...*

The bedspread rose above her, leaving the thick blanket and silk sheet in place. Slowly, gently, as if trying not to wake Willie, the spread hovered above the bed for a moment, then pulled together to form a small mountain of material.

Mary-Martha's lungs felt on fire, and her heart, instead of racing, slowed and threatened to stop. Her skin tingled. Once again she told herself it was a dream, just a nightmare.

Secrets and lies; lies and secrets—even with herself.

She wanted to scream. She couldn't. She tried to touch Willie, but her arms wouldn't move. Her legs wouldn't move. Paralyzed. She held a brief thought about the stories of alien abductions. Nearly everyone who claimed to have been abducted said they couldn't move.

Something else stopped moving. Her lungs. Mary-Martha couldn't breathe. She tried to open her mouth to gulp air, but her jaw wouldn't budge and her lips wouldn't part. She felt no air enter her nostrils. Suffocating; she knew she was suffocating. How long could she go without air? Minutes, that's all; mere minutes.

The mound of bed linen morphed before her wide eyes, twisting, turning, bulging, contracting until a shape formed.

The Face, draped in cloth, hovered above her. Although made of material, it looked like puffy flesh. Something twisted beneath it—something that smelled of evil.

Mary-Martha tried to gasp, but that required working lungs. Faster than it rose, the bedding dropped, but the Face remained. A small emergency light glowed nearby, painting weak illumination upon the Face. Brown-red-yellow skin pulled tight over a lumpy bone structure made the Face. It reeked of a thousand dead fish in the sun. Mary-Martha gagged, but her mouth remained glued shut.

The Face floated above her belly, rose a few inches, and then moved forward one inch at a time.

Her lungs burned for lack of oxygen. The specter advanced until it hovered a few inches from her face.

It smiled, revealing yellow, blocklike teeth that reminded Mary-Martha of piano keys.

"Are you a faithful servant?" the Face asked.

Mary-Martha didn't respond. Surely the voice would awaken Willie. Willie continued to snore.

The Face frowned and moved an inch closer. Mary-Martha could feel its breath on her cheeks.

"Are you a faithful servant?" The voice sounded like a rusty hinge on an old car door.

Mary-Martha nodded and hoped that was the right answer.

The Face smiled, forcing more sharp knives of terror into her brain. "The world shall call you blessed. You shall be the master of the messenger. Do you believe me?"

She nodded.

"And I will be your master."

Mary-Martha didn't move.

The suspended head tilted to one side as if questioning Mary-Martha's non-answer.

"And I will be your master."

Mary-Martha nodded. Air, she needed air. She cut her eyes to Willie. He continued to sleep. How could he sleep through this? Couldn't he feel the bedclothes move? Couldn't he smell that stomach-turning stench? Couldn't he hear the rasping, grating voice? The man who had promised to always protect her slept through her greatest time of need.

"Mary-Martha, master of the messenger, the world comes to bow at your feet—at my feet."

The head began to rise like a tired balloon with just enough helium to keep it afloat.

Darkness pressed in from the corner of her eyes. She was suffocating. In minutes she'd be dead, the victim of her own body's failure to respond to her need for air.

The Face rose a few more inches. "I am Lustar, your spirit guide. I am master of the master of the messenger. You will be my voice, the conduit of my wisdom."

Lustar? Lustar was fiction, a fabrication of months of planning. He wasn't real.

"I AM Lustar. Do you believe?"

Again she nodded.

"Our time has come. Be diligent. Listen to me. The messenger is close. You must find him and bring him to me."

The perimeter of the room drew in. She knew unconsciousness and death were moments away.

"We are one," Lustar said. "One are we."

The Face dissolved above her and showered down like a rain of fireflies. At the same instant, her mouth opened and her lungs inhaled air in great gulps, and with every inhalation she took in the glowing detritus of the Face. She turned her head, but the bits of the Face entered her mouth and lungs.

In her mind she heard the Face's voice, "We are one."

Next to her, Willie snored.

I N A HOTEL ON THE OUTSKIRTS OF THE EL PASO AIRPORT, Gabriel sat in an Executive Suites hotel room and watched the sun rise. His frustration level simmered just below the boiling point. The task before him seemed as slippery as a soapy eel. How could he find two people in Texas with almost no information? Sure he knew they were driving a pickup truck, but this was the Southwest and a corner of Texas where a pickup was required for citizenship.

He tried to think like two fugitives. Granted they weren't true fugitives, but they certainly seemed to be making efforts to avoid the law. He could admire that. Still, his job was to do the impossible.

He looked at his watch. He had slept four hours and assumed Howie was still sawing logs in the room next to his. Hoagland didn't like sleep. It was a necessity he surrendered to each night but for as little time as possible. To him, sleeping seemed very much like dying. A man got a limited number of hours to live. Sleeping away a third of life was the act of a fool.

His laptop chimed, and he exchanged the view at the window for that of his computer screen. A new e-mail had arrived, and it was a large one—four megabytes. He clicked on it and found what he expected, a short note:

> G—
>
> I did the best I could and found a few things that might help. See attachments. Usual password.

Later.

—TG

TG, Teddy Gold. A resourceful man Hoagland had called on several times for technical expertise, the same kind of expertise that landed the man in prison for five years.

Hoagland clicked on the first attachment, entered a password he had been given when he dealt with Teddy once before, and a still photo clipped from the news video he had recorded from CNN appeared. He could see the pickup and a blurry man in the passenger seat. The next photo showed a close-up of the man. He could see Teddy had toyed with the image until it was as clear as electronic enhancement could make it. It wasn't a perfect image, but he could see enough features of the bald man to be able to recognize him if he bumped into him on the street.

The next photo was of a group gathered around a crispy-critter that had once been a truck driver—the truck driver he had interviewed yesterday. The image showed several men, but two held his interest. One, naked and bald; the other, young and standing near the miracle man. Now he had faces for both men.

Another double-click made another photo appear on the screen. This time it was a close-up of the truck. Teddy had electronically penned a note in the upper left corner of the image: 1986 BLACK CHEVY PICKUP. BODY APPEARS IN GOOD SHAPE.

Double-click again and he was looking at a new photo. This one showed the back of the truck. The helicopter camera that had taken the video had been too high for Hoagland to pull the license number. It wasn't a problem for Teddy. He could make out most of the numbers. Again Teddy had inscribed a note in the upper left corner. Hoagland had strained to read the tiny print:

> INCOMPLETE LIC. NUMBER BUT GOT TWO HITS WHEN
> SEARCHING FOR 86 CHEVY P.U. WITH TEXAS PLATES—
> EDDIE FEELY OF BLINK, TX AND MARTY FELLMAN, SAN

ANTONIO. DMV RECORDS SHOW FELLMAN B.DAY IN
1958. EDDIE FEELY = 1985. FEELY BEST BET.

Hoagland decided Teddy was a true genius—a twisted genius
to be sure, but a wizard at accessing databases that didn't belong
to him.

The next attachment was another photo, a forced close-up of
the miracle man's companion. It too had a note: CHECKED OUT
FEELY. SEE ATTACHED DOCUMENT.

The next attachment was a Word document.

> As mentioned, Eddie Feely is your best bet for the young guy.
> Checked out a couple of sources. He has a record. Several
> arrests for disturbing the peace, assault, and public intoxica-
> tion. A real winner.
>
> Snooped some Texas cop databases. Feely was arrested a few
> days ago in Blink, TX. Blink…ya gotta love it. Anyway, they
> booked him for disturbing the peace and assault. The arrest
> info says they took him to the local hospital to receive treat-
> ment for a broken hand. Look at the photos. Do you see a cast
> on his arm? Maybe I got the wrong man, or maybe your healer
> did a little work in exchange for transportation. Beats me.
>
> Hope this helps.
>
> —TG

So, Eddie Feely liked to cause a little trouble now and again.
Hoagland filed that info away. He clicked on reply and wrote:

> Got it, TG. Good job. You can expect a five large in your
> Christmas stocking.
>
> —GH

"Blink, Texas," Hoagland said to the empty room. He went
online and Googled the name. In five minutes he knew more
about the small town than he could want. The best he could tell
it was little more than a truck stop off the freeway. The question

that plagued him was if the town merited a visit. His prey was traveling away from the place. He might be able to learn more about Eddie Feely and maybe a thing or two about the mystery man, but to do so he'd have to put several hundred extra miles between him and the man Mary-Martha tasked him to catch.

As he pondered this, the computer screen went blank for a moment then came back and chimed. A new e-mail had arrived. Perhaps Teddy had forgotten something.

Hoagland opened the e-mail, and the screen went blank again.

"What the—"

When it came back on, the e-mail software was gone, replaced by a familiar image: a shadowy man walking a deserted road—the same image he had seen in the *New York Times,* and like the full-page ad, the man was walking toward the viewer. Strange music poured from the speakers, a kind of music Hoagland had never heard.

"What is this?" He removed his hands from the keyboard as if he expected lightning to come from the keys.

The man continued to walk forward. "Time grows short. Look for the one I send you. He walks among you."

The shadowed man took several steps closer as if walking toward a camera.

"Listen to the message. Believe him."

Hoagland realized the last two lines were new.

The man walked out of the shadow, and Hoagland was staring at the bald man he had seen in the video footage—the mystery man; the Messenger.

The scene repeated itself. Hoagland snapped up the phone and dialed 4227, Howie's room.

"Yeah."

Hoagland could tell he woke him. "Get over here. Now!"

"What's up?"

"Now!"

Hoagland hung up and watched the video play over and over again.

The moment he hung up the phone, his cell phone chimed. He snapped it up. "No excuses, Howie."

"Gabriel."

His brain skipped a beat. "Mary-Martha?"

"Have you seen it?"

It was her all right. "Yes. I got one in my e-mail."

A knock on the door. Hoagland rose and opened it. Howie stood at the threshold with his shirt unbuttoned and zipping his pants. "I got here as fast—"

Hoagland cut him off with a raised finger and turned away. He heard Howie enter.

"Write this down," his boss said. She sounded different. Her voice had an undertone to it, and it made the hair on his arm stand erect.

"Hang on." He grabbed a pad of paper from the desk drawer and a pen. "Go ahead."

Mary-Martha gave him an address. "Roadway Motel. He's there."

"How do you know?"

"I know. One more thing: every fox has its hole." The line went dead.

"Was that her?"

"Yeah."

"What'd she say?"

"She gave me an address where the Messenger is."

"How did she find him?" Howie finished tucking in his shirt.

"She didn't say." Hoagland slipped the cell phone back in his pocket and began gathering his things.

"What else did she say?"

"Nothing, Howie; go and get your stuff."

"You sure?"

"Yeah, I'm sure. Why?"

"I've just never seen you scared before."

I'M TAPPED." EDDIE STARED WOEFULLY IN HIS WALLET. "I didn't have much to begin with when I left Blink, but I'm beyond broke now. Bank is tapped as well." He turned to Henick, who sat at the cheap hotel table looking at a Gideon Bible. "You got any scratch left?"

"Scratch?"

"Money. We need gas, and I could use a Breakfast Jack or an Egg McMuffin."

Henick reached into his pocket and withdrew two one-hundred-dollar bills.

"I hate that you have to pay for me. We're running through that five hundred Jake gave you pretty quick. When this is gone, we will be officially broke. That ol' truck of mine gulps gas like it was cheep beer."

"We will be fine."

"How do you know that?"

"I know."

"It's gonna take at least fifty to fill the tank. That should get us another three hundred miles on the road. If we eat light and stay in cheap hotels, we can last a couple more days. Unless we get some cash in that time, we are going to be walkin' wherever it is you're taking us and…what are you doing? You're lookin' at that Bible like you've never seen one before."

"You are right. I have not seen a Bible."

"You're kiddin' me, right? You of all people have never seen a Bible? If you're as old as you say, then I figure you must have known the guys who wrote it."

Henick grinned. "I was gone long before they were born."

"Here we go with the mysteries and cryptic remarks. I'd pump you for more info, but I know I wouldn't get it, then I'd get frustrated and say somethin' I'd regret later." Eddie reached for the remote and found it attached to the nightstand. "No one trusts anyone anymore." He pushed the power button and turned to CNN. "Let's see if they're still talking about you."

Henick didn't reply. He kept his eyes on the Bible.

A few minutes later, Eddie said, "Uh-oh. I think you had better see this."

An ebony-skinned reporter faced the camera. "Today computer users were surprised to find an unusual e-mail in their inboxes— a video similar to a full-page ad that appeared in the *New York Times*."

"Are you watching this, Henick?"

Henick stepped to his side. "Yes."

The reporter continued. "Everyone here at CNN received the same message, and we now have reports that this is truly a global phenomenon. Many of our viewers will recall a recent full-page ad that appeared in the *New York Times*. It was widely reported that the image in the ad would move on its own. That same image has been delivered to countless e-mail inboxes. Some experts have speculated that every e-mail user in the country, maybe in the world, received such an e-mail. Of course, that has yet to be confirmed."

The news anchor interrupted with a question. "How is that possible? I know I got one. My wife tells me she had the same thing on her computer this morning. How can a person send an e-mail to the whole world?"

"We don't know that it was sent to the whole world, but some experts think that is what happened. Of course, great effort is being made to track down the hacker who pulled what may be the world's greatest Internet prank."

The image of the e-mail played on the small television. Eddie watched as a shadowed man walked along an empty road, a road that looked suspiciously like Ranch Road 1232 outside of Blink, Texas.

With every step the shadow grew lighter until Eddie was staring at Henick staring back at him through the television. Strange music floated from the tiny, tinny speakers, then a voice: "Time grows short. Look for the one I send you. He walks among you."

Eddie looked from television Henick to real-life Henick. "Just when I thought you couldn't surprise me anymore, this happens."

Henick looked troubled. "It's time for you to go home."

"We've been through this, man. You're stuck with me."

"You must go."

"Go? Go home to what? I've never done anything right in my life until I started hanging out with you. I'm not going back to being the same ol' Eddie. I can't leave you."

"You must."

"Yeah, well, I won't."

"What I do must be done alone. You do not understand."

He turned to face Henick. "My momma used to read the Bible to me when I was young. A Bible like what you just been reading. I don't know much about such things, but I do know a little bit— maybe just enough to get me in trouble. When Jesus sent out His disciples, He sent them in pairs. Right? Don't answer. I know I'm right. And I remember something else. When they crucified Jesus, most of His disciples left Him. I ain't gonna be like them."

"I am not Jesus."

"Well, I figured that. I don't know what you are, but you're more than any man I've ever met. It's my job to stick with you."

"Your job?"

"Don't ask me to explain, but I know it's true. I know it right here." He taped his chest. "My heart tells me to stick with you. This is new for me. I can't remember a time when I stuck out my neck for anybody. I'm willing to do it for you."

There was a knock on the door.

EDDIE SNAPPED HIS HEAD AROUND AND STARED AT THE door. He then looked at Henick. Henick closed his eyes and lowered his head.

"Cops?"

"No—"

The door flew open, bits of wood from the doorjamb flew like missiles, striking Eddie's arm. "What the—"

Two men charged in, each holding a handgun with a silencer. Eddie was no gun expert, but he knew he was staring down a 9mm barrel of death. His heart seized then started galloping a moment later.

The first man was huge with enough muscle for two men. The second was smaller but wore an expression of delight that frightened Eddie even more.

The large man plowed into Eddie, knocking him to the bed. The cold metal of the silencer pressed behind his left ear with enough force he thought his skull would crack. He heard the door slam shut, then saw Henick pressed against the wall, the smaller man holding his gun an inch from Henick's face.

"You are hard people to find," the large man said.

"We're shy," Eddie replied, then regretted it when a fist landed on his face.

"You really want those to be your last words, pal?"

Eddie didn't answer. Something warm and sticky ran from his nose.

"OK, here's what's going to happen. We're all going to take a short walk to the car, then we're going to take a long drive. You will cooperate or you will regret it."

"Man, you need a new writer. You sound like an old movie hood." Eddie steeled himself for the next punch. Instead, something stabbed him in the back, and fire raced through every fiber of his body. His limbs jerked. His eyes slammed shut. He shook uncontrollably, then it stopped. The big guy carried a Taser.

"Any more smart remarks?" He hit him with the Taser again, and Eddie struggled to remain conscious.

Weeping. "My fault. It was all my fault, man."

Eddie opened his eyes to see Henick's hand on the other thug's chest. Eddie grinned. *I know what that's like.*

"Pull it together, Howie."

"My fault. It was supposed to be fun, nuthin' more than a little motorcycle ride."

"Howie, shut up!"

Howie didn't respond. He lowered his gun. "She meant the world to me, man. I mean everything. I woulda cut off both arms for her. I never shoulda done the meth."

"*Howie!*"

Howie turned his head to speak. "I can't help it, Gabe. I see it every day—every day. She was on the back of my Harley. I was going too fast. I was juiced, man, really juiced. I didn't see the truck…I lived…she didn't. It ain't fair. I shoulda been the one lying under the truck, not Julie—me." He collapsed.

The man Howie called Gabe released Eddie and turned his gun on Henick. Henick didn't move. Eddie did. He rolled on his side, brought up his left leg, then drove his foot into the man's side between his hip and rib cage. Eddie put as much force into it as possible. Air rushed from the man's lungs and his gun arm lowered.

Eddie tried to spring from the bed, but the Taser had left him weak. He pushed himself up on wobbly legs but didn't wait until his full strength returned; he didn't have time. With all the strength he could marshal, he threw a roundhouse punch to the right cheekbone of the attacker. The man's head snapped back. He grabbed the man's gun arm with both hands and brought his knee up as hard as he could. He hoped to break the man's forearm, but he lacked the strength. Still, the blow landed with enough force to make the man scream with pain.

The gun dropped to the floor.

Eddie reached for it, but when his hand was two inches from the weapon, he felt a sharp pain in the back of his neck. The pain ran like an electric current through his body. His vision narrowed around the edge.

He straightened and threw another right cross. The assailant blocked it. Eddie tried a left to the body. It never landed. Desperate, he reached for the big man's throat, but his hands were knocked away. The guy was toying with him.

Then came a left jab that landed square on Eddie's nose. Another jab hit just below his left eye. For a moment Eddie thought the man had slipped on a pair of brass knuckles but realized it was only the man's fists.

A body shot drove the air from Eddie's lungs. An uppercut snapped his head back. He raised his hands in a futile effort to protect his head, but the attacker didn't care. He punched, punched, punched Eddie's arms until Eddie could hold them up no longer.

Then the blows stopped. Eddie raised his head and peered through watery eyes. Henick stood between him and the bruiser trying to kill him with his bare knuckles. Eddie stumbled to the side and saw Henick's hand on the man's chest.

"Yes!" He tried to pump a fist in the air, but pain pulled him up short.

He waited but there were no tears. No confession. He watched as Henick pushed the man's chest harder. Nothing.

"Sorry," the man said. "It seems I'm fresh out of regrets."

A powerful right hand landed on Henick's cheek, and he crumpled to the ground. Eddie started forward when something hit him on the side of the head.

The room spun.

The lights went out.

"Honey, you're not going to believe this. I was just talking to Wendy and Ben." Willie walked into Mary-Martha's study. "Tuffy died last night. Apparently the dog went mad and kept crashing his head into the fence. I told you that dog lost its mind—"

Mary-Martha removed another robe from the special closet where she kept her "church wear" and placed it into a garment bag.

"What are you doing?"

"What's it look like? I'm packing."

"You didn't tell me you were taking another trip. Don't you think you should stay home a few days? I mean because of your fall."

"No. I'm fine. Better than fine."

Willie felt empty again. His wife took frequent trips. She called them "engagements," and she never took him along. Over the years he had grown used to it. Mystery was part of her personality. Late-night meetings, trips that lasted a week or more, unusual phone calls; he assumed it all stemmed from her control issues. Mary-Martha was only happy when in control. He could live with that, but this time something was different.

"You're taking all your robes? How long are you going to be gone?"

"We're going to be gone, Willie. You should pack. I need you to drive me somewhere."

"Where?"

"I'll tell you when we get in the car. The car has plenty of gas, doesn't it?"

"I filled up yesterday. Just how far are we going?"

"Just pack for a couple of weeks."

"A *couple* of weeks? You're kidding, right?"

"No. Go pack."

"I've got to get someone to look after the house, water the plants. I need to suspend mail delivery and the newspapers."

"My office will take care of all that. Just go pack."

"But sweetheart—"

"NOW!"

Willie took a step back. His wife was firm and argumentative, but she never shouted. More troublesome than her tone was her voice.

Willie was certain he had heard two voices.

KATHERINE ROONEY CLOSED HER CELL PHONE. "THAT was Flannigan. He got a report about a pair of men meeting the description of our Messenger and his friend."

"Really? That's a break." Gene Manford poured more cream in his coffee. The two sat in a Starbuck's knockoff coffee shop across the street from the Van Horn motel they had stayed in the night before.

"A motel manager in El Paso said the pair checked in last night. This morning he noticed the door to their room had been kicked in. The room was empty, and there are signs of a struggle."

"So our boy is in trouble."

"El Paso police are investigating. The manager said he got the same e-mail as the rest of us. The man in the video is the same man he saw in his lobby."

"El Paso is a good ways away."

"Flannigan has made arrangements. He's going to give us a lift in a patrol plane. It'll be cramped, but he can have us there in much less time that it will take to drive or to arrange for a charter flight."

"When do we leave?"

"He called from his car. I figure you have ten minutes to down that coffee."

When Eddie awoke, he was in the backseat of a large sedan with tinted windows. His head lay on Henick's shoulder. At first he struggled to make sense of his environment. The backseat part was easy; it was how he got back there that eluded him.

He sat up and raised his hands to his face. That's when he saw the gray duct tape around his wrists. He touched his face. It was swollen. His ribs hurt. His neck felt stiff. He closed his eyes for a few moments, then opened them. As he hoped, the act cleared his vision.

Outside, a vast expanse of flatland scrolled by. Eddie turned his attention to Henick. Dried blood crusted his nostrils and one eye was swollen.

"Do I look as bad as you?"

Henick turned and smiled. "Always."

"Cute. Now you get a sense of humor."

In the front seat sat the two who barged into the hotel room. The big guy drove; the smaller guy whimpered in the other seat. *Henick got you good, didn't he?*

"How long was I out?" Eddie asked.

The driver answered. "Forty-five minutes. You took quite a nap."

"Thanks to you," Eddie snapped.

"I do what I can." The driver glanced at the rearview mirror. Eddie could see his eyes. They seemed to float in darkness.

"So I take it you guys ain't the local cops. They usually announce themselves before busting in the door." Eddie looked at the door next to him. It was locked.

"Forget it, chump; the door can't be opened from the inside."

Eddie believed him. "I don't suppose you're willin' to tell us who you are and what you want."

"I got what we want. I haven't decided if you're a bonus or unnecessary baggage. I'm leaning toward the latter."

Henick looked at Eddie. "I told you to go home."

"That you did, so no need for you to feel guilty." He looked at the front-seat passenger. He continued to sniffle and wipe at his eyes. "Havin' second thoughts, buddy? Seeing yourself for what you are packs a real wallop, don't it?"

"Shut up! You want me to come back there? I'll show you a wallop."

A digital display filled one corner of the rearview mirror providing outside temperature and compass direction. An NW indicated they were headed north. Anything north of El Paso meant New Mexico. South would have meant Mexico, and that thought made Eddie more uncomfortable. The road was straight, two lanes, and lightly traveled.

"I don't suppose you want to tell us where we're going."

"You're right. I don't want to tell you."

"Shut up," the other man said.

"Howie, right?" Eddie said. "That's what your buddy called you—Howie."

"What of it?"

"Just like to know what kinda trash I'm traveling with."

Howie unsnapped his seat belt, turned in his seat, and reached for Eddie. Eddie pulled back. A second later the arm withdrew and Howie stopped moving. His partner had clinched his big hand around Howie's throat. Eddie could see the thick fingers constrict.

"Take it easy, Howie. Don't make me mess up a good, professional relationship. Understood?"

Howie croaked.

"Good. Now get ahold of yourself." He let go.

"Sorry, Gabe. I...don't know what's wrong with me. My brain, my emotions are fried."

"It'll pass. Just sit there and let me do the driving and thinking."

"OK, Gabe. Sorry." He began to cry again.

"Gabe? Is that short for Gabriel?"

"So what if it is?"

Eddie shrugged. "Gabriel is an angel's name. You ain't no angel."

"I'm guessing you're no angel yourself. You threw a couple of good punches back there. Still, you hit like a girl."

"I was going easy on you."

"Sure you were, sport. You're a real gentleman. Now tell me your name."

Eddie laughed. "Since my wallet is missing, I think you already know."

"Well, what do you know, you're not as stupid as you look, Eddie Feely. What I want to know is if that's your real name."

"Why wouldn't it be?"

"Because Gabriel Hoagland is just one of my names. It pays to have different names in my business."

"That a fact? And just what is your business?"

"Doing whatever pays me the most money. Now are you going to answer my question, or do I take the next farm road, pull you from the back, and put a bullet in the back of your head?" Hoagland uttered the words as if describing a trip to the store.

"Yeah, it's real. It's the only name I got."

"And what about your partner?"

"He's a big boy. Ask him."

"Henick."

"Henick what?" Hoagland pressed.

"Henick Jaredson."

"Odd name for an odd man." A car sped past them, making the most of the nearly empty, straight road. "What did you do to my partner?"

Henick shrugged. "He did it to himself."

"No, no," Howie said. "You did something to me. You messed up my brain. I can't stop crying, can't stop feeling guilty."

"That's right," Eddie said. "You killed your girlfriend. Do you see her in your dreams? You know, all munched up by the truck?"

Howie filled the car with curses and started to turn in his seat. Hoagland grabbed his shirt. "He's baiting you, Howie. Don't let him get under your skin. We got a job to do."

"Pull over, Gabe. Let me do this guy, right here and now. Take a side road. I can shoot him. I'll start with his knees and work my way up. We can let him bleed out."

"Not going to happen. Not now anyway. If she gives us permission, I'll let you do the deed. You can take as much time as you like."

For the first time since Eddie came to in the car he saw Howie smile.

"She?" Eddie said.

"Don't ask. It will only lead to a beating."

Eddie decided he had pushed enough. He was facing bad guys, but he didn't know how bad. Howie was little more than a thug, probably hired for his lack of scruples. Hoagland's response showed him to be calculating and controlled, and that made him more dangerous.

He turned to Henick. "How come Howie is such a mess? I mean, I know what it did to me, but I came out of it."

Henick spoke softly. "You are open to repentance. Your pain was the pain of your mother. He can't forgive anyone, so he can't forgive himself."

"But what about our chauffeur? I saw you do the same thing to him, but it didn't bother him."

Henick looked at Hoagland. "He is empty. He has no regrets, no love, and no conscience."

"How nice of you to notice," Hoagland said.

Henick ignored him. "He is a shell. His soul no longer thrives."

"Figures," Eddie said.

"He is to be pitied. He died a long time ago. What lives now has no value or purpose."

"That's it," Hoagland snapped. "Next one to speak gets Tasered—several times."

NOT MUCH IN THERE," THE EL PASO DETECTIVE SAID. "We're dusting for prints, but it's going to take some time to process."

"Why is that?" Manford asked.

Katherine answered. "It's a hotel room and a cheap one at that. There may be prints from a hundred different people."

"Oh. That makes sense."

"What about surveillance cameras?" Flannigan asked.

"We got a break on that one. The motel has several cameras. One for the lobby and two for the parking lot. A late model sedan pulled in about 8:45 this morning. Two men exited and kicked the motel room door in. Fifteen minutes later four men entered the car...actually, three men entered the car; one was carried."

"Not good," Katherine said. "License plate visible?"

The detective nodded. "I had to send the tape to our forensics department for video enhancement. You know how these low-end video cameras are. They were able to get enough of the plate to trace ownership to a car rental company. The car was rented to Gabriel Hoagland at El Paso International Airport."

"Gabriel Hoagland?" Katherine said.

"Before you ask, special agent, yes, we did a wants and warrants on the name. Nothing. My guess is he's working with false IDs and credit cards."

"Great," Manford said. "Where do we go from here?"

"I think we go up," Flannigan said. "Assuming they've left El Paso, we can search for them from the air. What about GPS tracking?"

The detective shook his head. "We checked. The rental car does have a tracking device, but it's been disconnected. I think we're dealing with a pro here. He seems to have thought of everything."

"Did you check to see if Gabriel Hoagland has a cell phone account?"

"You thinking of tracking his cell phone?"

"If he has it on and is anywhere near cell towers we can locate him."

The detective nodded. "I hear the Homeland Security people have been doing that for years."

Katherine pressed her lips together for a moment. "We can discuss warrantless cell phone tracking later. We have enough reason to convince a judge to grant a warrant if we need one, but first we need to know if he has a phone."

Flannigan spoke softly. "If he's smart enough to disable the GPS on the rental car, then he's probably smart enough to think about his cell phone."

Katherine's frustration rose to the surface. "We have to do something. It's clear that this guy and his friend have two hostages. That's kidnapping, and since he left El Paso, he's transporting his victim across state lines. That is FBI territory."

"He may have headed east across the state," Manford said.

She looked at her watch. "They have a two-and-a-half-hour head start. Every minute we stand around here, the more ground we have to cover." She turned to the detective. "Do you have air support?"

"Yes."

"Can you get some cooperation from other local agencies?"

"Sure. You want as many birds up as possible?"

"Exactly. We know the car type, the license, and the number of people on board. Let's get word out to other agencies." She turned to Flannigan. "That plane still available?"

"Your chariot waits."

The six-seat Cessna 206 climbed into a cloudless sky. Manford sat next to the pilot; Katherine and Flannigan sat in two of the remaining four seats.

"OK, Lieutenant, you've just kidnapped two men and decide to leave town; which way do you go?" Katherine spoke loudly to be heard over the aircraft's engine.

"That depends on my goal. I suppose I might head for Mexico. It's just over the Rio Grande. I could be there in a few minutes, but I'd worry about the border crossing. If the Border Patrol decides to inspect my vehicle, the gig would be up. Besides, we know one of the men is awake and alert to walk to the car. If he started making a ruckus, he could draw the attention of others."

He thought for a moment. "If I want to off my victims, I'd drive outside of the city and into the rural areas, maybe one of the farms, take a dirt rode, find a quiet place, and put a bullet in their heads."

"But they could have done that in the motel and not bothered with the kidnapping." Kathleen watched the ground recede. "No, kidnappers take a person because they want something from them or from their loved ones."

"OK, I see your point. I might head for the airport if I had a private plane waiting."

She shook her head. "Maybe, but airports are public places. Too easy to be seen."

"OK, OK, what do we have? We've alerted the Border Patrol, the airport police, and other law enforcement agencies." She sighed. "The rats could have gone anywhere."

"I need a direction," the pilot said. "Shall I continue north?"

"No, go east. Follow the nearest freeway."

"That would be US 180."

"Then US 180 it is."

"You have an idea?" Manford asked.

"No, just a hunch."

"Women's intuition?" Flannigan suggested.

"No, an FBI-educated hunch." She looked out the window and saw a ribbon of asphalt running east from the city. "Look. If it were me, I'd head north toward Las Cruces or some place like that, but this guy is smart, real smart. He has two captives in a large sedan. He knows that someone is going to notice a broken motel door. At the very least the manager is going to come knocking if the guests aren't out by noon. The broken door is a giveaway. Most likely, someone else would have noticed the door and reported it if the manager didn't."

"I can buy that," Manford said.

"So, if I'm the bad guy and I'm smart enough to disable the GPS tracking system on my rental car, then I'm smart enough to assume that security cameras caught me kicking the door in. So I have to assume the cops are going to be on my tail sooner rather than later. I need to leave. Do I take the major freeways? No, too many troopers. Do I take the small rural roads? No. My rental car might stand out. The fact that I'm in a rental car means that I couldn't use my own vehicle. I'm guessing they're from out of town, but being smart, they plan an escape route. So, I take, not the interstate, but the next size major road. There should be plenty of cars so that I don't stand out, and I can make good speed."

"You know that's not foolproof," Flannigan said, "but I can't come up with anything better." He pulled a cell phone from his belt, then leaned forward to the pilot. "Is this thing going to send us spiraling to a fiery death?"

The pilot laughed. "Hardly, Lieutenant. "I'm flying by eye anyway. On a clear day like this, the eyeball is still the best navigational instrument I have."

"Who you calling?" Katherine asked.

"I'm going to let the others know our course. El Paso police have two helicopters searching the city and surrounding areas. Las Cruces sheriff deputies can backtrack the I-25 south to El Paso. Maybe one of us will stumble upon these guys."

IT'S GOING TOO FAST."

"The plane?" Willie watched the ground below scroll by.

Mary-Martha turned from the window of the Beechcraft King Air C90GTi as it cruised southeast from Albuquerque at 250 miles per hour and faced him.

"Not the plane—the situation."

"I didn't even know the church had a private plane." He agreed things were moving too fast, but he doubted they were talking about the same thing.

"There are many things you don't know, Willie."

"Maybe you can bring me up to speed."

She returned her gaze to the scrolling ground twenty thousand feet below. "What do you want to know?"

He nodded in the direction of two thickly built men who sat in the two opposing seats. Both wore suits and silk ties; neither had said anything since meeting them at the airport and boarding the plane, and each looked capable of carrying a car on their backs. They gave no indication that Willie's question bothered them.

"I introduced you to Ron and Jessie."

"I don't recall seeing them around the church." The one named Ron looked at him, and Willie's courage melted like wax.

"You must have missed them. The church has thousands of attendees; you can't possibly have met everyone."

"Maybe, but I still don't know why they're here. For that matter, I don't know where we're going or why."

"As I said, there are many things you don't know."

"Could you be a little more forthcoming—"

"We're going to one of our alternate facilities, Willie. I have some business there—important business."

"You've always kept me at arms length when it came to church business."

"Consider this your induction to the Circle."

"The Circle?"

She sighed. "Willie, what you see at the church, the television shows, the newsletters, and the magazine—everything you see us do is just the tip of the iceberg. The organization goes much deeper and reaches a more enlightened congregation."

"More enlightened? How?"

"Those who know that the world is not what it seems, those who know that humanity is at a crossroads. So far, humankind has made all the wrong choices, traveled the wrong roads, and made the wrong friends."

"I know the spiel—"

She snapped her head around. "Never call my message a spiel. I see things you can't imagine. I talk to beings you can't fathom." She looked back out the window. "I've always known the Catharsis would come and made plans for it."

"What are you talking about? What catharsis?"

"Catharsis comes from the Greek, Willie. It means 'purification.' The purification is coming. I'll admit that I thought it would unfold differently, but then he came along."

"Who?"

"The Messenger. I didn't expect him or…"

"Or what?"

She remained silent. "I have a new spirit guide, Willie. I hear this one more clearly. He knows more. He reveals more. He makes me alive."

"You're spooking me out. I've heard you talk about spirit guides before. I even got comfortable with ascended beings like Lustar using you for a megaphone, but I can tell something is different."

She smiled. "Yes, Willie, I am different, more different than you know. You have been faithful to me, so I feel compelled to protect you."

"Protect me from what?"

"The coming Lie. The Catharsis. The Messenger."

Willie rubbed a hand across his chin and tried to force his thoughts to line up instead of bouncing around in his brain. He reached across the narrow aisle and laid his hand on her wrist. Her skin felt as cold as a cadaver's. "You're cold to the touch. Are you feeling all right?"

"I feel better than ever. You worry too much."

"This isn't helping."

"Trust me, Willie. It's all about trust. You trust me; thousands of others trust me. I trust my guide. The future is taking its new form. The old must pass away."

"Now you sound like a cult leader. You know what happened to them."

"They were pretenders, posers; we're the real thing."

"We?"

"My guide and me."

Willie looked at Ron and Jesse. Mary-Martha's words had no affect on them. *They drank the Kool-Aid.*

"What do you plan to do when we get wherever we're going?"

"I plan to meet the Messenger. Remember, my last revelation said I was the lord of the Messenger. It's time for him to meet his master."

Willie gave up asking questions. He had learned a few things but only generalities. He would learn the rest when they arrived at the "other facility." He spent the long, silent minutes worrying. Worrying was his foremost skill.

Words came over the onboard intercom: "We're on approach,

Reverend. Seat belts should be fastened. Please stow any loose items."

The nose of the twin-engine turboprop dipped. The aircraft had been descending for the last ten minutes; now the glide angle grew steeper. Out his window he could see scrub brush and desert terrain. He saw only one road, a wide dirt path, straight as an arrow. He also saw a high chain-link fence with a barbed-wire crown pass beneath them.

The Beechcraft touched down smoothly on an asphalt runway. Willie continued to look out the window. He saw no terminal and no other aircraft. He assumed they had just touched down at a private field.

The pilot taxied for a few minutes, then brought the craft to a stop. A few moments later the propellers stopped. The pilot emerged from the cockpit and opened the hatch, lowering a set of air stairs. Willie exited first and held out a hand to help his wife descend the steep steps. Ron and Jesse followed. The pilot exited last and then helped unload the luggage and carry it to the door of a long and wide metal structure.

"Do you need any help carrying these things into the building?" the pilot asked.

"No, thank you," Mary-Martha replied. "We can handle it from here. Please return to the airport."

"I assume you'll call when you need me," the pilot said.

"Yes, please remain on call, but I doubt I'll need you anytime soon."

They waited for the pilot to return to the craft, taxi to the runway, and lift off. Only then did Mary-Martha turn and enter a code into a keypad by the door.

The building had no windows, but Willie had detected a few skylights on the roof. The building looked weathered and nearly abandoned. He turned and took in his surroundings. He couldn't see another structure anywhere. He heard no traffic, just the sound of a few birds in the brush nearby. An eight-foot-high fence ran the perimeter of grounds enclosing the building and the single runway.

"Where are we?" Willie asked.

"East New Mexico." Mary-Martha pushed open the door and stepped in. Ron, or was he Jesse, motioned for Willie to follow. For some reason, Willie felt like a sheep being led to the slaughter.

The space inside the building was dim, lit only by light pressing through dirty skylights. He looked around and saw nothing but emptiness. The metal structure was completely empty. The only object in sight was a small metal shed—a tiny building within a big building. Mary-Martha marched straight for it, Ron and Jesse in tow.

The flat-roofed shed stood eight feet tall and had a single door. Mary-Martha tapped in a code on a second keypad and the door popped open, revealing a third door. This one differed from the previous door. It looked new and seemed to be made of thick black metal. Yet another keypad and a small glass lens provided further security.

He watched as his wife tapped in another code then placed her eye by the lens. The sound of a heavy latch surrendering its hold echoed in the empty building. The door swung in.

As soon as the door opened, a dank breeze poured between the jambs.

Willie took in his surroundings. "What is this place?"

Mary-Martha turned to face him. "It's home. Watch your step." She moved into the black, open maw.

48

THE DIRT ROAD WAS SMOOTHER THAN EDDIE EXPECTED, but it still jarred his kidneys. Hoagland sped down the lane as if it were a freeway. If it weren't for the luxury car's advanced suspension, Eddie was certain they would have rolled by now.

"I take it you're late," Eddie said.

"No cops on this road. It's private. I can do whatever speed I want."

"Fine by me. Dying in a car wreck can't be worse than what you got planned. At least you guys get busted up too."

"Just relax. I know what I'm doing."

"Sure you do." Eddie smirked. "You want me to drive?"

"I want you to shut up."

"OK, just making conversation. I mean, I know how to shut up. Just tell me to be quiet and I'll be quiet. No sir, I don't have to be told twice. I can zip it any time I'm told to—"

"SHUT UP!" Howie shouted, then returned to his crying.

"Easy, Howie. The kid think's he's smart, but he's not. He think's he's indispensable, but he's not."

"Yeah, yeah, I know," Eddie said. "I'm dead man riding."

"Keep talking, pal, and you'll be dead man buzzard food." Gabriel leaned over the steering wheel and craned his neck to look up. Eddie leaned against his door and stared in the same direction. He saw a twin-engine aircraft climbing through the air.

"She got there before us, Howie. She didn't waste any time."

"A friend of yours?" Eddie asked. "She travels in style."

Hoagland didn't answer. He pressed the accelerator closer to the floorboard.

"The proverbial needle in a haystack," Gene Manford said.

"We're fighting the odds here." Katherine continued her gaze at the freeway below. "OK, I think we would have caught up to them by now. We're making much better time in the air than they could on the ground."

"I had hoped one of our patrol units would have come across them by now." Flannigan spoke without taking his eyes off the ribbon of asphalt below him.

"Maybe we should double back and widen our search zone. Our guys may have left the highway already."

"We could, but we'd be guessing which way they went. If they did leave the highway, which way did they go: north or south?"

"It's all a toss of the dice," Katherine said. "I say we search farther north."

"That'll put us over the border into New Mexico," Flannigan said.

"Is that a problem?"

"Not really. It's out of my jurisdiction, but you're a fed, so you don't have that problem."

"OK, let's do that."

The pilot banked north, then a few minutes later completed the U-turn by angling west.

"I don't think they could have reached beyond this point." Katherine knew she was repeating herself, but thinking out loud always helped.

Minutes chugged by, and every one that passed stung Katherine a little more. Two people were in danger, forced into a car against their will and held by someone who knew what he was doing. Criminals were often a stupid bunch, but every once in a while one came along and surprised everyone with their well-thought-out plans and executions. Those guys were the most frightening.

"What's that?" Manford asked.

"Where?" Katherine leaned toward Manford.

"That dust cloud there." He pointed north.

"It looks like a dust devil to me." Disappointed, Katherine leaned back.

Manford shook his head. "I may be a city boy, but I'm pretty sure that isn't a dust devil."

"Could be a farmer working a fallow field," Flannigan said. "Those machines kick up a lot of dust."

"Where are the binoculars?" Manford began looking around the cabin. The pilot produced a pair from a space next to his seat. Manford raised them to his eyes and worked the focus knob. "I can't get a clear image. Too far and too much dust. I say we check it out."

"I don't know, Gene; that pulls us off our course." Katherine let her words carry the disappointment she felt.

"What course? You said this was all a toss of the dice. Let's throw the cubes that way."

Katherine thought for a moment. "Do it."

The plane banked.

Minutes later they had narrowed the gap separating the aircraft from the moving line of dust. Manford kept the glasses pressed against his eyes.

"Anything?" Katherine pressed.

"No, not yet. Let's move to the side some. Maybe I can get a better angle."

The pilot complied, guiding the craft a few hundred yards to the east, then taking a parallel course.

"It's no tractor, I can tell you that. Whatever it is, it's going too fast for a dirt road—hold it."

"What?" Katherine said.

"Give me a sec, will you?" Manford then spoke to the pilot. "Can you take us down some?"

"Can do."

The plane dipped, dropping several hundred feet.

"Bingo!"

"Let me see." Katherine reached for binoculars.

"It's a dark sedan," Manford explained to the others. "Just like we've been looking for. I can't get the tag numbers, but I did see a passenger in the front seat and one in the back. Obviously there's a driver, so that brings the occupancy up to at least three. If we could see the other side, I bet we'd see a fourth occupant."

"Manford?" Katherine said.

"Yes."

"I should never have doubted you. I owe you dinner."

"You're on. Now what?"

"Now we follow. Once we know their destination, we call for backup."

"It could take some time for backup to get here," Flannigan said. "This isn't the most heavily populated area."

"We call for it anyway. Then we decide what to do next."

Truth was, Katherine had no idea what to do next. All she could do was follow the car to see where they stopped. Airplanes were great for observing, but there was nothing you could do to apprehend the suspects—nothing sane anyway.

Finally, the car slowed and turned on a side road that led to a fenced area of barren land. The only structure visible was a large metal building.

"Who puts a building like that out here?" Katherine looked around. "No one is farming the land. I don't see any vehicles or planes on the runway."

"Maybe it's just a private airport owned by several locals," Manford offered.

"Or military," the pilot said.

"Military?"

He nodded. "I spent some time in the air force. Ten years to be exact. There are several military sites with underground facilities. They use some for continuation-of-government bunkers, others hold munitions, and others are secret facilities. They're more common than you might imagine."

"You think the military ran this abduction?"

"I doubt it," the pilot said, "although the military has done some strange things. I'm just saying it looks like one of those places with an underground vault or even underground facilities. Maybe someone bought a discontinued site. I've heard of people buying old missile silos and converting them to homes. One entrepreneur bought an underground silo to house his computers. He sells a service where businesses can store data somewhere safe."

"Underground..." Flannigan began.

"What?" Katherine said.

"OK, you're going to think I've lost my mind, but we're not all that far from Carlsbad Caverns. There are scores of underground caverns in these parts. Some think there are many more to be found."

Katherine rubbed the back of her neck. "And I thought the academy taught me how to face every situation."

EDDIE COULDN'T HELP NOTICING HENICK'S SILENCE. HE had uttered only a handful of words since Eddie had come to in the car. Yet to look at him, he showed no fear. He moved like a man on a long escalator—there was little he could do but wait.

His stoicism wore on Eddie's nerves. When frightened, Eddie knew only two things to do: fight and/or shoot off his mouth. He had been doing the latter, successfully antagonizing his captors, but it had gained them little.

The sedan stopped at a wide gate in a tall chain-link fence with razor wire running its length. "Reminds me of the youth detention center I spent a summer in." Hoagland exited the vehicle, stepped to the gate, opened a small metal box, and punched a number into a keypad. The gate swung open. Hoagland took his place behind the wheel and drove through. Eddie turned in time to see the gate close on its own.

Hoagland directed the vehicle along the side of a narrow runway and to the door of a large metal building. "OK, Howie, you get Mystery Man; I'll take the Mouth."

Howie sniffed and wiped away a few tears.

"Did you hear me, Howie?"

"What?"

Hoagland delivered a backhand that landed so hard Howie's head bounced off the headrest.

"What'd ya do that for?" He covered his face.

"Because I'm sick of your sniveling. You can't let her see you this way. I told her you were the best, and she believed me. The last thing I need is for you to show up like some love-lost teenage girl. Suck it up and suck it up now, or so help me I'll give you a whole new set of pains to cry over. Now get out and do as I say."

The men slipped from the front seat. A moment later, Eddie's door opened and Hoagland's beefy hand reached in, seized him by the front of the shirt, and yanked him from the backseat. Before Eddie could settle his feet on the ground, he felt Hoagland's knee drive into his right thigh. Scorching pain rose from the leg and galloped up his spine. Hoagland spun him, and Eddie felt a punch just above the right kidney.

Eddie dropped to his knees, then vomited.

Hoagland leaned over him. "Next time I tell you to shut up, you'd be wise to do it. Got it?" Eddie nodded. Hoagland pulled him to his feet.

Eddie leaned against the car trying to catch his breath. Henick rounded the car with Howie close by. Eddie noticed that Howie wasn't touching Henick.

"Watch 'em while I open the door." Hoagland stepped away.

"I'm sorry," Henick said. "I should have made you leave before all this happened."

"I wouldn't have left. I won't leave now—as if I could."

Henick raised his taped hands and touched Eddie on the shoulder. The pain in his leg and kidney disappeared.

"Thanks."

Henick smiled. "It is nice to have a friend in difficult times."

Eddie chuckled. "Yeah, it is."

"Let's go," Hoagland said.

Eddie and Henick walked to the open door. Howie followed behind silently. They stepped into the building, and when the door closed behind them, Eddie wondered if he had seen the sun for the last time.

"What's happening?" Manford asked.

"You don't want to know," Katherine said. "The big guy just inflicted some pain on our guy's sidekick. I don't know what the kid did, but he sure ticked his abductor off."

"Can you still see them?" Flannigan asked.

"They just went in the building. I don't think they saw us; we're pretty high. They shouldn't be able to hear the engine, and I didn't see them look up."

"So we sit it out until the cavalry arrives," Flannigan said.

"Yeah…maybe."

Manford turned in his seat to face her. "What do you mean maybe? You're the one who said we need backup."

"We do, but after seeing that beating, I'm concerned the abductees may not live long enough to be rescued."

"Why would they bring them all the way out here to murder them? There were a lot of desolate spots along the way where they could do the deed."

"That would leave the body in the open. Sooner or later someone would find it. If they kill the men in that building, secured as it is, the corpses may never be found."

"What do you have in mind?" Flannigan asked.

"What I really want to do is land on that strip and go after them, but they would know we're there the moment we touched down. At the very least they'd hear the engine as we land. They may even have security cameras. We just don't know enough."

"Can we land nearby?" Manford asked the pilot.

"Maybe. We might find another private field. They're not uncommon in open areas like this."

"Let's see if we can find one." Katherine looked back at the building. She had no idea how they would get in.

Eddie didn't know what to expect once he crossed the threshold into the building, but seeing another smaller building wasn't it. Nor did he expect to see the door of the inner building open to reveal another door. Most of all he didn't expect to see a long stone stairway leading from ground level to something deeper.

"Howie, you go first." Hoagland pointed down the dim stairwell. "You two next. I'll follow behind. That way I can push you down the stairs if you give me any grief."

Howie started down the steps, Henick went next, and Eddie followed. Ideas of escape scampered through Eddie's brain. Could he move fast enough to upend Hoagland? Maybe he could dive low at the man's feet, causing him to trip and fall face-first down the stairs. Of course, if he fell too far, he'd hit Henick and perhaps injure him. If he didn't fall far enough, then he would have just succeeded in making an already mad man furious.

Howie was the unknown. He had stopped whimpering, but the last time Eddie looked in the man's face, he could see it was all about to start over. Henick had done a number on the man. Grief had brought Eddie to his knees; regret had melted Howie's armor.

The staircase was much wider than the door they entered through. Eddie guessed the door was a security precaution added later. The ceiling hung eight feet overhead, and a long row of fluorescent lights ran down the middle, illuminating the hallway. Smaller lights at the base of the walls cast bluish light on the treads. There was enough light to move down safely but not enough to read by.

Howie led the way one step at a time. He seemed in no rush; no doubt the darkness outside reflected the blackness inside him.

At first Eddie counted the steps, but he lost count when he reached three digits. Wherever they were going, it was deep below the surface.

Time had no reference in the corridor. No one spoke. The only sounds were footfalls and breathing. Step followed step; tread led to tread; riser after riser passed underfoot.

At least this way they won't have to bury us.

The staircase ended in a large empty room. As Howie moved into the room, lights came on. Eddie blinked against the glare. When his eyes adjusted, he saw something he never expected: a cavern that rose several hundred feet above them and expanded in every direction. Stalactites hung from the ceiling; limestone stalagmites stretched for the ceiling.

"Whoa!" Eddie said.

"For once we agree," Hoagland said. "The place never fails to impress me."

"Incredible." Eddie was surprised by his own surprise.

"This way." Hoagland led them to the side where an electric golf cart waited. Eddie wondered how they got the cart down the stairs, then decided they must have brought it down in pieces.

Hoagland stepped to a small phone mounted to the wall, lifted the receiver and spoke, then returned to the cart. He took the driver's seat and Howie the front passenger spot. Henick and Eddie were shoved to the backseats.

As the cart pulled away, Eddie wondered if he could get his arms around Hoagland's throat but dismissed the idea. He might successfully choke the man into unconsciousness, but Howie would certainly jump in. He doubted Henick would help. He didn't seem the fighting type. Failure to choke his abductor to death would result in a beating that would certainly be his death. And who knew what they'd do to Henick. No, Eddie would have to take this ride until the end. *Where was Deputy Pardee when you needed him?*

The cart traveled down a concrete path that divided the ever-expanding cavern into two parts. Water dripped from the ceiling and fell into pristine pools that shimmered in the artificial lights spaced along the path. Despite the danger, Eddie couldn't stop staring at the remarkable sights around him.

He thought for a moment. They had headed NW from El Paso. The time of travel seemed right too, best he could judge.

"Carlsbad Caverns?"

"No, but close."

Eddie didn't press the issue. It didn't matter. He knew this would be the last sight he'd see. It didn't take a genius to know that the important commodity here was Henick, not him. He had no idea why he was still alive and not lying dead in the motel room.

As the cart moved, Eddie caught glimpses of side rooms. Some were filled with shelves and stacks of boxes. He guessed the boxes held food and supplies—maybe construction material.

The path turned right, and they rolled through a narrow, natural tunnel and came out on the other end.

He had visited Carlsbad Caverns once as part of a school outing. The caverns were amazing, but more stunning to his twelve-year-old mind was seeing a large open expanse with a snack bar, tables, and a bank of restrooms. Smack-dab in the middle of one of the caverns someone had set up shop and sold hot dogs and potato chips. If they could do that, surely somebody with some money and influence could build a stairway and road down here.

Hoagland stopped the cart near a massive pair of gothic wood doors. Eddie waited to be told he could leave the cart. Henick apparently had the same thought. Hoagland opened the doors, looked inside, then returned to the cart.

"Out of the cart," he snapped.

Eddie looked at Henick, then shrugged and slipped from the seat. They walked to the twelve-foot high doors, and Hoagland opened them.

They stepped inside.

Eddie gasped.

He was standing in a church—no, not a church, a cathedral.

Rows upon rows of chairs made up the congregation's area. An acrylic pulpit stood in the center of a wide, ornate stage. Television cameras were situated throughout the space. Golden light filtered down onto the stage.

"Keep going." Hoagland shoved Henick and Eddie down the aisle. The floor sloped down to the stage area, reminding Eddie of a movie theater except far more grand. When they reached the first row, Hoagland told them to sit, and he stepped to one side. He didn't sit, and Eddie couldn't help noticing the man stayed in striking distance. It was like sitting in a chair with a coiled rattlesnake looking at you from a few feet away.

Howie went to the other side of the aisle, sat, and lowered his face into his hands. He started crying again.

A movement on the right side of the stage caught Eddie's attention. A woman with coal black hair moved onto the stage. She wore a long gold robe. Although the woman was twelve, maybe fifteen years older than Eddie, he considered her a beauty.

She moved to front and center of the stage with the smoothest gait Eddie had ever seen. Then he realized why.

…her feet hovered two feet above the platform.

He looked at Henick and for the first time saw him tense. This was a bad sign.

50

THE AIRCRAFT BOUNCED ALONG THE DIRT RUNWAY JUST ten miles from the secured runway they had followed the sedan to. Katherine had doubts about landing on such uncertain ground, but the pilot assured her that it was done all the time. Only after they landed did he bother to reveal that this was his first time.

They exited the aircraft and turned toward a set of buildings a short distance away. A man in a Korean War–era Jeep sped toward them, hitting the brakes at the last minute. Dust filled the air as he leapt from behind the wheel. He brought a shotgun with him and leveled it at the new arrivals.

"This is private property. You ain't got no right landing here without my permission."

The man looked like he had lived seventy very hard years. "Just take it easy—" Flannigan started.

"Don't tell me what to do, Mister. I live out in the boondocks for a reason. I don't cotton to no strangers."

The pilot who had helped Katherine disembark rounded the aircraft. The old man took a look at the uniform and lowered the barrel a touch. The pilot didn't wear a Sam Browne belt with gun and other police items. He didn't need them to fly, but he did wear a pair of overhauls with a fabric badge sown over his chest.

"You New Mexico sheriffs?"

The pilot shook his head. "I'm a Texas State Trooper pilot. My passengers are all law enforcement."

"What'd I do?" He seemed frightened.

"Nothing that we know of," Flannigan said. "I'm Lieutenant Michael Flannigan, Texas Highway Patrol. This is Agent Gene Manford of the FCC and Special Agent Katherine Rooney of the FBI."

"FBI? What's the FBI want with me?"

Katherine smiled. "We need your help. I'm going to reach for my badge, so just ease up on the trigger." She removed her badge case and showed her shield and ID. Manford and Flannigan did the same.

The old man lowered the gun, then put it in the back of the Jeep. "What kind of help?"

Katherine stepped forward. "We followed a car that was carrying two kidnap victims. We tracked them from the air and saw them pull into a private airport nearby—"

"The old Patterson place?"

"I don't know who owns it."

"Me neither, but old man Patterson had claim to it for a lot of years."

"Old man Patterson?" It amused Katherine that a man on the north side of seventy would call another man old.

"Don't know his first name, but I grew up calling him old man Patterson. He died twenty or twenty-five years ago. Didn't have no family. Last I heard, the state put the property up for auction to get the back taxes. I have all the property I need, so I didn't pay it no never mind. Heard tell someone in the state got a good deal."

"When was the last time you were over there?" Katherine asked.

He shrugged. "Can't remember. I know I ain't stepped foot on the place since Patterson kicked the bucket." He chortled. "Patterson always talked big, saying how he was gonna make some serious money with that place. Yeah, right. I thought I'd make some good cash by running air races out here. My dream died about the same time he did."

"How did he plan to make so much money?" Katherine asked.

"Well, with the cavern of course."

Katherine tried to make sense of that. "Cavern?"

"Yes, cavern. Carlsbad Caverns is just forty or so miles that way." He pointed southwest. "Of course, old man Patterson's cavern ain't nearly as big as the Carlsbad ones, but it's a good sight more than a hole in the ground. He gave me a tour once. Acres and acres of cave. Much larger than mine."

Katherine looked at the others then turned back to the old man. "Mr. um…"

"Oh, sorry. Name's Buster Young."

"Mr. Young—"

"Call me Buster."

"All right, Buster. You say there's a cavern on this property?"

"Sure. There are lots of caverns in New Mexico. Some don't amount to much; some become real tourist attractions. Of course, in these parts, Carlsbad Caverns is the granddaddy, but that don't mean there ain't no other caves." He chuckled. "I liked old man Patterson, but he could be a tad greedy. We talked a little business back then, but nuthin' came of it. I don't think he wanted to share any of the proceeds he thought he was gonna get."

In the distance a sharp whine pierced the air. Katherine chose to ignore it. Her subconscious screamed louder than whatever made the distant whine.

"Let me know if I'm way off the mark here, Buster, but if I understand you, Patterson's property is over a large cavern; your property has a cavern as well, just not as large. Right so far?"

"Yup."

"And you and Patterson talked about doing business together."

Her heart dropped into fourth gear. "Please tell me that the two caverns connect."

"You FBI types are smart. The two caves are sorta connected."

"Sorta?"

"There's a small opening between the two but not large enough to let tourists through. I tried to talk him into blowing open a larger hole, but he wasn't keen on the idea."

"Tourists can't go through the opening, but a man or woman could if they wanted to?"

"Sure. It ain't easy. You have to do some belly crawling, but it can be done."

"Buster, this is important. Lives may depend on it. Can you take a few of us through your cavern to Patterson's?"

"No, ma'am, I can't." He looked sad. "I'd love to help you out, I truly would, but I'm way past my climbing and hiking days. I can still fix an airplane or two, but crawling through limestone caves passed a decade or more ago."

Katherine closed her eyes and tried to weigh the wisdom of trying to find the opening herself. Buster must have picked up her thoughts. "And don't even think about trying it by yourself. You'd get yourself killed for sure. Walking is hard enough down there; dragging out a corpse is worse."

"There has to be a way to do this."

Buster started to speak, then stopped and turned his face skyward. The whining had turned into a drone. "My daughter could take you there. She knows more about that cave than anyone alive, including me."

"Is she here?"

"Nope."

"Is she nearby? How long would it take her to get here?"

Buster delivered his next words through a wide grin. "I'd say about five minutes."

"Five minutes?"

He pointed skyward. "Here she comes now."

Katherine gazed into a cerulean sky and saw a small red aircraft flying toward them. It took a moment before she realized she was watching a brightly painted biplane. Before she could speak, the small craft pulled into a steep climb until it completed a full loop. It followed the maneuver with two barrel rolls.

"She likes to show off for company."

The trooper pilot asked, "Is your daughter married, Buster?"

"Nope. Why?"

"'Cuz I think I'm in love."

51

In the five minutes it took Natalie Young to land, Buster filled Katherine in. "That there is a Waco UPF-7. Nat and I rebuilt it with our own hands. When we started, she was only ten. We flew it on her eighteenth birthday. Been babying the thing ever since. Only about eighty of those gems still flying. The rest are rusting in museums."

"She's been a pilot since she was eighteen?"

Buster shook his head. "Got her license when she was sixteen. Of course, I was out of the navy by then and crop dusting for a living. I've never seen anyone take to flying like her."

"Flying isn't my need at the moment."

"She's still your woman. She's a park ranger and works the caves for the National Park Service. She comes out here on her days off to see if I've croaked. Been trying to get me to move in with her, but I ain't ready to leave all this."

Katherine didn't know what "all this" referred to, but it wouldn't take much to get her to leave whatever it was behind.

Natalie worked her way out of the historic plane and removed a leather helmet and goggles to reveal long, brown hair and deep blue eyes. Military-issue green overalls covered a narrow frame. She wore a white silk scarf around her neck and tucked into her shirt. Her smile could shame the stars. As much as Buster looked like an old desert rat, Natalie looked runway-model perfect. Katherine felt a twinge of envy that evaporated in the heat of necessity.

Her father spoke first, then Katherine told her about the need to get into the other cavern. First she gave a few facts, then prepared added pressure with the "lives at stake" line when Natalie said, "Let's go."

She led them to the metal work shed that had been designed for aircraft parking for the air race park that never was. Inside one of the bays, near the center of the floor rested a manhole cover. Natalie tossed her goggles and leather helmet on a dirty work bench and grabbed a three-foot-long metal bar with a vicious-looking hook on one end and a handle on the other. She slipped the hook in one of the holes.

"Let me help you with that," Flannigan said. Before he could finish the sentence she had yanked the heavy metal disk from the opening. Air rushed past them and into the hole, whistling as it poured over the edge.

"OK, here's what you need to know." Natalie's voice rode on sweet tones but still carried a no-nonsense quality. Katherine didn't know how to take her and didn't have time for a get-to-know-each-other tea. "This is the safest access into the cavern below. Don't misunderstand me. I'm not saying it's safe, just the safest way we have in. The first thing we have to do is descend 125 feet to the upper level of the cavern. That's 125 feet of straight descent down a metal ladder. From there, things get tough. If you have a fear of heights or are claustrophobic, I need to know now. No heroes. I'm good at what I do, but I don't want to have to drag someone back, so be honest."

She waited. "I take it by your silence that none of you suffer from those conditions—or that you're lying to me. To my knowledge there is only one opening between this cavern and Patterson's, and the path there is tough. Much of it will be on our bellies. Can you do that?"

They answered yes in near unison.

"Who's going and who is staying behind?"

"What do you mean?" Katherine asked.

"I mean, I don't have gear for everyone. I can take three of you.

This isn't a tourist tour. I have enough equipment for four people; one set is mine. I'll let you do the math."

"Not a problem; only two of us are going," Katherine said. She turned to Flannigan. "That is, if you're with me."

"I wouldn't miss it."

"OK," Katherine said. "Tell us what we need to do—"

"Hang on a sec," Manford said. "You're not cutting me out of this."

Katherine turned to him. "Listen, Gene, we don't have time to argue. Flannigan is a weapons-trained officer of the law. With all due respect, your FCC training hasn't prepared you for this."

"You're telling me the FBI Academy has a How to Rescue Hostages From a Limestone Cavern course? I'm going."

"No, you're not. I'm responsible for the people on my team. I need Trooper Walton to guide our backups in. You can help with that."

Manford turned to Natalie. "I'm going."

"Look," she said. "I don't care who goes as long as they understand I'm in charge from the time my foot hits the first rung of that ladder until you guys wiggle through to the other cavern." She moved to a set of lockers and pulled out two sets of overalls and handed one to Katherine. "That pant suit isn't going to do."

"I'm not worried about my clothes getting dirty."

Natalie raised an eyebrow. "I'm more worried about your clothing getting my cave dirty." She faced the others. "Listen up, people. I know what you're doing is important. I want those men rescued as much as you do, but this cave is pristine. To my knowledge, only I, my father, and a few other rangers have been in it. I intend to keep it that way. So do your best not to leave any evidence that you have been there. Don't touch the limestone formations. Try not to disturb any of the pools."

Natalie looked at Katherine's feet. "Sensible shoes for your situation; lousy for what you're about to encounter. I have an old pair of boots that may fit you." She pulled a pair of brown, ankle-high hiking boots from one of the lockers. They were covered with dirt, and some of the leather over the steel toes had been worn off. "Put these on. I know they don't look like much, but you'll thank me later." She addressed Flannigan and Manford. "There are boots in the locker. I don't know if they'll fit or not, but try and find something close. Dress shoes on damp surfaces and sharp rocks are dangerous."

They slipped on the coveralls and boots. Manford found a pair of boots just his size. Flannigan wasn't so lucky: his boots were a size and half too large. Two extra pair of socks given him by Buster helped fill in the space.

While they dressed, Buster went to a generator near the rear wall and turned it on. "Most of my power comes from solar panels and two wind turbines. Works great for my little place, but sometimes I need a little help from this generator. You're going to need it more." He moved to a metal box mounted to the back wall, opened it, and threw a large switch. A dim light oozed from the manhole.

"Thanks, Dad." Natalie stepped forward with a set of safety belts. Each belt was made of leather and nylon with large metal clips on each side. "OK, put these on. The latches should be over each hip."

Katherine and the others did as instructed.

"The ladder is like most other ladders you've seen. It has metal rungs fixed between a pair of metal stiles. Unlike most ladders, there is a third element: a vertical safety bar on each side. After you've descended a few steps I want you to hook one of your latches to the bar. There's one on each side of the ladder. A horizontal stop-bar is spaced every ten feet. Should you slip, your safety hooks will be stopped by the bar, keeping you from falling to the cave bottom and taking the people below with you. This means that every ten feet you'll have to unhook the latch. Before you do, latch the hook on the opposite side. In other words, if your safety belt is hooked to the bar on your left when you reach a stop, connect the right hook before disconnecting the left. After you do two or three of these it will become second nature."

Buster handed Katherine and the others a red, hard-plastic helmet with a light attached to the front.

"You will need to wear your helmet at all times. The light on the helmet is one of three lights each of us will carry. The other two are waterproof flashlights."

She paused. "Look, are you sure there's no other way to do this? I should spend a lot more time prepping you for this."

Katherine shook her head. "I wish there were, but we saw one of the captives take a beating. I believe their lives are in danger."

"OK, let's go."

After Natalie checked their equipment, she demonstrated how to slip through the manhole.

"So who's next?" Manford asked.

"I'll go next," Katherine said. "Ladies first and all that. Just don't step on my hands with those big boots of yours."

"Wouldn't dream of it."

"You really should stay." Katherine tried one last time to convince him.

"I'm going, and speaking of going, I think you should start down the rabbit hole. Natalie doesn't seem the kind who likes to wait."

"You got that right," Buster said.

Katherine sat on the floor, swung her legs into the hole, and took hold of the metal ladder. Once on the rung, she hooked herself to the vertical safety bar. She took a couple of deep breaths as if she were plunging beneath the water. She wondered if it had been a mistake to lie about her claustrophobia.

EDDIE HAD TUSSLED WITH HOAGLAND AND SEEN NO fear. Nothing seemed to bother him until the lady in the long gold robe floated two feet above the stage. The sight was enough to back the man up, and since Eddie's first thought was to flee screaming like a little girl, he couldn't blame him. Two men followed her on to the stage, then walked down the steps that joined the floor with the cave. They took positions behind Henick and Eddie. Another man stood in the wings just off the stage.

The brief evidence of fear Eddie had seen on Henick's face had disappeared. He showed no signs of terror. Instead, he looked like a man who had lost a dear friend. That didn't make Eddie feel better.

"Do you know her?" Eddie asked.

"Not her. I do know him."

Eddie snapped his head back to the gliding woman. "She's a man?"

"No."

"You know, Henick, it's bad enough I'm scared out of my gourd; I don't need your cryptic talk to confuse me."

"Shut up," the man behind Eddie said. He wasn't as big as Hoagland, but he seemed to have the same attitude.

The woman floated to the edge of the stage then over it before stopping several feet from the front row. Her feet were now five feet above the sanctuary floor.

"Welcome to the Church of New Revelation Sanctuary," she

said. Eddie thought there was something odd about her voice. "It's beautiful, isn't it?"

No one spoke.

She raised a hand and pointed at Henick. "You are the Messenger."

Eddie couldn't tell if it was a statement or a question.

Henick stood. "I am Henick Jaredson, servant of the Most High."

Eddie noticed that his friend stressed the syllables of his name differently: Heenock Jaredson.

The woman seemed puzzled for a moment. "Hee-nock Jared-son." An expression of understanding washed over her face as if someone had just whispered a stunning truth in her ear. "Welcome, Enoch, son of Jared. I know you. You are he who never died."

Henick nodded. "I am as you say."

"I am Mary-Martha Celestine, founder and leader of the Church of New Revelation. I am...*the lord of the Messenger.*"

"No." Henick said.

"You doubt my words?" She rose another two feet, and her face darkened as if something above her shadowed her features.

"You are not Mary-Martha Celestine. You were named Shirley Lennox. You are more than she."

"*I am who I say I am.*" The orbs of her eyes flashed the color of jade.

"Um, Henick." Eddie touched Henick's arm. "Maybe it would be best not to tick her off."

Henick ignored him. "The Messenger has only one Master."

"*Your faithfulness to Him is foolish. Look where it has landed you.*"

"I am in His will, and that is where I wish to be."

Mary-Martha laughed from a dark place in her soul. The sound of it seemed beyond what a human body could produce.

"*I am your lord now, Enoch. You are mine to do with as I please. You may have lived millennia, but you are not immortal.*"

"I have never feared death. I have lived both sides and found joy in it. You know nothing but hatred."

Her jaw clinched. Eddie expected to hear the crack of a jawbone breaking into pieces.

"*I have the right to hate. He may have loved you, but He despised me.*"

"Come out of her."

"*No. She has sought my kind for years. She has been my puppet for so long she no longer knows her own thoughts from mine.*"

"Come out of her."

"*Your message ends here, Enoch of old. Look around. She built this to be her sanctuary, a place to bring her followers. A place to hide when her deeds became known. This place is your tomb. Here you are. Here you die.*"

The voice no longer sounded female—or human.

"*I want to hear the message. I want to hear the full measure of it. I want to know what pathetic plan He thinks will work after so many failures.*"

"You will hear it when the time comes." Henick's voice remained firm and calm.

"*I will hear it now.*"

"Honey?" The man in the shadowy wings stepped on the stage. He looked the same age as the floating woman. He also looked as fragile as a snowflake. His hands shook. "Shirley."

"*Go away, little man.*"

"I want my wife back."

"Willie, don't— Leave!"

Two voices. One person. Eddie struggled to believe his eyes and ears. The man on the stage took another step forward. He was either crazy or supremely brave, Eddie decided.

Willie straightened his spine as if tapping into a hidden reservoir of courage. "I want my wife back."

"Willie, do as it says—*She's mine now. She is lost to you.*"

Eddie glanced at Henick and saw the concern on his face.

"I won't leave without her," Willie said.

"*You will do as I say*— Willie, step back."

"Fight him, Shirley. You have to fight him. I want you back. I need you. I love—"

Something dark and mistlike shot from Mary-Martha's body and struck Willie. Eddie watched Mary-Martha fall from her suspended place and land awkwardly. First she moaned in pain, then she screamed, "Willie!"

Whatever left her slammed into her husband; he staggered, then screamed. Someplace in the shriek was laughter.

Willie fell to the stage and writhed. Mary-Martha struggled to her feet. "Help me, Gabriel."

Hoagland sprinted to her side and helped her to her feet. She hopped on one foot. Eddie assumed the other to be sprained or broken.

A chilling scream came from Willie. Eddie stood and saw the man's skin bubble as if being boiled from within.

"Willie. Willie! WILLIE!" Mary-Martha started forward, but Hoagland held her back. "Let go. I have to help him."

"He's beyond help now," Hoagland said.

"What have I done?" Mary-Martha shuddered and convulsed into sobs.

Henick started forward, but the man behind him grabbed him by the back of the shirt. "You're not going anywhere, pal." Eddie slapped the man's hand away. The thug behind Eddie punched him on the side of the head. Eddie felt his knees go weak, but he remained on his feet.

Henick turned and placed his hand on the man's chest. Within a second he was weeping into his hands, saying something Eddie couldn't make out. He did hear the word *daughter*.

The other man seized Henick by the throat. "What did you do to him?"

Eddie started for the man but stopped when he saw Henick's hand come up to touch the man's chest. He dissolved into tears.

Eddie didn't even try to understand the man's mumbling.

Willie stopped moving. Mary-Martha screamed his name over and over. "I'm sorry, Willie. I'm so sorry."

The same darkness that shot into Willie returned to Mary-Martha. "Willie—" She turned her gaze to Henick. "*Tell me the message or he dies.*" She pointed at Eddie.

THE SOLID FLOOR OF THE CAVERN FELT GOOD TO KATH-erine. The descent down the ladder had taken all the concentration she could muster. She did her best to avoid thinking about the climb back up.

The cavern was stunning. Katherine figured it was larger than it looked. The few lights driven by the generator above pushed the blackness only so far. She estimated the ceiling to be one hundred or more feet above her. "I thought there would be more...you know...stuff hanging down from the ceiling."

"Stalactites?" Natalie said. "There are plenty of those in the other chambers. Stalactites and stalagmites are formed from dripping limewater. There hasn't been much water in this chamber for centuries. You'll see some soon enough."

Manford and Flannigan arrived a few moments after Katherine put boot to ground. "We should go. We have five miles to cross in as little time as possible."

"Five miles?" Natalie said. "Oh. Patterson's place is about five miles from here. You think the distance underground is the same? We have maybe a mile and half to go before we reach the access point. The chamber under Patterson's place reaches a good ways under our property line. I suppose a good real estate attorney could make an issue out of that, but Dad never saw the sense in it."

She faced the others. "OK, now the hard part begins. We have light for about 500 yards. After that we'll be carrying our own

it easily." Natalie paused for effect. "As long as he crawls on his belly."

"Um, great," Katherine said.

"The passage is about thirty feet long, narrows in the middle, then empties about four feet above the adjoining cavern's floor, so be careful on the exit. I'll go first so I'll be there to help."

Natalie didn't wait for a response. She stepped to the small opening, lowered her head, and crawled in.

Katherine felt the need to throw up.

"You want me to go next?" Manford asked.

"No, why?"

"Because you look ready to keel over."

"Don't be silly. I'm fine."

Flannigan stepped to her other side. "With all due respect, Agent, it's nice and cool in here, and you're sweating like you've marched a few miles through a sauna."

"It's just the hike."

Manford lowered his voice. "You're a tad on the claustrophobic side, aren't you?"

"No—maybe a little, but I don't want Natalie to know it."

Manford sniffed and ran a hand under his nose. "I think she already does. She doesn't seem to miss much."

"I'm not turning back." Katherine directed her light to the opening.

"I'm not suggesting you do; I just want you to know that we're here for you."

"That's very gallant, Manford, but I'll be all right."

"Good," Manford said, "because you may have to be there for me. Shall I go next?"

"No. If I don't go next, I won't go at all."

"Thirty feet sounds like a lot," Flannigan said, "but it's only a few body lengths. Take them one at a time."

"Thanks, guys. I'll be fine." She walked to the hole. She didn't feel fine.

A breeze moved through the opening, and that gave her some hope. First it meant that Natalie had made it through, and they were about the same size. There was a good chance she wouldn't be an underground stopcock. Second, it meant she would have plenty of air even if she did get stuck.

She took several deep breaths and crawled into the narrow tunnel. As promised, the opening was large enough for her to crawl easily but soon narrowed. Fearful that she would wedge herself in if she kept her arms beneath her, she stretched them ahead of her like a diver launching herself from a diving board.

Through the narrowest section she pushed with her feet and clawed with her hands. She wondered what maniac would attempt this without knowing what lay ahead.

Her heart slammed against her sternum; her breathing grew more rapid and shallow. She could taste dirt.

Push. Pull. Grunt. She inched along, pressed down more by fear than rock. She reminded herself that although she couldn't rise to her knees, there were still several inches of free space around her.

She pressed on until her hands no longer felt the base of the tunnel. Something grabbed her wrists and pulled. A moment later she stood by Natalie.

"Congratulations, Agent Rooney. I would have bet a week's salary you wouldn't have even tried."

"Thanks for the vote of confidence."

"Any time."

Manford appeared next, with Flannigan on his heels.

"If I never do that again, it will be way too soon," Flannigan said.

Katherine whispered. "OK, we need to consider this hostile territory. Let's keep our voices down. I've noticed these chambers have a pretty good echo." She turned to Natalie. "I'm not sure what's ahead—"

"Save your breath, agent. I'm not letting you wander these caverns unescorted. You'd get lost in no time flat, and how would

I explain that to my supervisor? Besides, many park rangers are peace officers. I happen to be one. Had I known I would be doing this today, I would have brought my weapon."

"Next time I'll try to give you more notice." Katherine smiled. "OK, we're looking for four men; two are hostages. There may be others as well. Once we find them, I take the lead."

"Agreed," Natalie said.

54

EDDIE TOOK STOCK OF THE SITUATION. HE STOOD IN front of a woman with two voices who hovered over the floor. Three of her henchmen sat in the padded chairs of an underground church building, weeping from regrets only they fully understood; a man had just died in front of his eyes. Only he, Henick, and Hoagland were still remotely normal—if Hoagland could be called normal.

Henick—Enoch, as the crazy woman called him—refused to be cowered by threats. It all seemed to hinge on Henick's message. What Mary-Martha wanted with it was beyond him.

"Let her go," Henick said.

Mary-Martha laughed. "*She is of no importance to you. She is your enemy, yet you plead for her life.*"

"No one deserves you," Henick said.

"*She had plans for you, you know. She was going to use you, just like me, except her vision is so small. She wants to be great among her people. She built this place to protect her and her most faithful followers. At first she planned to pretend to be the messenger but realized you'd show up someday. My plan is so much grander.*"

"Your plan failed a long time ago. You influenced many but not me; not then, not now."

"*Tell me the message, Enoch.*"

"Go ask God yourself."

She flew through the air and touched down a foot away from

Henick. Eddie backed up and bumped into Hoagland, who clamped a huge hand around Eddie's neck.

Mary-Martha spoke. This time the interloper's voice could be heard without the dual tonality. Eddie assumed the real Mary-Martha had given up. Maybe she was fighting back. There was no way to know.

"You care about your enemy, but your kind has never cared for me or mine."

"Such decisions are not mine to make."

"Not yours to make?" She nodded, then grabbed Henick by the front of the shirt. Eddie expected her to strike him. Instead she rose from the ground again, dragging Henick with her. She rose slowly; Henick offered no resistance. Ten feet, fifteen feet, twenty, thirty and more until she reached the ceiling of the cavern sanctuary.

She let go.

Henick fell.

"This helps," Katherine whispered as they moved from the dark cavern through a small opening and into a much larger space. Lights cast beams through the clear air. She switched off her helmet lamp.

"Look at this," Manford said. He moved to a fenced area. "Military rations, boxes and boxes of them."

Flannigan joined him. "It looks like someone was preparing for a long stay."

"There's enough food here to feed an army." Katherine looked at a small sign attached to the fence: 25F. "Twenty-five F. Does that mean there are twenty-four other storage areas like this? Does F stand for food?"

A corridor ran just to the left side of the food locker. The others followed as she moved slowly down the small hall. To one side were banks of metal lockers, each with a large padlock.

Flannigan sniffed the air. "Smell that? Smells like gun oil."

"Weapons?" Natalie said.

"Based on the number of lockers, these guys are preparing for a war." Manford said.

"No, a siege." Katherine removed one of the flashlights Natalie had given her and shone it through the upper vent in the metal door of the locker. "Rifles. Remember David Koresh and the Branch Davidians?"

"A little," Manford said.

Katherine explained. "They lived in a compound in Waco, Texas. Several former members described a large number of weapons. When ATF agents investigated in 1993, a firefight broke out. Four agents were killed. They held out for weeks. Finally, agents tried to break the stalemate with tear gas. A fire broke out. Some think the tear gas canisters started it. Many think the cult group torched their own place. More than eighty members died, including many children. They believed the arrival of federal agents was the beginning of the apocalypse."

"How can someone like Koresh get people to follow him like that?" Flannigan asked.

"He's not unique. In the late 1970s Jim Jones and the People's Temple killed a congressman and several others there investigating the cult's activities. They had moved to Guyana. Before it was all over, 913 people committed suicide by drinking punch laced with cyanide. The list is longer than most realize.

"One thing is clear," she continued, "this isn't good."

"I wonder how many people are down here," Flannigan said.

"Not many," Natalie said. "I spend a lot of time in caves like this. If there were a crowd down here, we'd hear it."

"So maybe we're just dealing with a handful of people," Manford said. "I like those odds better."

Katherine unzipped her coveralls and removed her weapon. Flannigan did the same.

The sound of Henick's body hitting the stone floor, the crack of bones breaking, echoed in the expansive cavern. He lay on his back unmoving, arms and legs at odd angles.

Eddie screamed and ran for his friend. He dropped to his knees, reached forward, then stopped. Bones protruded from Henick's lower legs. Blood oozed from his nose and mouth. More blood pooled beneath his skull.

"No, no," Eddie mumbled. His vision blurred as tears welled then poured from his eyes. "Oh God, oh God."

Henick opened his eyes. "God hears. God knows."

"Hang on, man. Stay with me. You're going to be OK."

Henick smiled and slowly moved his head from side to side.

"Yes, you are, man. I've seen it. The fire. You walked into and out of the fire. I saw your skin heal. You can do this."

Mary-Martha floated down and hovered in a prone position a few feet above Henick. *"The message. Tell me. I may let you live."* One voice delivered the words, the other wept softly.

Eddie watched Henick's eyes turn to the floating figure.

"Leave him alone."

Mary-Martha gave no indication she heard him.

"The message, Enoch son of Jared, or learn what death is."

Henick grinned. Blood poured from his mouth as he did. He coughed. "Too late. Too late."

Mary-Martha's face went slack. She rose a few more feet and turned her head to the side, as if listening to something in the distance.

"No."

"Yes," Henick said.

She rose and moved back over the stage. *"Too late."*

"Too late," Henick whispered.

She shrieked, rose to the ceiling, her head shaking. As Eddie watched, Mary-Martha's face changed into something hideous, then the same dark mist that left her to enter her husband's body shot from her chest.

The body of Mary-Martha fell from the ceiling to the stage below. Again, the sound of breaking bones and flesh impacting a hard surface turned Eddie's stomach.

The mist formed a gargoyle figure, then dissolved into nothing.

"It's gone, Henick. Henick? Come on, man. Don't leave me. You can do this. I know you can."

Eddie saw the bravest thing he had ever seen: Henick raised his broken left arm and reached for Eddie's chest. Instinctively, Eddie pulled back.

"Rory Stover says, 'Hi.'"

The image of the boy in the hospital stabbed Eddie's mind.

"Don't leave, Henick. Stay here. We need you. I need you."

"Someone…else…to say…" He moved his hand another inch closer to Eddie's chest. Eddie leaned forward until Henick's fingers touched his sternum.

A moment later, Eddie whispered, "Mom?"

The shriek led Katherine and her team to the chamber. She motioned for Manford and Natalie, neither of whom carried a weapon, to stay back. She and Flannigan slipped into the chair-filled chamber. The sight of the underground church sanctuary distracted her for a moment, but only for a moment.

"Federal agents! Hands up. I want to see hands."

A motion to her left near the stage caught her attention. A large man drew a gun.

"Don't do it!" Katherine shouted.

He raised the weapon. The trigger beneath Katherine's finger moved. The sharp report of gunfire bounced off the hard walls.

Acrid smoke from spent gunpowder hung in the gently moving air.

The big man took two steps back then collapsed.

"On the ground! Everyone on the ground!"

Three men who looked to Katherine to be weeping moved to the aisle and lay face down. She could hear their sobs.

She heard another sound. The young man she had seen in the video knelt hunched over a body, holding a hand to his chest. He laughed. He cried.

Flannigan had approached the body of the man they shot, his gun still pointed. A moment later he turned to Katherine and shook his head. He walked to her. "What happened here?"

Katherine looked around. "I have no idea."

Katherine had never been so happy to see sunshine. Doug Walton had done his job, leading a dozen New Mexico State Police and federal agents to the Patterson site. Katherine remained below only long enough to help secure the crime scene. Manford, Flannigan, and Natalie stayed with her. As soon as she felt she could professionally do so, she and her team followed another FBI agent from the cavern sanctuary and to the surface, happy to have a direct way out. The thought of going back the way she came unsettled her.

They had just stepped from the large metal building and into the New Mexico sun when Manford's cell phone beeped. He dug it out of his pocket.

"Four messages," he said. He selected the earliest and listened. He stopped midstride.

"What?" Katherine asked. He furrowed his brow.

"Check your cell phone."

She did and found a message. She couldn't believe her ears.

"What?" Natalie asked.

"Do you have a cell phone with you?" Katherine asked.

"I left it in the plane."

Katherine pressed a key to replay the message and handed the phone to Natalie. Flannigan had his phone to his ear.

Manford saw that his other three messages were from his office. He entered the phone number and stepped away. He placed a finger in his other ear. Katherine had noticed that the signal on her phone was weak. They were close to being too far from a cell tower to have any signal at all.

When Manford returned, he looked hollowed, empty of strength. "That was my office at the FCC. The message we just heard went out to every cell phone and appeared in the message boxes of every landline. The same message is being given over every radio frequency and television station, including satellite and cable. It's appearing on television and in movie theaters. It has shown up in many newspapers, and the guess is it will appear in every one. There are even reports that commercial pilots heard it over their FAA frequencies."

"Every form of media," Katherine said. "How is that possible?"

"It's not possible," Manford said. "Citizen-band hobbyists are complaining that message is on every channel." He ran a hand through his hair. "Not possible. Trust me, I know this stuff. It just isn't possible."

Katherine walked to one of the officers. "Excuse me; did you guys have any trouble with your radios earlier?"

"You mean that lame broadcast? Yeah, someone got on our frequency. Whoever it is has bought himself some big trouble."

"Somehow I don't think so," Katherine said.

EPILOGUE

EDDIE FEELY FELT UNCOMFORTABLE IN HIS SPORTS COAT. It was new and the first time he had worn it. He thought he should dress up a little before appearing on television. Trixie helped him pick it out. She had accepted his apology and said she believed him.

The studio was dark except for stage lights that stabbed Eddie's eyes. He sat at a modern-looking glass-top table. Across from him sat Peter Lawrence, seventy years old, hunched in the shoulders, gravely voice, but with a mind more keen than most men a third his age.

"Help our audience understand this, Mr. Feely—"

"Folks just call me Eddie."

"All right, Eddie. You traveled with the man everyone calls the Messenger."

"Yes, for a few days."

"Why did he pick you?"

"He didn't. I picked him. He tried to send me home several times."

"But you stayed with him anyway. Why?"

Eddie shifted in the seat. "It's hard to describe. I just knew I should be with him."

"How did you meet?"

Eddie smiled. "I tried to bust his nose. Instead, I messed up my hand." Eddie filled in a few of the details.

The interviewer wouldn't let up. "That's an odd thing for a disciple to do."

"I wasn't his disciple. He touched me and changed me." Eddie didn't feel the need to explain why he was grinning when he said, "…touched me…"

"As you know, a great many skeptics are saying this is a hoax. What do you say to them? What message do you have?"

"I have no message. I was a tagalong, nothing more. The message came from God. I can't add to it."

"But what about the skeptics?"

Eddie shrugged. "What about them? Look, I ain't…I'm not a Bible scholar. I'm no preacher. I'm just a guy who met one of God's own prophets. There have always been skeptics, so we shouldn't be surprised there are so many now. There are those who will believe and those who will not."

"You said earlier that the Messenger was Enoch from the Old Testament. Do you really believe that?"

"Yes. I called him Henick. He pronounced his name Hee-knock. That sounded like Henick to me. He never corrected me."

"Enoch is the man who never died."

"Right. Genesis 5:24—'Enoch walked with God; and he was not, for God took him.'"

"And you expect the world to believe that?"

Eddie shook his head. "I ain't got no expectations. You can believe or not. I choose to believe what I know to be true. The world has seen the video from the highway pileup. The news media have interviews of people who had contact with him. The evidence is there."

"But this is so hard to believe."

"Who said belief was easy?"

Lawrence sighed. "So this Messenger delivers his message over the media. His face appears in newspaper ads that the editors didn't put there and the ads move; he appears on movie screens, television sets, the Internet; he delivers the message via cell phone, landlines, radio, just about everything. Why do things that way?"

"I'm told there are six and a half billion people in the world. Can you think of a better way of reaching them?"

"No, not really."

"It's similar to what you do here," Eddie said. "You broadcast to the world. God enabled His messenger to do the same with other media."

"The message was simple. Some think God would have delivered something a little more profound."

"The Bible is filled with profound teaching, and you know how much the world pays attention to that. If we can't handle the simple, what makes us think we deserve the profound?"

"What should we get out of the message?"

"Just what you heard: free will is a gift, but we've made it a curse. God is giving us some time to make right choices—to choose Him through Jesus. The message told us that every free gift we've received we've misused or destroyed. It's time to take a new approach—God's approach. As the message said, time is short."

"So this Enoch is the new Jesus."

"No. There is only one Jesus. Enoch, like the rest of us, is His servant. Nothing revealed in the Bible has changed. Christ is coming again. Enoch's arrival reminds us of that."

"So when does Jesus come back?"

"I have no idea. All I know is that Enoch showed me faith. I plan to live in that faith. I hope the world does the same."

"My understanding is that Enoch died. Tell us that story."

"No. Enoch's purpose was to draw attention to Jesus, not himself. I plan on honoring that."

"I assume he was buried or cremated. Can you tell us anything about that?"

The question snapped Eddies thoughts back to the soul-burning moment in the cavern as Enoch lay dying. He recalled his friend touching his chest, recalled seeing the image of his mother in heaven. When he opened his eyes again, Enoch was gone. *Enoch walked with God, and he was not, for God took him.* The thought hesitated then changed. *Enoch walked with us and is not because God took him—again.* "No."

"Can't or won't."

"You choose."

Peter Lawrence turned to the camera. "When we come back, we'll take calls from you out there in TV land. What about you? Are you a believer? We'll be right back."

The director said, "And we're clear. Two minutes, people."

"Are you ready to take some calls, Eddie?"

"I'll do my best."

"You really believe your friend was the Messenger of God?"

"I have no doubts."

"I wonder," Lawrence muttered.

"You wonder what?" Eddie could almost see the wheels in the man's head turning.

"How many television interviews have you done in the last few weeks?"

Eddie shook his head. "I can't remember. Lots, I can tell you that."

"How about radio?"

"Even more," Eddie said. "Newspapers, magazines, Internet. It's been pretty crazy."

Lawrence scratched his chin. "And in all these interviews you've repeated everything that happened and the message Enoch brought?"

"Of course. I know the world heard it a dozen different ways, but I plan on repeating it whenever I can."

"You see, that's just the thing. From where I'm sitting, it seems that you're doing the messenger work now."

Eddie didn't know how to respond.

Lawrence leaned forward. "You read your Bible much?"

"I'm learning. I've been reading in the New Testament."

"You might want to do a little study in the Old Testament. You know Enoch was just one of two men who never died."

"Two men?"

"I spent a few years in Sunday school as a child. As I recall, the Bible mentions two men who never died. Enoch was the first. The other was Elijah."

If you liked *Enoch*, you will LOVE this...

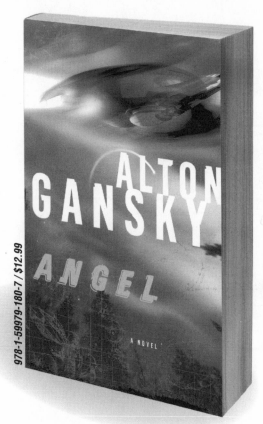

978-1-59979-180-7 / $12.99

A wise stranger has come to save our world. Miracles happen around him, spectacular promises are made, and wisdom flows forth from his lips. But is he too good to be true?

Alton Gansky is a master of the "what if" that spins an ordinary world into an extraordinary adventure.

—ANGELA HUNT, author of *Uncharted*

VISIT YOUR LOCAL BOOKSTORE.

REALMS
A STRANG COMPANY

8149